ALEX DELAWARE NOVELS

Jigsaw (2026)
Open Season (2025)
The Ghost Orchid (2024)
Unnatural History (2023)
City of the Dead (2022)
Serpentine (2021)
The Museum of Desire (2020)
The Wedding Guest (2019)
Night Moves (2018)
Heartbreak Hotel (2017)
Breakdown (2016)
Motive (2015)
Killer (2014)
Guilt (2013)
Victims (2012)
Mystery (2011)
Deception (2010)
Evidence (2009)
Bones (2008)
Compulsion (2008)
Obsession (2007)
Gone (2006)
Rage (2005)
Therapy (2004)
A Cold Heart (2003)
The Murder Book (2002)
Flesh and Blood (2001)
Dr. Death (2000)
Monster (1999)
Survival of the Fittest (1997)
The Clinic (1997)
The Web (1996)
Self-Defense (1995)
Bad Love (1994)
Devil's Waltz (1993)
Private Eyes (1992)
Time Bomb (1990)
Silent Partner (1989)
Over the Edge (1987)
Blood Test (1986)
When the Bough Breaks (1985)

BY JONATHAN KELLERMAN AND JESSE KELLERMAN

Coyote Hills (2025)
The Lost Coast (2024)
The Burning (2021)
Half Moon Bay (2020)
A Measure of Darkness (2018)
Crime Scene (2017)
The Golem of Paris (2015)
The Golem of Hollywood (2014)

OTHER NOVELS

The Murderer's Daughter (2015)
True Detectives (2009)
Capital Crimes (with Faye Kellerman, 2006)
Twisted (2004)
Double Homicide (with Faye Kellerman, 2004)
The Conspiracy Club (2003)
Billy Straight (1998)
The Butcher's Theater (1988)

GRAPHIC NOVELS

Silent Partner (2012)
The Web (2012)

NONFICTION

With Strings Attached: The Art and Beauty of Vintage Guitars (2008)
Savage Spawn: Reflections on Violent Children (1999)
Helping the Fearful Child (1981)
Psychological Aspects of Childhood Cancer (1980)

FOR CHILDREN, WRITTEN AND ILLUSTRATED

Jonathan Kellerman's ABC of Weird Creatures (1995)
Daddy, Daddy, Can You Touch the Sky? (1994)

JIGSAW

JONATHAN KELLERMAN

JIGSAW

AN ALEX DELAWARE NOVEL

BALLANTINE BOOKS
NEW YORK

Ballantine Books
An imprint of Random House
A division of Penguin Random House LLC
1745 Broadway, New York, NY 10019
randomhousebooks.com
penguinrandomhouse.com

Hardback ISBN 978-0-593-49771-5
Ebook ISBN 978-0-593-49772-2

Printed in the United States of America

randomhousebooks.com

1st Printing

First Edition

BOOK TEAM: Production editor: Dennis Ambrose • Managing editor: Pam Alders • Production manager: Sandra Sjursen • Copy editor: Laura Jorstad • Proofreaders: Michael Burke, Karina Jha

The authorized representative in the EU for product safety and compliance is Penguin Random House Ireland, Morrison Chambers, 32 Nassau Street, Dublin D02 YH68, Ireland. https://eu-contact.penguin.ie

To Ori

JIGSAW

CHAPTER

1

We all know the one-liner: A true friend is someone who'll help you hide the body.

For the most part, I like people. Have never experienced social anxiety though I've helped others deal with it. I choose to think empathy's been enough for my patients and so far no one's complained.

Despite all that, I've got two true friends: the woman I love and live with and a homicide detective with whom I've worked on scores of horrific murders. What Milo Sturgis calls "those cases."

So there you have it: a lifetime of relating but only two people who'd help me hide a body. Three, if you include Blanche, the little French bulldog to whom Robin and I have been catering for years. Dogs are way above us emotionally and canine love's unconditional but I'm not sure what Blanche could accomplish in a pinch.

I see her and Robin daily. My contact with Milo is a different story. Occasionally social—Robin and I having dinner with him and the man he lives with—but mostly work-related.

The worst in people brings out the best in Milo and me.

I hadn't heard from him in over a month, had assumed none of "those cases" had surfaced. But when he finally called on a Monday afternoon, he sounded low and I began to wonder.

"What's up?"

"Can I come by?"

"Sure."

Seven minutes later he was at the front door, meaning he'd phoned from the road, hoping I'd be available.

Today, he'd lucked out. I'd just finished a morning of child custody consults and phone chats with attorneys and judges, had planned to wind down with a run. Not just for the exercise. Looking out for speeding cars on Beverly Glen heightens my senses and I return to the house adrenalized like a fox who's avoided the hounds.

Now that energy was pinging like a series of manic texts.

I heard the engine of his unmarked Impala and opened the door. He trudged up the stairs and walked in looking the way he'd sounded. His suit was gray and wrinkled, his shirt gray-beige and wrinkled, his tie limp and brown. Pink-soled desert boots were scuffed glossy at the toes.

Green eyes that could be startlingly bright were bleary. Bison-shoulders drooped, causing his gut to protrude. His default pallor had bleached to chalky, heightening the cruel legacy of the acne pits and welts that brocade his face.

He stood there for a second, rolled enormous hands into fists, and tugged at spiking black hair before loping past me toward the kitchen.

Improvising at our fridge is another of Milo's defaults. When he fails to do so he's usually distracted by a strong lead.

Today was odd. No evidence of progress in his walk but he still didn't forage, choosing instead to settle heavily at the table and shake his head like a weary, wet mastiff.

I said, "Coffee?"

"Experience is supposed to make you smarter."

I kept silent.

He said, "Not true?"

"It can help."

He growled. "Put it this way: What am I always preaching to the junior D's about?"

"Avoid assuming."

He clicked his tongue. "Go to the head of the class. Yeah, coffee sounds okay."

I pulled out a bag of Ethiopian beans Robin had just roasted and ground and loaded the machine.

When I produced cream and sugar, he said, "No thanks, black. To match my mood . . . where's the pooch?"

"Out back with Robin."

"Probably for the best. Just read an article, dogs can sniff out the stink of stress. Don't want her to suffer my reek."

I laughed reflexively.

He smiled. "Yeah, I'm whining. Figured if anyone would have something supportive to say it would be you."

I switched to a plummy voice. What screenwriters have determined shrinks should sound like. "Sounds like you're upset."

He broke into laughter.

The coffee machine beeped.

"Perfect timing," he said. "At least someone's got it."

I poured, we drank.

He drained his mug, chose to inhale this time before blowing out audibly.

"Okay, confession time. Doctor, I have sinned."

I said, "Second cup?"

"If it ain't sacramental wine, no thanks." He inhaled deeply. "Okay, coupla weeks ago I get a morning call on a body. Apartment not far from the Westmont mall. Female victim named Sophie Barlow, sitting at *her* kitchen table. Her head's tilted back, rounding her neck."

He demonstrated.

I said, "Postmortem gravity would tug it down. What was on display, cutting or strangulation?"

"The latter. Ligature mark's ringing her neck, her eyes are riddled with petechial hemorrhages, and on the table in front of her is a long shoelace, probably from a sneaker."

"More display."

He nodded. "In answer to your next question, she's fully clothed, no obvious signs of a sexual assault or a struggle, I'm figuring she was taken by surprise from behind by someone she trusted. Which leads me you-know-where."

"A domestic."

"Backing that up is a plastic bowl on the table in front of her that was used for an ashtray. In it are a couple of Marlboro Gold butts. The fact that there's no actual ashtray or cigarettes in the entire place suggests Sophie's not a smoker. So her guest is. By itself that doesn't mean much, the butts could come from any visitor and why would the killer leave obvious evidence behind?"

"Like you always say, stupid criminals."

"Thank God for them. So I was hoping that's where it would end up. The techies tag and bag the butts and I call in some markers at Hertzberg and manage to get a relatively quick analysis. Meaning ten days for a basic DNA. A sample showed an unknown male, no surprise, someone smoked those cigs. But without a suspect, no big deal yet. Then wouldn't you know it, we get a CODIS hit. Local guy, Michael Heck, has a bit of a felony record, turns out to be Sophie's ex-boyfriend."

He reached into a jacket pocket, drew out an enlarged DMV photo, and slid it across the table. Good-looking man, faint smile, late forties, with a meaty chin, thick wavy dark hair graying at the temples, and narrow, acute-blue eyes.

Keeping it in a pocket was interesting. Normally Milo totes case material in a battered, olive-green vinyl attaché case. Not enough on this case to justify it?

I said, "What's a bit of a felony record?"

"Assault charge sixteen years ago when he was in the service, basically a bar fight in Oceanside that got pled down to misdemeanor. Unfortunately for Heck, that was after Prop 69 so the arrest was enough for DNA. Bingo, we arrest him and lock him up, he looks shell-shocked but lawyers up. It looked to be an easy one, that's why I didn't call you."

I said, "Given what you had, it sounds more like logic than tunnel vision."

"Thanks for the therapy," he said. "Yeah, one would think and one would be wrong . . . you know, a second cup doesn't sound half bad."

I drank but despite his request Milo didn't, circling his mug with both huge hands and staring past me.

"So what changed everything?" he said. "Nasty old reality. Two days after Heck's arrest, a woman shows up unannounced at the station asking for me. I go downstairs, see a young redhead in a white Armani suit and big heels pushing an impressive wheelie bag. Moves fast, talks fast, shoves her business card at me fast. Wanna guess?"

"Attorney."

"Bettina Bel Geddes, Esq., big Century City firm. Corporate litigator but she's representing Heck in the criminal case, announces it like it's gonna win her a Nobel. I say, 'How can I help you?' She says, 'You can't but I can help you. Let's go up to your office, if you're smart enough, you'll pay attention.' All this in front of Demetria, the civilian clerk. *She's* looking at me like, *Who's this piece of work?* I coulda shined Bel Geddes on, but she's too damn happy. Won-the-lottery happy. We go upstairs, minute we're out of the elevator, she starts orating."

I said, "Her client's innocent."

"Expressed with smug self-righteousness," he said. "She claims Heck's got an ironclad alibi for the time of the murder, opens the wheeler and sets out to prove it. Hundred and twenty miles from the crime scene, at a hotel in La Jolla with another woman, and Bel Geddes has time-stamped CCTV footage to prove it along with a readout from those high-tech key dealies hotels use to monitor comings and goings."

"Heck came but didn't go."

"Didn't leave his room once. And if the camera and the door stuff wasn't enough, Bel Geddes also has a stack of time-stamped room service receipts, affidavits from hotel staff, more footage from the parking lot, and a clear shot of Heck and some blonde checking out and finally leaving two days later."

"Party time," I said.

"From the booze receipts I'd say serious party."

"Who's the woman?"

"Married, so Heck won't say."

"Noble of him."

"Apparently, he's up for sainthood and waiting to hear from the Vatican. All the camera picks up on her is a brief shot in the lobby. She keeps her head down, which fits with a naughty wife. Has white-blond hair that has to be a wig. In any event, Heck's cleared so how the hell did his cigarette butts get on Sophie's table?"

"He could've paid her a prior visit and she never cleaned up."

"According to Bel Geddes, Heck hasn't been there for a coupla months and the look of Sophie's place backs that up. Neat, clean, organized. Leaving a random stash of stale tobacco doesn't fit."

"Someone got hold of Heck's old smokes and planted them?"

"I know," he said. "It's screenplay stuff but I haven't found a better explanation. Accessing the butts wouldn't be tough if you had access to Heck's trash. Which fits with something personal. Against Heck or him *and* Sophie Barlow."

"With an alibi like that, why wouldn't Heck tell you right away instead of lawyering up and sitting in jail?"

"I posed that to Ms. Bel Geddes. She looked at me like I had brain damage and said, 'Because only stupid people talk to you guys.' "

"Two days in lockup is smart?" I said.

"Guess a felony record could make you careful. That and all those true-crime shows. Nowadays, even the stupid ones are clamming up. And Heck's no moron. Business degree, works as an administrator for a law office."

He lifted his mug. Sipped. Drank deeply.

I said, "Could Heck be smart enough to hire someone to kill his ex *and* leave the butts behind? Knowing he'll be arrested then released due to his alibi?"

"Kind of a warped double-jeopardy thing? But unlike real double jeopardy it wouldn't really insulate him from future charges, Alex."

"But it could prevent any warrants or affidavits for his home, phone, or financials."

He thought about that. "I guess anything's possible. *If* I can find a motive for Heck wanting Sophie dead. Bel Geddes claims there isn't one, the two of them parted on friendly terms."

"What do Sophie's friends say about the relationship?"

"Haven't gone there yet," he said. "Still acclimating to the time zone at Square One." He sighed. "The whole thing's crazy. Which is why I'm here."

His phone tooted something baroque. He glanced at the screen, said, "Alicia," and clicked in. "What's up, kid?"

For the next minute or so he listened and said nothing, eyes widening, head pitched forward.

"Gimme the address . . . okay, be there in twenty."

Clicking off, he scooped up Michael Heck's photo and turned to me. "Still free?"

"I am."

"Good. Time for a ride-along."

CHAPTER 2

This crime scene was twenty-five minutes from my house but seven minutes from the West L.A. station.

Yellow tape fenced off a one-story bungalow on a block of nearly identical structures five streets south of the monstrous mall at Westwood and Pico.

Many of the small, simple houses shouted pride of ownership. This one didn't.

Mint-green stucco had faded to sludge-gray sallow in spots. The lawn was skimpy and bristly, green conceding to brown. A gray asphalt roof sported black rectangles where shingles had fled. A dirty, older beige Lexus sat in a cracked, weed-choked driveway.

Black-and-whites positioned perpendicular to the street extended the cordon beyond the death house, walling in two neighboring properties on either side. Parked in front was a black unmarked Ford. Detective Alicia Bogomil's ride.

A few neighbors gaped from a distance but like most L.A. streets, this one reacted to daylight with isolation. The only other people in sight were uniformed officers doing what everyone else does with spare time: practicing self-hypnosis by phone.

No vans from the Hertzberg crime lab or the coroner had arrived. Same for the compact cars coroner's investigator used.

Nothing but the initial police presence said a recently discovered body.

Milo said, "Let's find Alicia."

Before we took a step, she emerged from behind the Lexus and strode toward us. Trim and purposeful, hair clipped shorter than the last time I'd seen her and tipped with magenta and peacock blue, she wore black slacks, a black leather jacket over a black T-shirt, and black flats. Looking like anything other than what she was.

We'd met her working private security for a hotel where a hundred-year-old woman had been murdered. She'd been a major factor in closing the case and Milo had encouraged her to apply to the department. Then he'd helped fast-track her to detective.

"One of the smartest things I ever did," he told me shortly after. "Super smart and that work ethic!"

Now she was frowning. "Wouldn't have called you, L.T., but it's a strange one." Her lean avian face canted toward me. "Glad you're here, Doc. Same reason."

Milo said, "Thanks."

"Sir?"

"You rescued me. We were just conferring on Sophie Barlow."

Alicia smiled faintly. "That one. Okay, let me show you this one."

The three of us gloved and bootied and Alicia led us past the Lexus toward the rear of the green house, keeping up a steady pace while reporting.

"It started a couple hours ago when a neighbor—I took her statement and had her go back to her place but she'll be available—this neighbor called in a possible welfare check on the occupant because she hadn't been seen in a while and mail was piling up. I found three days' worth but it was a pretty big pile so I could see the neighbor's point."

Milo said, "Anything interesting?"

"Like what?"

"Warnings from the Black Hand."

Alicia laughed. "Unfortunately not. All I saw were circulars and catalogs and other junk. I bagged it, it's in my trunk."

"How long is a while since she'd been seen?"

"Neighbor thought at least a week but she doesn't really pay attention to comings and goings. Since it was an elderly living alone, Dispatch sent two of ours—Santos and Meade, they're in that first Oreo whenever you want them. No answer to their door-knock so they came back here."

She swung her arm toward a shallow strip of yard enclosed by block walls. No trees or shrubs, just a clothesline on rusted metal posts, the rope limp and filthy.

Milo looked at the back door. White and warped and set with a high fanlight window.

Alicia said, "Same thing there, so they checked that out."

"That" was the garage. A single-car structure with old-fashioned barn doors painted deep green and left open, revealing a floor-to-ceiling hoard.

Cardboard cartons were stacked to the rafters, as were black garbage bags stuffed to corpulence. Bound stacks of browned newspapers and an assortment of flimsy luggage created additional towers. A collection of rusty bicycles had been stacked into a tenuous minaret. Four grubby mattresses stored vertically pushed against random pieces of scrap wood and an equally unstable pile of transparent plastic bags crammed with matted clothing.

The only object privileged with breathing room was a chipped white deep-freeze on the right wall, plugged in and chugging. Alicia walked to it. "Ready?"

Milo said, "Do it."

"Here we go. Again." Biting her lip, she lifted the freezer lid with apparent tenderness.

Inside was another oversized plastic bag. Unlike the garment receptacles, this one was clouded to translucence by condensation, ice flecks, and brownish-red smears.

The contents blurred, like something preserved in aspic, but still visible.

Two scrawny, gray-white human arms had been severed from the gray-white torso on which they'd been placed. The limbs were folded across each other in a cruel parody of stubbornness. Both legs were bent under at the knees but appeared intact. Same for the sunken-cheeked face topped with long, wispy white hair that stared up at us with a gaping toothless mouth and inert black eyes.

Milo turned away.

Alicia shook her head. "Yeah, it's horrific. Meade threw up over in a corner of the yard and Santos held it in but was feeling sick when I got here and embarrassed by it. She's new, maybe she feels she needs to prove herself."

"Getting sick just proves she's human."

"That's what I told her."

Milo returned his attention to the frozen body, leaning in, careful not to touch anything. "Looks like the arms were cut off pretty cleanly. I can see dismembering in order to fit someone inside. But she's small and bending the legs did the trick so why bother?"

Alicia said, "Some kind of sick message?"

Both of them looked at me.

I examined the white porcelain front of the deep-freeze, then the sides. Plenty of nicks and dents but no blood. I said so.

Alicia said, "Nothing I can see."

"What led Meade and Santos to open it?"

"It wasn't any great deduction, it was just there so Santos flipped the lid. She didn't expect to find anything."

Milo said, "Good reason to feel sick. Victim's the occupant?"

"Haven't verified it yet but the age and dimensions fit." She pulled out her pad. "Five-two, a hundred pounds. Seventy-two years old, poor thing. Who would *do* that?"

Milo produced his pad. "Name?"

"Martha Joline Matthias."

His eyes rounded and his arm dropped. The pad slapped against his thigh and for a moment he seemed to lose balance. "Oh Lord."

Alicia said, "You know her, L.T.?"

"Know her and worked with her. She was one of *us.*"

CHAPTER 3

We were still near the deep-freeze when the coroner's investigators showed up. Not the usual solo or pair. A team of four, paper-suited and gloved and looking purposeful.

Alicia said, "I told them the situation, said they might want backup."

Two of the C.I.'s were familiar. Gloria Mendez, a former nurse, and Tom Blessingame, a former Torrance cop who'd despised retirement. The other two were tense young men who seemed surprised to be there.

Alicia explained the situation.

Gloria said, "See what you meant. Okay, we'll figure out how best to do it and let you know once we're done."

Nice way of saying scram.

Milo, Alicia, and I returned to the front of the house. Fewer neighbors were in sight. Uniforms continued to push buttons, breaking for occasional conversation with one another. The sun was egg-yolk yellow, the air crisp and too pleasant for this situation.

Milo said, "Have you been through the house yet?"

"Not extensively without a warrant, just took a quick look-through with a couple uniforms in order to clear it. It's like the garage."

"Hoarder's palace."

Alicia nodded. "Except for the kitchen, I guess she needed the space to prepare food. Rest of the house, it's up to the ceiling with just a couple of skinny aisles for walking through. It's amazing nothing fell and crushed her. When you knew her, was there any indication she was like that, L.T.?"

"Didn't know her enough to check out her housekeeping," he said. "But she always seemed put together."

"So maybe she changed in old age. Not that uncommon, right, Doc?"

I said, "It happens." Thinking about dementia, deterioration of the brain's frontal and prefrontal lobes, the variety of changes that could cause. I've seen severe cognitive decline but also humorless people suddenly enjoying jokes because their inhibitions have been stripped away.

Brand-new obsessions, as well, which could explain the hoarding.

Milo said, "Someone managed to get in there and make sure her death wasn't accidental. Any blood in the kitchen?"

"Not that I saw," said Alicia. "The whole place smells stale. You know, musty. But none of *that* smell that I could tell. Still, we're going to need time to plow through all of it. Any chance I can have Moe and Sean?"

"Captain okays it, sure. She doesn't, I'll help."

"Teamwork leads to dream-work? Thanks, L.T. So she was one of us, huh?"

"Literally," he said. "Westside station, Homicide. One of the first women to do it. When I started out she was already a veteran. Then—ten or so years ago she transferred to something small-time at another station. Theft, Fraud, not sure."

"That's a come-down," said Alicia. "She ever say why?"

"Nope, just there one day, gone the next."

I said, "Ten years ago she was in her sixties. Maybe the hours got too tough for her."

Or she'd sensed her own decline and wanted lower stakes. No sense bringing that up at this point and complicating matters.

Milo said, "It's probably too ancient of a history to be relevant."

He tapped a foot, looked around and frowned. "Martha and I didn't hang out much but she treated me well."

Alicia nodded but I wasn't sure she got it.

I did.

The unspoken words: *As opposed to.*

Remembering the bad old days when gay cops didn't "exist" in LAPD.

Given that state of affairs, Milo had never advertised his sexuality but neither had he hidden it. Police departments have supersonic grapevines and he'd suffered through a whole lot of whispered innuendo and not-so-covert comments, homosexual porn stuffed into his locker, the occasional spit-gob of vile graffiti, and social isolation that intensified when a partner dropped him, egged on by a wife's religious views.

Either that destroys you or you push through it. Milo's solution had been to cast aside comradeship and learn to go it alone as he overachieved his way to a solve rate better than anyone else's. Finally accomplishing an uneasy stability that carried him into changing times.

Alicia said, "Did you work cases together?"

"Nope. She had her own load and was only there for a year or so before moving on."

"Anything you can tell me about her family?" Her tone had changed. Bye-bye deference to a superior, hello investigative probing.

Milo said, "Widowed, husband had also been on the job. Wilshire patrol, I think. By the time I met her, he was gone. Heart attack or stroke, something along those lines."

"Any kids?"

"Not that she ever mentioned."

Alicia smiled. "This is different, no? Interviewing you."

Milo smiled back. "Live long enough, everything happens." He turned to me: "Same question as before: Why cut off the arms?"

I said, "If you're looking for something psychologically profound I don't have it."

"Yet," he said.

Alicia said, "Second the motion on yet."

I said, "Appreciate the optimism."

Milo said, "Caught it from you."

Alicia said, "Doc, could disabling the arms be a symbolic way of weakening her?"

"Sure."

"But maybe not?"

I shrugged.

She laughed. "Okay, I'll hold off bugging you until we know more." She turned to Milo. "Want to start with the neighbor who called in the welfare check or Meade and Santos?"

"Let's start with Meade and Santos. Gonna be a shorter conversation, then they can join the canvass."

Alicia looked over at the idling uniforms and grimaced. "I know, it hasn't started. Sorry, got caught up back there."

"Understandable. Which ones are Meade and Santos?"

"They're inside their car, the first one, closest to mine. Last time I checked just sitting there looking stunned."

"No phone games?" said Milo. "Guess *Grand Theft Auto* can't compete with reality."

CHAPTER 4

Officer Katherine Santos was a mid-twenties, six-foot blonde with stooped posture. Maybe a tall person's habit, maybe the stress of a first homicide scene. Freckled and sturdy, she had a strong jaw but a weak mouth. Officer Stephen Meade was ten years older, thin with a black buzz cut and small dark eyes that flitted around like houseflies.

The two of them had sprung out of their cruiser before we got there.

Milo introduced himself and me, avoiding the doctor bit and keeping my presence ambiguous. Neither uniform seemed curious about that. Or anything else. Both looked drained and grim.

He said, "Quite a thing to discover, guys."

Meade said, "Last thing I expected, sir. Kathy's first but she's the one who thought smart and opened the freezer."

Santos shrugged, nodded.

Milo said, "Good work, Officer."

She blew out air. "I almost didn't. But then I figured it was there, let's check." She lowered a hand to her abdomen and let it sit there. "*Last* thing I expected. There she was. Right on top. I couldn't believe it. I mean . . ."

Meade said, "Like out of a movie."

Santos said, "Not the kind I watch."

Milo said, "Your intuition was good, Officer."

"You say so," said Santos. "Sir."

Meade said, "I'm figuring you could probably go years and never see that." Looking to Milo for confirmation.

"You're figuring right, Officer Meade. So. Where does the neighbor who called in the welfare check live?"

Meade pointed south. "Four houses down, the white one with the brown roof. Mrs. . . . um . . ." Snapping a finger to no avail.

Santos said, "Winslow. Genevieve Winslow."

Meade looked up at her. No resentment at being out-remembered. More like grateful for the save.

Milo said, "We'll be heading over there. Everyone else on the block needs to be canvassed. If that's not productive, extend it . . . what do you think, Detective Bogomil, a block in either direction?"

Alicia said, "Good start. We can always go farther. Especially if someone out there has security footage."

Milo turned back to the uniforms. "You guys are in charge of organizing the canvass."

"Us?" said Meade.

"Any reason why not, Officer?"

Meade stood up taller. "No, sir. Thank you, sir."

"Me, too, sir," said Santos. "Thanking you, I mean. We're on it, sir."

They stood there for an uneasy moment then she saluted and walked ahead of Meade to the adjoining cruiser. By the time she was addressing a pair of phone-wielding comrades, Kathy Santos's back had straightened and her mouth had transformed.

Strong as her chin.

Genevieve Winslow was sixtyish with lilac-shadowed eyes, magenta lipstick, and hennaed hair streaming from beneath a wildly patterned green-and-chartreuse silk scarf. Her dress was loose, long, a print of wildly patterned red-and-blue silk, her footwear acid-green plastic sandals. Half a dozen bangles clinked on each arm. Her fingernails were polished pearlescent gray, the thumbs augmented with glitter. Black toenails showed themselves in the open toes of the sandals. Like tiny little mussels perched on pale rocks.

Despite all that flamboyance, her house was thinly furnished in tones of beige, gray, and white. Bare walls, functional seating, bright lighting.

Wanting to showcase herself?

She said, “Hi, ready for you!” and ushered us to a coffee table set up with salted nuts, crackers, and bottled water.

Before any of us could sit, she said, “Anything you want to ask is fine. I’m an open book.”

Alicia said, “We appreciate your initiating the welfare check on Ms. Matthias.”

“Just being a concerned citizen.”

“You were concerned about Ms. Matthias.”

“Is that her name? I just knew her as the strange old lady who lived down the block.”

“Strange how, ma’am?”

“Ma’am, eh?” said Genevieve Winslow. “Like in one of those western movies? Or *Dragnet*—I met Jack Webb once. When I was waitressing at the Brown Derby. He was wearing *that* tie and flirted with me.”

We smiled.

Alicia said, “Ms. Matthias was strange . . .”

“She never talked to anyone, I call that strange. Most you could get out of her was when you passed by and tried to be friendly and said hi, she’d look down at the ground and give this kind of grunt.”

She demonstrated, producing a wet sound from deep in her throat. “Small little thing but she could sure grunt.”

I glanced at Milo. Stone-faced.

Alicia said, “So you knew her from seeing her on the block.”

“Not often,” said Genevieve Winslow. “I like to get my steps in every day. I’d go past her house and usually there’d be nothing but sometimes she’d be taking out the garbage. Or unloading groceries from her car. The mail, too, she'd be out there picking it up like clockwork. That's why when I saw it on the stoop I wondered if something was off. You hear about it all the time. Elderlies falling and no one's there to help them."

Alicia said, "Thanks. So you saw the mail and . . ."

"And nothing, Detective, end of story. And by the way I think it's great they've got women doing the job. We have a lot to offer by way of sensitivity and deep perception."

Alicia smiled. "The mail made you wonder . . ."

"Obviously," said Genevieve Winslow. "It was unusual. Unusual makes me wonder. I knocked on her door, nothing, rang her bell, nothing, looked in a window, nothing—she's got these opaque drapes, you can't see inside. So I called 911 and they told me it wasn't an emergency, next time try the non-emergency number but they'd put it through anyway. I thought that was rude, here I'm trying to help and I'm getting corrected."

Alicia said, "Sorry for that. And again, thanks for calling."

"So she's not okay," said Genevieve Winslow. "All those police cars and now detectives."

"Unfortunately not, Ms. Winslow."

"She's totally gone?"

Alicia looked at Milo.

He said, "Afraid so. Have you ever seen anyone visiting Ms. Mathias?"

"Never. Not once."

"Any deliveries?"

"Never. Not once. This day and age, you want to reduce your footprint so you cut back on your driving and use Grubhub and also the stores deliver. I get everything delivered so I can concentrate on my work."

Her eyes begged for a question.

Milo said, "What work is that?"

"Used to act. Now I write. Memoir-based fiction."

"Ah."

"Finishing up my latest, going the self-publish route again."

"Good luck."

She waved that away. "One makes one's own luck."

He smiled. "So Ms. Matthias didn't take deliveries."

"Not that I saw. Always the car, unloading her groceries and grunting if you said hello."

Milo said, "Any idea where she got her groceries?"

"Sure do, saw the bags, not a supermarket," said Genevieve Winslow. "That discount place—Stark and Miner on Pico. I tried them once but the quality wasn't up to standards."

She stuck out her tongue. "You can penny-pinch on other things but food should be quality. I guess she didn't care. Which fits the way she kept her house, right?"

"You've been inside the house?"

"No, no, of course not, the outside. Dried-out lawn, no flowers. That roof of hers coming off in pieces? Not that I want to speak ill of the . . . deceased but obviously her standards were low. Did she harm herself or was she . . . you know."

Alicia said, "We really can't get into details."

Genevieve Winslow smirked. "There's my answer. Well that's just terrible. Right here on the block. Horrible. Should I be frightened?"

"It's always good to be careful but there's no reason—"

"I have an alarm and stout dead bolts and perfectly legal pepper spray in several locations. Have a dog, too, but he's at the vet and only weighs nine pounds. But he can produce a growl. Not for nothing, he's not stupid. But when he's motivated he can growl."

She smiled with pride. Then she blinked. "Kind of like *her,* now that I think about it. Small body, big voice."

Alicia said, "Sounds like you've taken plenty of precautions."

"If *I'm* not on my side," said Genevieve Winslow, "who will be?"

Alicia glanced at Milo.

He punted to me.

Informational relay race.

I said, "Has your dog growled recently?"

"He did four nights ago." Lilac lids fluttered. "Oh. See what you mean. So maybe . . . forget it, I know you're not going to tell me anything." She hugged herself. "This is creepy."

I said, "What time four nights ago?"

"Late. I'd fallen asleep out here with my laptop and Balthazar woke me with his barking and his growling. He was up by the front window, pawing the sill. I got up and checked but there was nothing out there. Wow. Now I *am* frightened."

Alicia said, "Is that unusual behavior for Balthazar?"

"You bet. We're usually back in the bedroom sleeping and he never makes a peep. I was out here because I'd been wrestling with a tough chapter and dozed off."

"Nothing sets Balthazar off when you're in the bedroom."

"Such as?"

"An animal."

"No, no, never," said Genevieve Winslow. "Balthy is *totally* animal-friendly. Even squirrels. He'd lick one to death, it's just people he doesn't like. Wow. This *is* alarming."

"No reason to be alarmed," said Alicia.

"Easy for you to say."

I said, "Sounds like Balthy was a great sentry. Great addition to all your other precautions."

"Well, yes. I guess. But I'm going to install cameras. Been thinking about it, now I've made the decision. If it's not too expensive. You recommend that, right?"

"Can't hurt," said Milo. "So your dealings with Ms. Matthias were casual."

"Not even that," she said. "More like random. But I don't like to see anyone in any sort of peril so I called you people. Apparently at the wrong number."

Alicia said, "And again, thanks for that."

"No thanks required," said Genevieve Winslow without a trace of sincerity. "Virtue is its own reward. A famous Roman said that. Cicero. As in Open Cicero."

CHAPTER 5

We left Genevieve Winslow standing in her doorway.

When Alicia looked at her, she shut the door.

"What do you think of her, Doc?"

I said, "Unconventional."

Milo said, "Not for L.A. Yeah, she's an odd one but I don't see an indication she had anything to do with it. And she doesn't seem to actually know much."

Alicia said, "It was pretty much dead-ending until you brought up the dog, Doc."

Milo said, "Little growler hearing something four nights ago."

"Which fits with the mail piling up. So maybe we've got time of death."

A figure emerged from Martha Matthias's backyard and hurried toward us.

Tom Blessingame holding up an index finger.

Milo said, "Got something?"

"Just the opposite. After taking a careful look we decided not to touch it. Too much risk without a pathologist on-scene. So we called for one and Dr. Lopatinski's coming over."

"Beautiful."

Blessingame looked confused.

"She's the best, Tom."

"Oh. Good."

"What's her ETA?"

"Didn't ask."

Blessingame returned to the rear of the house and Milo speed-dialed.

"Hi, Basia," he said. "Yeah, just found out . . . appreciate it . . . any idea when . . . great, see you then, bye."

He clicked off. "Fifteen to twenty. She was at the U. lecturing."

"Awesome," said Alicia. "Basia rocks."

"She's also meticulous, meaning her evaluation's gonna take time. Where are the techies?"

"Last I checked, on their way."

"Why don't you get the victim's warrant so it'll be in place when they arrive. Then see if Moe and Sean can help us scavenge."

"Us? You're going to participate?"

Milo grinned. "Man of the people. And you kids are my people."

Alicia grinned back, produced her own phone, and stepped a few feet away.

I said, "What a dad."

He said, "Closest I'm gonna come to parenting."

A shouted "Sirs!" from the south swiveled us.

Katherine Santos jogged our way with the easy stride of a practiced runner. No heavy breathing but flush-faced.

Excitement.

"Got something, sir," she said. "A neighbor says the victim has a daughter who's a 5150."

LAPD code for a mentally ill person eligible for a seventy-two-hour involuntary hold. The criterion: danger to self or others.

Milo said, "She's caused problems?"

"Don't know about that, sir," said Santos. "I just meant she sounds pretty crazy."

"Thanks. Where's this neighbor?"

"Across the street, two down, the yellow one."

"Name?"

"Hawkins. Mister."

"Excellent, Officer. Keep going."

Santos returned to the canvass and Alicia came over. "Warrant in the works. What was that all about?"

Milo told her.

She said, "A crazy person. That would fit with cutting Mommy's arms off and deep-freezing her. The yellow house, huh?"

"Let's go."

Lionel Hawkins was eighty or so, Black, short and stocky and white-haired and dressed in a starched blue shirt, pleated khakis, and shiny black oxfords. From the decorations on his wall, a man with dual devotions: the marines and the Dodgers.

Evidence of the former included a *Semper Fi* banner, stock shots of Iwo Jima and attack helicopters, and a photo of a young man in full dress. From the picture's faded pigment, probably Hawkins himself, but maybe a son.

No food prep on his coffee table, no theatrics to his dress or décor. A well-kept, unassuming house with a vague aroma of tomato soup filtering from the kitchen.

Milo made the introductions.

Hawkins said, "I figured you'd be here once I told that lady officer. Don't know what I can add, though."

Both Milo and Alicia had their pads and pens at the ready.

Milo said, "No problem, sir, but if you don't mind repeating?"

"Sure, but there isn't much to tell," said Hawkins. "Basically what I said was I haven't seen her a lot but there's this strange-type gal who sometimes visited her. I'm assuming a daughter because the age is right, about fifty, same as my two sons."

"Strange, how?"

"Weird. Walks stiff, doesn't look at you. Once I said hi, and she didn't answer. Like in her own world, you know? And she always goes over to— Don't know her name, your victim."

Alicia said, "Martha Matthias."

"Martha Matthias," said Lionel Hawkins. "All these years and I never knew that."

Milo said, "How long have you been living here?"

"Ten years after I retired from the corps, which makes it eighteen years ago. She was already living here. Martha Matthias. Okay."

"How did the woman we're assuming is the daughter act?"

"She didn't," said Hawkins. "Just walked. Like you didn't exist. Like she'd walk right through you. Her body posture was all wound up—knees, head bunched up."

He demonstrated.

Alicia said, "How was she dressed?"

"A dress," said Hawkins. "I think. Don't ask me colors. Not a pretty dress. A dress, that's all I recall. Didn't see her much. Either of them for that matter."

"You figured this person was mentally ill."

"Trust me, so would you if you saw her," said Hawkins. "I mean you don't need to be a psychiatrist."

"Did she look homeless?"

"Was she dirty? No, can't say that. Just weird. But maybe—and *they're* all nuts. I don't truck with that woke stuff about un-homed or whatever they're calling it nowadays. They're nuts plain and simple."

A pained expression took hold of his face. He touched a cheek hard. As if he'd been clawed without warning.

"I've got a nephew like that. Drives my sister and brother-in-law crazy." Feeble smile. "So to speak."

Milo said, "So this woman . . ."

"That's all of it," said Lionel Hawkins.

"How many times have you seen her at Martha's?"

"Actually there? Couldn't tell you. Not often. Mostly I see her coming and going. Once in a while I happened to see her go in."

"What time of day?"

"Normal time," said Hawkins. "Daylight. Never paid attention."

"Not at night?"

"I wouldn't know if it was. Go to sleep at nine and get up at six to do my push-ups."

"When's the last time you saw her?"

"Not for a while," said Hawkins.

"Weeks?"

"Maybe. Can't say. Could be a month."

"Nothing more recent."

"All these questions, she the one who did it?"

"We're not even close to that, sir," said Alicia. "In fact, this is the first we've heard of her."

Lionel Hawkins said, "Well, I can't be the only one who noticed her, someone crazy like that. The way she walked was enough to figure it out."

"Figure what out, Mr. Hawkins?"

"Stiff, not normal, the brain all scrambled up. Maybe on drugs, too."

He made a churning motion.

Alicia said, "When you did see her enter Ms. Matthias's house, was it through the front door?"

"Nope, always the back. And that's all I can tell you."

"Thank you, sir."

"Now *I've* got a question for *you.* Do I need to be keeping my .38 at the ready?"

"There's no sign anyone's in danger," said Milo. "I'd just continue normal precautions."

"Normal," said Hawkins. "Too bad she wasn't. Neither of them, actually."

"She and Ms. Matthias."

"I never saw her much, either. Which is kind of a symptom, right? Being a hermit? Shutting yourself in? The one time I tried to be friendly—shortly after I moved in—I'm taking out the garbage and see her doing the same. I wave and shout out hello. She ignores me. At first I'm thinking it's, you know, my complexion, welcome to the neighborhood. Then I thought, Hey, all the other neighbors are pretty friendly so she's either a racist or weird. Then when I saw how she lived I moved closer to weird. *Then* I saw the daughter and said, You got that right, Lionel. Making a kid like that, she'd have to be weird."

We returned to the sidewalk in front of Martha Matthias's house.

Alicia said, "Interesting."

Milo said, "When I get back I'll get hold of Martha's retirement docs and see if any dependents show up."

"Dependent as in heir, L.T.? Oldest motive in the books."

A silver Jaguar XE approached the cordon. A uniform went over and talked to the driver, allowed the car to nose in next to Alicia's unmarked.

A petite woman with short blond hair got out and retrieved a good-sized roller bag from the rear. She had on a maroon knit dress and yellow pumps, smiled and waved at us. Wide smile enhanced by perfect teeth. On to a new adventure. Dr. Basia Lopatinski's default approach to life.

When she got to us, Milo said, "Different one, Basia."

"My guys told me." Pleasant lilt to her voice. Faint Polish accent.

"Will you be able to determine TOD?"

"No way to tell without examining her, I'm talking down to the cellular level. Even with that it could be tough. If she was frozen shortly after death there's likely no decomp or insect visitation and rigor's certainly not going to be a factor."

"Ah."

Basia reached up and patted his shoulder. "All is not lost, Milo. One positive aspect of a frozen body is cause of death is likely to be well preserved. Same for identifying factors though I understand that's not an issue here. And there are other variables that could possibly tell us something. For example, if she was thawed and refrozen, there'll likely be ruptured blood cells. That's what I meant by cellular. And of course, the arms. We'll do tool-mark analysis and try to get you logical possibilities."

"We've got a possible TOD of around four days."

"How so?"

He told her about the barking dog.

She looked unconvinced. "Well, we'll see."

Running her hands over her dress, she tapped the roller bag. "Time for impermeable and disposable. So much for fashion."

CHAPTER

6

Time stretched.

Milo and Alicia grew antsy but when he said, "Gotta let Basia do her thing," she nodded and returned to her phone. Confirming the victim's warrant and the availability of Detectives Moses Reed and Sean Binchy for the toss of the house.

Milo said, "Good, tell them to head over."

His phone-work had been less productive. Trying to access Martha Matthias's retirement papers and coming up against multiple-choice voicemail at human resources that ended nowhere.

He growled. "Don't these bastards ever work?" Glanced toward the house, like a kid wondering whether to broach the cookie jar. Tapping his foot, he walked a few feet away and paced for a while. Had just returned when two crime scene techs arrived.

Alicia told them to hold off until the pathologist was through.

One of them said, "Pathologist? Must be a juicy one." Unperturbed, they returned to their van, phones out, fingers clicking.

Milo returned, left, paced some more. Alicia looked grim.

The waiting game. Crime Scene 101.

Twenty minutes in, information began to trickle in from the canvass. Three other neighbors had noticed the staggering woman on their block but none had paid her much attention or had linked her to Martha Matthias.

The common belief: The homeless were everywhere, city government was useless, ignore the mess.

Closed-circuit cameras were located on eight homes over a two-block stretch. Five were focused narrowly on entrances and failed to cover the street, one was a dummy, and two were inoperative due to computer glitches.

Just as that had settled in, Gloria Mendez came out and said, "Want to take a look?"

I followed Milo and Alicia toward the rear of the house, wondering if what I was about to see would stay with me. Sometimes terrible stuff does, etching mental pictures in my brain that come back from time to time during unexpected moments. Sometimes, though, the pictures don't register. I haven't found any correlation to anything and I'm not sure what the inconsistency says about me.

Nor do I care. Introspection's the enemy of getting the job done.

When Milo and Alicia saw the body, they winced simultaneously.

Removed from its plastic sheath and laid out on a white forensic tarp, Martha Matthias's corpse was small and shriveled and beyond sad, with long but wispy white hair fuzzing the peripheries of her sunken face and trailing to frail, bony shoulders. At first glance, looking considerably older than seventy-two, but death was a sadistic stylist.

Her eyes had frozen to vacant dark disks. Pale-pink liquid seeped beneath her and had begun to pool in the upturned corners of the tarp created by the C.I.'s.

This one probably would stay with me.

Especially the arms, lying to the left on a smaller tarp.

Cut cleanly, still frozen into L-shapes.

Basia, white-garbed, hooded, gloved, and bootied, said, "We have to thaw her anyway, might as well start early. Obviously the arms are the only disarticulated limbs. And they were staged on top of her. It's the first time I've seen that, generally dismemberment focuses on disposal of hands and head in order to obscure identification. This is strange."

She looked at me.

I shook my head.

"Well," she said, "it certainly seems psychopathologic to me. Some kind of message, maybe the arms have special meaning to this maniac. In terms of clinical guesswork, there's no apparent evidence she's been thawed and refrozen but I can't say for certain until I examine her blood vessels. In terms of the instrument used to sever the arms, I'm going to wait until my tool-mark guy weighs in to give you an educated guess but I see small serrations."

Alicia had been looking away. Now she forced herself back to the arms. "A saw?"

"Most likely," said Basia. "But nothing with big teeth—not a chain saw or a circular saw or even a band saw. All of those would inflict a lot more ripping damage."

Milo said, "A jigsaw?"

Basia considered that. "Something along those lines. Have you found anything like that in the house?"

"We haven't tossed the house yet," he said.

"So no definitive death scene." She looked back at the garage. "It certainly wasn't here."

"We're assuming it's in there but who knows?"

Alicia said, "We just got the victim's warrant, will get started once we're out of your way. It could take time, the interior's crammed just like the garage."

"A hoarder," said Basia. "Do we know anything else about this poor woman?"

Milo looked at Alicia. Alicia nodded.

He told Basia.

It takes a lot to shake her. She blinked, stared at the body, shook her head, blinked some more. "A detective. Wow. She must've deteriorated mentally. How old is she? I'd guess at least eighty."

Alicia said, "Seventy-two."

"Rapid aging could be consistent with dementia," said Basia. "Which isn't to say there aren't plenty of fully functioning people that age or older . . . a detective. Oh my. Did either of you know her?"

Milo raised a finger.

When he didn't add more, Basia said, "Well, enough of my questions, it's answers you want from me."

Her Apple watch beeped a text. "Drivers are here, let's get her to our place."

A pair of burly crypt attendants marched forward with a gurney. One of them looked unimpressed by what he saw. The other stared wide-eyed and openmouthed before a nudge by his partner blanked his expression.

As they carted away the remains of Martha Matthias, Milo eyed her house's rear door. "Time to get in there. Sorry, Alex, this one's too complicated, I'll have a uniform take you home."

I said, "I'll see if Robin's free to pick me up, save your troops for the canvass."

Robin answered after one ring. "Of course, baby. He's protecting you? Must be bad."

"It's different."

"That terrible word," she said. "Well, at least your karma's good on a small scale. I was just leaving House of Hardwood so I can be there in ten."

"Great, thanks."

"Can't remember the last time I drove you anywhere," she said. "Guess *different* has spread its wings."

I waited at the northern perimeter of the yellow tape, a block up from the murder house. Robin's truck pulled up nine minutes later. Gorgeous woman behind the wheel of a starkly utilitarian vehicle, her auburn curls loose.

The truck's bed was empty. Unproductive search for exotic wood?

Then I saw the bag on the passenger seat, next to Blanche. I lifted and deposited both in my lap, leaned over and kissed Robin. The bag rattled. Inside were small, dark rectangles.

She said, "Ebony and rosewood leftovers, perfect for bridge blanks. They call me when they have stuff no one else can use."

"Good karma for both of us."

She eyed the squad cars. "As opposed to whatever happened here."

I kneaded Blanche's neck as Robin drove.

A few minutes in, she said, "Is it something you feel like talking about?"

I gave her basics.

She said, "A cop he knew. That's got to be tough for Big Guy. Not to mention the rest of it." She shuddered. "It does sound like the work of a crazy person so maybe that daughter or whoever she is will be the one and he'll wrap it up quickly."

I said, "Hopefully."

I thought: *Even so, the relief will be short-lived. There's still Sophie Barlow, a quick solve that's turned into anything but.*

A mile later, Robin said, "After seeing that, don't imagine you want to talk dinner."

I said, "I'm pretty hungry. What're you in the mood for?"

She shot me a quick sidelong glance.

Been with this guy for years and he still surprises me.

She said, "Sushi."

CHAPTER 7

It took a couple of days for Milo to call me.

"You have any time to come by? If not, I'll go to yours."

I'd just finished a morning consult. Acidic custody case. It's rare for me to have aggressively warring parents in the office together but these two had claimed they'd "raised their consciousness" and really wanted to work things out. That hadn't ended up well.

I said, "I can be there in thirty."

"I'm not going anywhere."

Milo's workspace is a windowless closet one floor above the big detective room.

That and his ability to work cases as a lieutenant had been negotiated with a corrupt police chief about whom Milo had damaging information. The chief, nearing retirement, assumed the pathetic allotment would drive a pariah to quit. Soon after, the chief was dead of a heart attack on the fifth hole of a Rancho Mirage golf course.

Milo continues to enjoy the solitude as he closes murders.

When I got there the door was open. He scowled, grunted, and hoisted his bulk from his desk chair, waited until I'd settled before sinking back down and making the chair cry.

I'd squeezed into my usual spot. The only spot, really, and not much of that: a hard chair in a corner behind the desk. If Milo wheeled back carelessly, I'd be the one to get dented.

He tapped a blue binder but kept it closed. Rotating slowly, he faced me.

"Okay, first off, the prelim autopsy, Basia's not sure when the final will come through. Probable cause of death: strangulation, no ligature marks so maybe manual, but with the freezing, no way to be sure. Basia said it wouldn'ta taken much force, Martha's hyoid and what was left of her thyroid cartilage basically crumbled. Overall condition of the body was malnourished and fragile. Basia also doesn't see any signs of thawing and refreezing so our working guess on TOD is reasonable. Apart from the dog barking and the mail at the door, it fits with last time Martha was seen away from her house."

I said, "A week ago."

"Six, seven days," he said. "Four days before she was found, that discount grocery place. No video there but they remembered her as a nice old lady who kept to herself and bought mostly frozen food. I'm still waiting for her financials and her phone-dump to come through. Phone as in landline, no mobile account."

He turned back to the desk, opened the blue murder book, flipped a page but paid it scant attention.

"The crime scene," he said, "is likely the bathroom. There's only one in the house. It had been cleaned up but there were minute blood specks on the wall above the tub and around the drain. Luminol picked up splotches in the tub itself and a whole lot more was found down the drain. Basia's tool guy can't be sure what was used to remove the arms but something like a jigsaw would fit. No tools in the house but if we ever find something, we can do a wound match."

I said, "Using a pig carcass."

"How do you know that?"

"You told me years ago."

"I did? What case?"

"No case. You were getting philosophical—pigs and humans, Orwell—"

He'd colored around his jowls. "I do that a lot, huh?"

"I find it educational," I said. "Seeing as Martha paid cash, did you come across any money in the house?"

"Funny you should ask, that was my next revelation. Yeah, Alicia found a big manila envelope with a little over five thousand in hundreds and fifties stashed between some old newspapers in the bedroom. Martha's pension was just short of four a month and she got another twelve hundred from Social Security so looks like she kept around a month's worth on hand."

"Makes sense if you pay in cash. Nothing else?"

"Place is such a mess it'll take a while to go through. There was a cigar box with some jewelry in a box under her bed. Looked like costume junk to me but Darlene will check at the lab. Her TV was an old thirty-incher still attached to a roof aerial. Not even basic cable, just local stations, and there doesn't seem to have been a computer, anywhere. It's like she was living in the past, Alex."

I said, "Maybe she'd freeze-framed."

"To what?"

"A happier time."

He thought about that. "When I knew her she always looked okay. Not super talkative but quietly pleasant. But who knows, she mighta been living weird even back then and keeping it to herself."

"Do you recall any friends at the department?"

"Nope." Crooked smile. "Maybe that's why she talked to me. Pair of outcasts."

"Any reason for her to be an outcast?"

"Other than being female, not that I knew," he said. "And honestly, Alex, she was treated well by the other D's. Respected for her work but I guess it didn't translate to socializing." The smile widened. "It happens."

I said, "Your finding no other money doesn't mean someone else didn't."

"The killer scored buried treasure? I guess it's possible but you'd really have to know where to look or take a long time rooting around. We'd been in there half a day before the envelope showed up."

"Not the usual toss."

He shook his head. "Godawful. Junk piled high, mouse droppings, mildew, dust you could finger-paint in. The mouse stuff got us nervous. Hantavirus or some other creepy-crawly. Once we saw it, we left and called for hazmat masks, which delayed everything another coupla hours."

I said, "Martha was able to live with it."

"Crazy, huh? Maybe she'd built up immunity. Or was damn lucky. Alicia was right. It's a miracle nothing toppled over on her."

I said, "Someone familiar with the house could've had an easier time finding buried treasure."

"The daughter—or whoever the woman who visited her was," he said. "Yeah, she's who we're concentrating on. I'm betting she *is* a daughter because I finally accessed Martha's retirement forms and there's a single dependent listed. Lynne Matthias, forty-six, which would fit age-wise. No address listed but no criminal record shows up. You're thinking a family reunion that went bad?"

I said, "Happens all the time. The woman was seen going toward the back of Martha's house. Any indication she ever stayed for a stretch of time?"

"Next to the bed there was a rolled-up futon."

"Any sign of recent usage?"

"Nope, dusty but not caked on, so maybe occasional usage."

"Mother and daughter bunking in together," I said.

"Then it goes *really* bad," he said. "Gotta find this woman."

I sat there as he logged on to the DMV, then local crime files. He'd already searched for info on Lynne Matthias but data's always coming in and it doesn't hurt to be careful.

No payoff this time.

He checked out L.A. County death certificates and came up empty.

I said, "Maybe she got married and uses another surname."

"She's listed under Matthias in Martha's personnel file."

"That was a while back. She could've married after the file was set up. Or it was wishful thinking on Mom's part."

"Meaning?"

"She's still my kid."

"More like delusional," he said. "Then again, Martha lived in *that* place."

He tried marriage records. Several Matthiases had attempted wedded bliss but no Lynne.

But Martha showed up twice.

Fifty-one years ago, Martha Joline Anderson, twenty-one, had married Pablo Gutierrez, twenty-two, at a Catholic church in Saugus. Five years later, just turned twenty-six, she'd been wedded to Richard Lee Matthias, thirty-three, at the L.A. county courthouse.

No notice of dissolution. Back to the death files where one showed up for Pablo Gutierrez. Four years after marrying Martha, he'd perished in an industrial accident at a construction site in Vernon. A year later, she'd wed Matthias.

I said, "Traditional church wedding, then widowed at twenty-five. Was she a cop by then?"

He checked. "Yup, still a rookie."

"Richard's the uniform you were talking about. She likely met him on the job, married him shortly after Gutierrez died."

"A precinct affair? Makes sense."

"When did Matthias die?"

"By the time I knew her, he was gone, hold on." He typed fast. "Here we go, *TBL* obituary. Twenty-two years ago, age fifty-seven, cardiac disease."

Thin Blue Line, the Police Protective League's magazine. Members-only access.

I said, "Martha was only fifty when she was widowed for the second time. Maybe that's when her life began to change."

"Fine, she got stressed and kept it to herself. But why would she change in *that* way?"

"You know what I'm going to say."

"Yeah, yeah, human beings are complicated. But be a pal and throw out a theory, any theory."

I said, "Any kind of obsessive behavior is an attempt to reduce anxiety. Martha may have had a tendency that ballooned under stress. The other possibility is some sort of early dementia was settling in and she realized it. That might explain the transfer out of Homicide."

"Wanting to deal with the small stuff," he said. "Well, if she was slipping, I sure didn't notice. And same question: Why change in that way, specifically?"

"We're pals, Big Guy, but that doesn't change things."

"Yeah, yeah, no way to predict how any individual is going to react." He shut his eyes. Rubbed his face like washing without water. When the green irises reappeared, they were fixed in a forever-stare.

"People," he said. "We're basically bags of question marks."

Opening a desk drawer, he removed another blue binder, opened it to the center, and handed it over.

"Long as we're talking ignorance, check this out."

White label on the front cover. *Barlow, Sophie,* followed by a case number.

He'd earmarked two pages of crime scene photos, all variations on a theme.

A woman sitting at a kitchen table. Smallish, beige table in a smallish, beige kitchen. Matching chair with a blue upholstered back. Slender brunette, wearing a white, ribbed tank top. Her right arm was clear, her left brocaded shoulder-to-wrist by a jungle of floral tattoos.

Pale complexion but no way to know what her skin had looked like in life.

Her head had been tilted back offering a full view of a long, graceful neck, ringed by angry pink deepening to coral red in spots.

The positioning also exposed her nostrils and a mouth slightly ajar that flashed a ribbon of white teeth. Dark hair was long and wavy. A rear shot showed it streaming over the back of the chair like a shower of sooty icicles.

On the table before her was a red plastic bowl. A directional arrow had been drawn in white, focusing attention on the bowl's contents. Two cigarette butts. White paper, brown filter.

I said, "Just as you described."

"For what that's worth."

Turning back to his desk, he busied himself with his keyboard. Wanting some sort of wisdom from me.

I said, "Tell me about her."

"Thirty-eight years old, originally from Tulsa, widowed ten years ago, moved here, worked as an office manager at a real estate firm in Encino."

"Any kids?"

"Nope."

"Any love interests besides Heck?"

"Excellent question, no idea." He swiveled around. "Gotta start doing some serious digging on her. Was about to when Alicia called about Martha."

"Dual priorities."

"Two whodunits," he said. "What deity have I offended?"

CHAPTER 8

Despite Milo's taste for isolation, there are times when the tiny office gets to him.

He shot upright without warning, said, "Walk?" and left before I could answer.

I followed him into the corridor and down the stairs. We exited the station and headed south, avoiding the businesses and traffic on Santa Monica Boulevard and entering a residential stretch of modest houses.

Bungalows, stucco cubes, mini Spanish Revivals. Not much different from the neighborhood where Martha Matthias had lost her life.

I said, "In terms of Sophie, Tulsa can be a tough town."

"I know, meth," he said.

"Maybe she left for more than the weather. Knew the wrong people back home, tried to distance herself but it caught up with her."

"You see some vengeful speed-cooking freak taking the time to set up Heck with his own DNA? Those types break in, smash, slice and dice. And if she did hang with a bad Tulsa crowd, it never got her into any trouble I can find. Same for her ex. Firefighter, solid citizen, coupla citations for bravery. Killed in a car crash."

"On the job?"

"Nope, wrong place, wrong time. Driving home from a convenience store and a wrong-way drunk got him on the highway."

"You've talked to Sophie's family."

He nodded, jammed both hands into trouser pockets, and leaned into a nonexistent wind.

"Not much family, just a sister in Tulsa and a brother in Boise. He knew nothing about Sophie's personal life but the sister suspected Heck because she met him once and didn't like him. Too slick." He laughed. "Her exact term was 'too darned L.A.' "

I said, "Another mark against him at the outset."

"Yup. And I wasn't interested in being dissuaded."

Half a block later, he said: "If it was only about Heck's alibi, I'd still be on him because what's to say he didn't hire someone? But with the planted cigarettes, it just feels like someone tried to set him up. I know he could be pulling a double bluff like you said, Alex, but getting yourself booked into County for two days smells more like screenplay than reality. Place is ganged up the wazz, once he was in there was no telling what could've happened."

I said, "Nothing interesting in his finances and his phone?"

"Nope. Bless me, Father, for I have sinned."

"What's the transgression?"

"Never saw his records because with the DNA handed to me I was concentrating on getting him locked up and didn't jump on the warrants as quickly as I shoulda. Then all of a sudden he's cleared and I lack grounds."

"Have you spoken to Heck since he was freed?"

He stopped and looked at me. "I put this guy in jail for murder and he's gonna help me?"

"Probably not," I said, "but there's an off chance he might want to come across helpful."

"Why?"

"If he's clean, he might actually care. If he's dirty, nobility would be a great façade. Either way, he was Sophie's ex and could know something relevant."

"Sorry, I don't see it."

He resumed walking, picking up speed. Then halted again and looked down at his pocket. Tweed pulsated. As if a small animal had been caught there.

Out came the phone. "Hi, Basia . . . that was quick, *jenkooyeh* . . . okay . . . got it . . . sure . . . well, we can't always be surprised."

He clicked off.

I said, "Polish for thank you?"

"Close as I can get to pronouncing it, the actual word has all these Z's and J's. Saint that she is, Basia came through and prioritized the autopsy. COD is strangulation, amputation was postmortem. TOD can't be fixed beyond a week or less and the tool-mark guy kept working and confirmed a coping saw, a jigsaw, or something similar. Probably not a jeweler's saw, the teeth appear to be a bit larger but nothing he'd testify to. We're waiting on the tox screen but preliminary bloods show nothing."

He stared at the phone. "Welcome to the circus as I juggle two balls and drop both of them."

Half a block later, he sighed and scrolled to a preset number. "Okay, Mr. Heck, let's see if you're noble."

Six rings were followed by a resonant baritone. Salesman's voice.

"This is Mike *Heck,* sorry I'm not *free* at the moment but I *do* want to hear what you have to *say. Really.* So *please* communicate."

Milo said, "Mike, this is Milo Sturgis. I'm probably the last guy you want to talk to, but any help you could give me on Sophie's murder would be deeply appreciated. That's straight talk, not an attempt to hassle you."

Click.

"Okay?" he said, sounding peeved.

Like a kid with no talent forced to practice violin.

I kept my mouth shut as we headed back for the station.

Rather than unlock his office door, he stood in the corridor. "No reason to keep you while I do grunt work on Sophie. Maybe Martha, too, if Alicia needs me for something."

I said, "Call if something comes up."

"Don't I always?"

As I turned to leave, he said, "What's that brain skill you're always talking about—being able to organize a bunch of stuff effectively?"

"Executive function."

"Can you get there from gofer function?"

More activity beneath the tweed, this time macerated Mozart.

He produced the phone, checked the number on the screen, grimaced, and switched to speaker.

"Hi, Bettina."

A woman's voice, tight, slightly nasal, said, "When did we get on first-name basis?"

"Hi, Ms. Bel Geddes."

"Whatever. Michael has just informed me of your call. Are you serious?"

"I explained—"

"Unbelievable," said Bettina Bel Geddes. "You trump up charges against my client, subject him to the horrors of incarceration, and now you expect him to help you?"

Milo said, "We're not in court, Counselor. No need to orate."

"*That,*" said Bettina Bel Geddes, "was downright rude."

"You're right, sorry," he said, rolling his eyes. "The thing is, I'm still trying to find out who strangled Sophie Barlow to death and seeing as your client was so adamant about being close to her once upon a time *and* about harboring nothing but good feelings toward her, I figured he might want to help. But up to you."

"It's up to Michael."

"Of course. And I can certainly understand him refusing. On the other hand, seeing as he feels he was framed, he might want to find out who did that to him."

"He doesn't *feel* he was framed, he was," said Bel Geddes.

"Even more to the point."

A few seconds of dead air, then "I don't like the tone of this, Mr. Sturgis, and to be frank, I don't trust you."

"Got it," said Milo. "Sorry for bothering you and your client."

"That said, I'm going to have a serious discussion with Michael because that's what we're about: the pursuit of truth."

A second eye-roll was followed by spinning an index finger in circles. "Thanks very much."

"Don't thank me until there's a reason for gratitude."

Click.

Milo looked at his closed door as if it were impenetrable. "I'll walk you to your car. Fresh air. And maybe that bakery—the Italian place—has humble pie."

We took the stairs back down and were outside the station when Bettina Bel Geddes called back.

"Counselor—"

"I know what I am. Here's the deal: Michael will meet with you under controlled circumstances. Meaning I will be there and so will Michael's therapist in order to ensure that Michael's mental health will be protected during what could turn out to be a duplicitous renewal of the trauma of false arrest and imprisonment."

"No problem," said Milo. "Who's the therapist?"

"A noted clinical psychologist named Dr. Wendy Allemande."

He looked at me. I grinned and gave a thumbs-up.

He said, "That's absolutely fine. In fact, I'd planned to have our consulting psychologist present."

"Who's that and why?"

"Dr. Alex Delaware and for the same reason. We do not want Mr. Heck subjected to any more trauma."

"That," said Bettina Bel Geddes, "sounds like utter bullshit."

"How about this, Counselor. Ask Dr. Allemande about Dr. Delaware. If she has bad things to say, he won't be here."

"I don't know, Mr. Sturgis, this whole thing is bizarre. You wanting to rake it up again."

"Just seeking the truth," said Milo.

"Sure you are, just like the first time," said Bettina Bel Geddes.

"Well, let's hope you've got a better grip on the concept. I'll conduct my due diligence and inform you of my decision."

The moment the connection was broken, he said, "Forget pie, I could use Prilosec. So you like this Allemande."

I said, "Smart, ethical, and a former student."

"You're kidding."

"Supervised her when she was a fourth-year grad student."

His turn to grin. "Small world when it comes to shrinks. You buy that crap about safeguarding Heck's mental health?"

"Not a chance," I said.

"What then?"

"My bet is Bel Geddes is working up a civil suit for wrongful arrest and wants to document Heck's reactions to further police contact."

"Building up a case for PTSD."

"And having her own expert there to document it."

"Okay," he said, "I'll be gentle as a cuddly lamb on tranqs. If I can have my expert there. Meaning it's probably not gonna happen."

But it did.

CHAPTER 9

Milo gave me the details that night at nine.

"As she charmingly put it, tomorrow at two, take it or leave it."

"Her office."

"Surprisingly no, a private room at Chelsea Club. Ever been there?"

"Couple of years ago."

"How'd that happen?"

"Can't say."

"Got it, some hoohah-patient. Some life you lead. Rick was offered a membership but turned it down. Anyway, are you free at two?"

"I am."

"Great. Don't need to give you the address."

The West Hollywood branch of the Chelsea Club chain sits on top of a twenty-story building on Sunset just past the point where the lick-the-sidewalk cleanliness of Beverly Hills gives way to the civic neglect of the Strip.

The clubs are hyped as invitation-only lairs for the young, talented, and fabulous. In reality, invitations are generated by member recommendations, and ability to pay is the main qualification.

Milo's assumption about a patient inviting me there was wrong. My dinner host had been a young, newly appointed family court judge who appreciated my assistance in helping her maneuver a big-ticket film-biz divorce. She'd brought her boyfriend and I'd brought Robin. Technically, I could've talked about it, but I keep my work in the "other" world buttoned up.

Robin and I had gone there expecting a dim, luxe, exclusive vibe heavy on décor, possibly soured by a snooty front desk. Wrong on all counts. The hosts were young and bland, the ambience bright and architecturally undistinguished.

The main room was a vast space surrounded by glass. Despite the sweeping dimensions, the place was crowded and noisy, mostly occupied by twenty- and thirty-somethings in designer leisure-wear perched at cocktail tables or sprawled on long couches.

Meager conversation as nimble fingers played laptops. The noise came from piped-in music. Soft-sell hip-hop, the type parents didn't mind.

As we neared our table, Robin said, "College dorm for the privileged. But the view's amazing."

I arrived five minutes early on Thursday for the meeting with Bel Geddes and Heck, found parking on a nearby side street, and entered the black glass structure. A sleepy-looking security guard passed me through to the direct Penthouse Elevator after a two-second look-over.

A quick, silent ascent deposited me into the massive room. In daylight, astonishing view on three sides. The same tables, chairs, couches, and several bars, one staffed by a guy washing glasses. The only other people were two men in maintenance uniforms operating humming carpet sweepers and a young woman sitting several feet behind the host lectern, captivated by her phone.

Chelsea's hours were generous: nine a.m. to midnight. But at two p.m. the lunch crowd was gone and the cavernous space had the bereft look of abandonment.

The hostess saw me, scrolled a bit more, then got off her phone and walked to her station wearing a programmed smile. Young, lovely, perfect body. I wondered how many auditions she'd been on recently.

I told her why I was there.

She said, "Yes, Alex, that's in the Thames Room. You're the second to get here, I'll take you."

"Taking" meant walking me halfway and pointing to a door.

I opened it on Milo, sitting on the left side of a pale-wood, surfboard-shaped conference table and listening to his phone.

Plain-wrap meeting place, maybe fifteen by fifteen, with white walls and bland nature photo-posters mounted on each of the four walls.

No view here. Windowless.

I sat down next to Milo. He listened for a few more seconds, said, "Thanks," and put the phone down.

"Anything interesting?"

"Alicia's back at Martha's going through the rubble again. She found some more money but nothing huge. Coupla hundred. The fact that Martha hid it all around is interesting."

I said, "Maybe there was a bigger stash that the bad guy took."

He nodded and waved a hand around the room. "Glamorous, huh? Think Bel Geddes is trying to tell me something? Panoramas are for the good guys, you get stuck in a closet."

"Big closet." *Especially for you.*

"Funny thing," he said, "it actually was a closet back when Delaney owned the building and this was his penthouse. Maybe he kept his shoes here."

"You knew Delaney?"

"Knew of him," he said. "Unsubstantiated rumors."

"Nasty stuff?"

"Financial stuff." He waved a hand dismissively.

The door opened and the hostess ushered three people in. They'd merited a complete escort.

Dr. Wendy Allemande didn't lead the pack but your eyes go to who you recognize and she looked exactly as she had when I'd seen her at a faculty meeting last year. Five-five, late thirties, pretty and zaftig, with curly brown hair and an open, lightly freckled face. In the classroom, she went for jeans and simple tops. Today she was dressed for the courtroom in a charcoal pantsuit, a white silk shirt with a ruffled front, and gray suede shoes with two-inch heels.

Our eyes met. She shot me a quick smile tinged with anxiety. Not unlike the look she'd given me when I served on her doctoral committee and she was about to take her orals.

Just behind her was Michael Heck. Five-ten, thickset and powerfully built, with a deep tan not suggested by his DMV photo. He wore an unstructured tweed sport coat over a nutmeg-colored T-shirt, black skinny jeans, brown Nikes. His eyes avoided us as he followed Wendy and the leader of the pack.

Bettina Bel Geddes's strut was fashioned to let the world know she was in charge. Ditto for her jewelry: diamond earrings, gold bangles, a serious diamond ring on her left hand. Five-foot-five or so in bright-yellow sandals with four-inch heels, she was a green-eyed redhead and had pushed that fact with a cardinal-red skirt suit. The skirt ended six inches above her knees. A lot of women have stopped wearing stockings but Bel Geddes had opted for black hose nubbed by tiny red roses.

Her face was smooth with the calculated beauty of an anchorwoman. The eyes were sea-green, nothing like Milo's traffic lights. Perfectly mascaraed, with a penchant for flashing that she employed as she studied me. Raising her eyebrows, she shook her head and sat down at the head of the table.

"If you're Delaware, there's no need for introductions."

I smiled.

Bettina Bel Geddes said, "Okay, then let's get going," and drew a tiny tape recorder out of her purse. "I'll be recording these proceedings."

Milo produced a nearly identical recorder from his attaché case. "Great."

Bel Geddes said, "Hmm. I suppose I can't stop you. Though you could always just request a copy."

"Easier this way, Counselor."

"Hmm. All right, we proceed."

Click click of both recorders. Smooth duet, as if choreographed.

Bel Geddes said, "*Mister* Sturgis." Meaningful stare. "Before I allow you to question Michael I'm informing you of the ground rules. You will be respectful of Michael and nothing you broach will imply any sort of wrongdoing on Michael's part. We all know where *that* led. Abject failure to find the real killer and severe psychosocial ramifications for Michael."

She looked at Heck, frowned when he remained impassive, and turned to Wendy.

"A brief summary, please, Dr. Allemande."

Wendy glanced at me and licked her lips. "I'm still evaluating but the gist is that Michael has experienced some of the common sequelae of incarceration—"

"Needless incarceration," said Bettina Bel Geddes. "A brutal process based on incorrect assumptions."

She frowned again as Wendy said, "Basically, there have been problems with sleep and mood."

I nodded.

Heck began drumming his fingers on the table. Not comfortable with being described as a patient.

Bel Geddes said, "How *are* you sleeping, Michael?"

"Getting better."

"But not back to normal."

"It can get a little sketchy," said Heck.

Bel Geddes said, "In any event, we've documented post-traumatic symptoms."

"Not PTSD," said Heck. "When I was in the service I saw plenty of guys with that but I wasn't one of them. This is more like . . ."

Bel Geddes said, "The sequelae of injustice. Which is a form of PTSD, albeit different from what was observed while offering service."

Taking a moment to let that sink in.

No one reacted. Including Heck.

"All right then. It took an unwarranted incarceration based on utterly faulty assumptions to bring you to a place where you hadn't been before."

Heck sighed. "Whatever."

Knitting sculpted eyebrows, Bel Geddes turned to Wendy.

Wendy said, "That's about it."

"So far."

No reply.

The Queen of All Frowns took over Bel Geddes's face. Amazing what anger can do to beauty.

"Okay," she said, turning to us. "What is it you need to know from Mike?"

Milo said, "Whatever he thinks could help us."

Heck said, "Sure."

Milo said, "Great, Mike, and thanks a ton for doing this. I could understand if you didn't want to—"

Bel Geddes said, "Talk about an understatement."

Heck said, "I want to. I wanted to help right from the beginning because I care—cared about Sophie. We weren't a couple anymore. But we stayed friendly and I'd never do anything to hurt her."

Tears welled up in his eyes. Heck swiped them away with a sleeve. Angry at displaying emotion. No attempt to milk the situation.

I told myself: *Oscar winner or innocent.*

Milo might've been feeling the same thing, because now it was his turn to frown. He pasted on a smile. "Got it, Mike. Can you think of anyone who might hurt Sophie?"

"I mean," said Heck. "I guess you guys always look for someone close. Which makes sense. I guess. Unless it's one of those serial killers who prey on strangers."

Fixing his eyes on Milo.

"Mike, we're not even close to guessing. That's why you're here. And yes, we do look at the victim's inner circle. We had no idea you were in it until your DNA—"

Bel Geddes said, "Ancient history. Move on."

Milo said, "Mike, who else was in Sophie's inner circle?"

Heck, relieved not to be talking about himself, said, "When we were together, she had a couple of friends. Ashley was one, don't recall the other. Maybe something with an M. Don't know their last names."

As Milo copied, Bel Geddes huffed. "You don't even know her friends yet?"

Milo ignored her. "Do you have numbers for them, Mike?"

"Nope, sorry, it wasn't like that."

"Like—"

"Hanging out with them. I just met them a couple of times, both when Sophie and me were having drinks and they came in. Sophie told me they were her friends and they sat down and had drinks with us and I got to know them a little. Ashley's a flight attendant. For . . . Southwest, I think. The other—Maria, I'm pretty sure that's it, she does something in the industry."

Milo said, "Films and TV."

Bel Geddes huffed again. *Like there's another industry?*

Milo said, "Were they by themselves?"

"The first time, yeah," said Heck. "The second time they were with guys but I couldn't tell you their names because they just talked to us for a few minutes then went to their own table."

"Double date."

"Guess so."

Bettina Bel Geddes said, "This is drifting far from any content I can see as relevant."

Milo said, "Mike, how long had you and Sophie been apart when she died?"

"Month and a half," said Heck. "About."

"So fairly recently."

"Yeah, but that was the formal time. When we actually discussed it and decided to just be friends. But we both knew, it had been happening for a month or so before that."

"Drifting apart."

"Yeah," said Heck. "You know. You can like someone and you think maybe this is the one but then you realize the friend thing works better."

"Did you have contact with Sophie after you became just friends?"

"Nope," said Heck. "I mean on the phone, yeah, but after we had the talk I wasn't at her place and she wasn't in mine."

"How long did you guys date?"

Before Bel Geddes could interrupt, Heck said, "Couple of months."

"May I ask where you met?"

"Cocktail lounge at the Mayfair in Beverly Hills. That's where her friends showed up so it was probably a regular place for them. I just happened to be there for a business meeting. Then that was over and I stuck around to have a couple of beers."

"Got it," said Milo. "Are you aware of who Sophie dated before you? And after you broke up?"

Bel Geddes fidgeted with her hair. Itching to find an objection but unable to do so.

Wendy shot me another collegial smile. I smiled back.

"I know she was married before and that he died in a crash," said Michael Heck. "But that's about it. We never talked about exes and once we broke up we didn't stalk each other."

Milo said, "I'm asking because someone tried to set you up by getting hold of your cigarette butts and planting them."

"Yeah, it's crazy. Scary. No one ever broke into my place, sir. I've got an alarm and it was never tripped."

"I'm assuming you tossed your butts out with the rest of your trash. What's the garbage-collection situation at your condo?"

"You put your crap in a couple of dumpsters and some private service takes it away." He paled. "You're saying someone was spying on me and saw me dump my garbage? That's *fucked.*"

Milo said, "Another possibility would be you were smoking outside and left the butts on the sidewalk."

The color returned to Heck's face. More pink than before. Rose-colored highlights on bronze. "I guess I do that sometimes."

"Any particular place?"

"Work. I guess. You can't smoke in the office so you go outside. You think someone was spying on me *there*?"

"Don't know, Mike."

"Why would anyone want to fuck me over?"

"The million-dollar question, Mike. Do you have any theories?"

"No," said Heck. "That's the thing. Been racking my brains but I can't come up with anything. You think it could've been some new guy Sophie was seeing who got jealous? Because like I said, Sophie and me stayed friends and we called each other but I have no idea who she was dating."

"How often were the phone calls?"

"Every so often . . . maybe, couple a month? She was a really nice girl. You think some jealous asshole got hold of her phone and saw my number on it and traced it? That's so fucking *twisted.*"

"We'll check out every possibility, Mike."

Bel Geddes huffed.

Heck said, "Hope you do, man. This is freaking me out."

"Incarceration can do that to you," said Bel Geddes.

"That's not what I mean. The whole thing of spying on me when I had no idea." He turned to Milo. "You got me totally wrong, sir, but I can see it, you had DNA. But now that we know it was bullshit you need to find out who did it. To Sophie and to me, 'cause it's obviously the same person."

"We'll do our best," said Milo.

"The royal plural?" said Bel Geddes.

"Anything else you want to tell us, Mike?"

"Can't think of anything."

"If you do—"

"He'll notify *me* and I'll notify *you,*" said Bel Geddes.

Heck's lips tightened. Not happy being treated as a dependent.

"Okay, then," said Milo. "That's it. Thanks, Mike."

As he began to rise, Heck said, "There is one thing but it's probably nothing."

Bel Geddes gave a start. "We need to discuss anything substantive, Michael."

"It's no big deal."

"Michael—"

"I'm not a two-year-old."

His voice had taken on a hard edge that Bel Geddes didn't challenge. She looked chastened, even a bit frightened, and I wondered if the lawyerly aggression was a thin veneer.

Milo said, "We're listening, Mike."

Heck said, "You know what I do, right? My career."

"Administrator at a law firm."

"Exactly. I oversee the basics at Rifkin, Wolfram and Sapir, over in West L.A. Fifteen lawyers, little bit of everything. Before that, I worked for Spitz, DeMarzio, Duncan and Baggs in Century City, they did workman's comp."

He leaned forward. "But. Before those two, I worked for Darren Alberts."

Bel Geddes said, "Be careful, Mike," but her voice lacked conviction.

Heck said, "I am being careful. I did nothing wrong, why should I be ashamed to talk about it?"

"It's best, Mike, not to hand bait to a poacher."

"Huh?"

Bel Geddes contented herself with an eye-roll once Heck's back was turned.

Milo said, "Darren Alberts."

"Total dirtbag," said Heck. "But I guess you know that."

"What'd you do at Alberts's firm?"

"Just what I do anywhere. Organization, making sure files are in order and bills are paid promptly. Sometimes they throw in some marketing—contacting media. But not for Alberts, he did all that stuff himself. Loved the attention. I was there for three years and never gave what they were doing a thought. Then calls began coming in, then people started talking, you know? Once I smelled what was going on, I said and gave notice. Thank God it was just before."

"Before what, Mike?"

Bel Geddes said, "I think what Michael's alluding to is patently obvious—"

Heck said, "Before the whole thing went tits-up. Even with that, I was questioned by you guys. And I had no problem saying exactly what I knew. Which was zero—nothing. But you guys kept at me. But no big deal, when you're telling the truth, you're mellow."

Milo glanced at me.

I said, "What made you think about the Alberts firm with regard to Sophie?"

Bel Geddes's eyes widened.

Before she could speak, Heck said, "I really don't know. Just searching. Grasping at straws. Someone tried to ruin my life. So I guess I could see someone at Darren's possibly being pissed at me. Because A, I quit just before all the problems, and B, maybe they found out the police talked to me even though I had nothing to tell the police but thought I did."

Milo said, "Who, specifically, do you think might be pissed?"

"That's the thing, I really can't think of anyone. Darren ran that place differently from a normal firm. Basically he was the emperor and everyone else was like . . . his peasant. Or serf, whatever you want to call it. So normally, I'd say if it was anyone it would be Darren but he's senile. So that's what's confusing me."

"Any employees in particular we should be looking at?"

"Racked my brains and couldn't think of anyone."

"One-man show," said Milo. "But the little I know about Darren's case says some of the people doing the serious lifting might not have been office folk. Like the doctors he relied on."

Heck said, "Doubtful. Stuff like that would never be at a desk."

"You never saw any sketchy people come into the office?"

"Sure I did," said Heck. "What I assumed were the people Darren was representing. But I didn't pay attention— Oh man, should I be scared?"

"I can't tell you that, Mike, but seeing as someone tried to frame you, you might want to be careful."

"Oh shit," said Heck. "Here I am, wanting to put it out there because I really want to know who killed Sophie. And not gonna lie, I want to know why he set me up. But now I'm thinking it's not over." His cheeks puffed as he exhaled.

Bettina Bel Geddes said, "I'm assuming you're talking about criminal types, Michael."

"Why not, takes one to know one," said Heck. "Darren was a really bad guy so makes sense he'd hang with really bad guys. But I had no contact with them. Not ever."

He rubbed his brow, kneading the spot between his eyes until it pinkened. "You know, this has really got me thinking. I'm going to get the hell out of Dodge. At least until you can tell me something that makes me feel better, Lieutenant."

Milo said, "Whatever you need to feel safe, Mike."

Bel Geddes muttered, "Gee, thanks for granting permission."

"The thing is, Mike, even if someone was out to get you, can you see them sacrificing Sophie just for that?"

"Sacrificing." Heck's lower lip trembled, causing the soul patch to bounce up and down. "That sounds horrible. Oh man, I hope I didn't cause her—"

Bel Geddes said, "Oh no. Do *not* go down that street, Mike."

She looked at Wendy. Then back at Heck.

"All this is nothing but pure pie-in-the-sky supposition and you are already dealing with enough stress, Michael. So we've got *much* to accomplish in order to restore your sense of well-being."

"Yeah, sure, great, whatever," said Michael Heck, rising. "Meanwhile, I'm still getting the hell out of Dodge."

He left the room quickly. Bel Geddes took a moment to recover before hustling after him. Disoriented by having to follow.

Wendy was the last to leave. She wanted to say something but was smart enough to keep her mouth shut.

CHAPTER 10

Milo said, "Thoughts?"

Before I could answer, the hostess stepped in wearing a permafrost smile. "The room's reserved, guys."

"Big-time meeting? Industry honchos?" said Milo.

The question threw her. Like most people who casually lie she was unprepared for challenge.

"Um . . ."

He flashed a wolf grin that scrubbed her face clean of intention and we walked past her. No escort in, ditto out.

Both of us had parked around the corner, on a pine-shaded Beverly Hills street lined with mansions. Wide swath, smooth and nearly silent; hard to believe the high-end dorm was a brief walk away.

As I walked Milo to his unmarked, he said, "Same question."

"To me, Heck comes across credible."

"Yup. And I put the guy in jail. Did you feel what I did? Ol' Bettina's definitely setting up a big civil suit."

I said, "No doubt and that might be the reason she let him stay in jail for two days. And he put up with it. Either he was part of the plan or disoriented. Or maybe both. He agreed with Bel Geddes then experienced what County's like."

"Yeah, he does look edgy. Wonderful. Can't wait for the subpoena."

"Meanwhile, he did give you some info you might be able to use. Sophie's friends and his time with Darren Alberts."

"Baron Darren, Lord and Master of Scumbaggery. It took, what, to uncover him—a decade? I thought he was headed for prison but Heck said he's senile. You hear anything about that?"

"I did," I said. "Major dementia, he's in a care facility."

His eyebrows dipped. "How come you know that and I don't?"

"Three neuropsychologists evaluated him. One's a friend."

"Honest friend?"

"All three are, including the one hired by the defense. Everyone agreed Alberts has deteriorated to where he needs special care."

"Convenient. So you're saying he's too messed up to pull off a fake-DNA thing."

"That would be my guess but I can try to find out. And even if Alberts wasn't directly behind it, someone else at his firm could've tagged Heck as a snitch and decided to get even."

"Someone gets back at Heck by strangling an innocent woman?"

"Targeting a loved one? We've seen that before."

"I guess," he said, "but ten years ago feels like ancient history to me, Alex. Sure, call your friend. Please. Thank you."

He salaamed. I laughed.

"Meanwhile," he said, "my first priority is talking to Sophie's girlfriends." He frowned. "Kind of thing I shoulda done right at the beginning."

I said, "If you feel like beating yourself up, I can't stop you. But the truth is you didn't screw up, you got had, just like Heck did."

He stared at me. "What was that, tough love?"

"Talking truth to power."

His lips began spreading in a smile. That died when his cell squawked atrocious Mahler.

"Hi again, kid . . . what? You're kidding. That's insane. Oh yeah, definitely."

He clicked off and strode to the Impala's driver's door. "Alicia just found more money at Martha's place. Not like before, this was a paper bag hidden behind stacks of *National Geographic* and stuffed with a hundred hundreds."

"Serious stash."

"And there are still plenty of places left to search in that dump so maybe it'll come down to burglary."

"Burglary plus disarticulation?"

"Okay, someone who knew she had dough and hated her for whatever psychy reason. A crazy daughter would fit that nicely, right? And the fact that Lynne Matthias can't be found makes her look dirty. I'm heading over there now. Want to see it for yourself?"

"Sure."

He walked to the rear of the Impala, popped the trunk, and produced a heavy-duty plastic zip bag. Inside was a neatly folded, hooded white coverall along with paper booties and rubber gloves.

"Here you go. Dress for success."

CHAPTER 11

Martha Matthias's house remained an active crime scene, the front door sealed by yellow tape. But a whole new mood had set in.

None of that first-call tension, no flashing lights, no flotilla of black-and-whites.

No uniformed presence at all.

Parked directly in front of the house and spanning its width was a massive, unmarked white van roomy enough to transport the contents of a McMansion. Rear doors propped open above a sloping metal ramp offered a view of a long, dim space. Nothing inside but flat-packs of unassembled cardboard boxes. Piles of them.

A couple of burly guys in blue coveralls stood on the sidewalk near the van's cab, smoking and pretending to ignore us.

Milo said, "Hey, guys."

Dual nods. Bored. The badge flash didn't change that.

He said, "You from the crime lab?"

The older man said, "Nah, we got a contract to bring stuff they can't. This time they said we'd be taking boxes back but they didn't say boxes of what."

His partner looked at him. "It's a crime scene, dude, what do you think, floral arrangements?"

He took a deep drag on a non-filter cigarette. "We been here three hours forty-two minutes. County wants to pay us to wait, bring it on."

Milo turned away and glanced across the street where three mini-vans were lined up. Like the rental behemoth, white. But not anonymous. Blue letters proclaiming *Police* ran along the bottom. In case you missed that, up above near the roofline, *Crime Scene Unit* was painted in black.

Behind all that were two sedans with fat black-wall tires, both maligned by paint hues guaranteed to gag a private buyer. Wet Cement Gray, Swamp Mud Brown. Behind the brown car, a dented blue late-model Mustang.

Milo said, "Wonder who scored the cool wheels," and donned his forensic suit. I did the same and just like the first time, we headed to the back of the murder house.

Alicia stood midway between the rear door and the garage, talking to a woman. Both of their suits were dust-streaked. Alicia's mask was down but the other woman's wasn't. Above the seam, her eyes were chocolate brown, her complexion coppery gold. A few feet away on the lawn was a four-wide, four-high stack of assembled boxes, each sealed with crime scene tape.

Alicia said, "Hey, L.T. This is Cheryl Najarian, supervisor at Hertzberg. Lieutenant Sturgis and Dr. Delaware, our psych consultant."

Cheryl Najarian said, "Assistant supervisor. Nice to meet you, Lieutenant." The mask canted toward me. "Psych? Makes sense, from what I've been hearing the whole case is kind of crazy."

Milo turned to Alicia. "How'd you find the money?"

"Wish I could say it was a brilliant deduction, L.T. I'm rifling through piles and piles of old magazines, had been doing it for an hour-plus and boom, this bag just falls into my hot little hands. When I saw what was inside, I brought it out here and Cheryl phone-filmed as I counted."

Najarian walked behind the stack of boxes and brought over a sealed, padded envelope that she tapped.

"Ten thousand. It's not a record, not even close with the dope money we get. But hiding behind junk? That's a first."

She turned to me, eyebrows arching.

Even without seeing the bottom of her face, I knew the look.

Give me a diagnosis.

Time to disappoint someone I'd never met. I said, "Different."

The eyebrows dropped. "Ya think?" *Who needs this guy?*

Alicia said, "That kind of money sure firms up a motive. Martha kept serious cash around and someone was aware of it. Maybe at the time of the murder they found some dough but didn't realize there was more."

Milo said, "Someone who knew her well enough to find it."

"That's what I'm thinking, L.T. As in crazy daughter. Who I still can't find any info on."

"Moe and Sean are inside searching?"

"Along with two of Cheryl's techs. We were all doing it, stepped out to get some fresh air."

Najarian said, "Emphasis on fresh." She lowered her mask on a pleasant oval face.

Milo said, "Who scored the Mustang?"

Alicia grinned. "Only thing that was available in the impound lot today. Poor, poor pitiful me."

Najarian said, "Great song."

Milo turned to her and smiled. "You didn't want to drive the moving van?"

Cheryl Najarian said, "When we heard about the situation from the team who got here the first day, we figured we might have to bring the house's total contents for analysis. The only vehicles we have with that capacity are the big motor vehicle transports and they're all tied up. So I authorized a company we sometimes use. I'll personally follow them back to make sure the evidence chain stays intact."

"Appreciate it, thanks," said Milo. "Not sure you'll need to analyze every scrap, though."

"Fine with me, Lieutenant. What criteria should we use?"

"The likelihood of something evidentiary coming up. What do you have so far, Alicia?"

"Like I said before, the bathroom was the crime scene for sure and it's been gone over thoroughly. Techs found additional serious blood in the tub plus more blood and tissue in the drain all the way down to the trap. That's what's over there in those boxes. The other place they swabbed thoroughly was the space Martha used for a kitchen, but that produced nothing. Now they're working on the one bedroom set aside for sleeping. The rest of the house is unbelievably filled with crap."

Milo said, "Cheryl, if we did bring everything back, how long would it take to go through it?"

Najarian frowned. "If I've got ample staff—which is a big if—two weeks minimum. You want us to get all OCD? Months."

"Okay, how about this. Take random swabs throughout the house and if nothing shows up, I can't see trucking tons of old paper over."

"Not going to argue with that, Lieutenant. We've got serious storage issues."

"Ever been in a situation like this?"

"I haven't but one of my instructors worked the Oklahoma federal bombing. Total nightmare."

"I'll bet," he said. "Now that I think about it, maybe the swabbing shouldn't be random. First off let's see if any more money shows up. Is most of the hoard paper?"

"All of it is," said Alicia. "Newspapers, magazines, random receipts—I found some going back twenty-plus years."

"Crazy," said Najarian.

Milo said, "How about this: If we find money, we sample paper close to the stash—say, a three-foot radius. The same goes for personal documents—letters, wills, insurance policies, photos. And obviously anything with blood or body fluids."

"If I was smart, I wouldn't bring this up," said Cheryl Najarian, "but fluids aren't always visible early on. So how're we going to be sure we're not missing something? I mean I'm not thrilled about schlepping tons of garbage, but . . ."

Milo closed his eyes, opened them, tapped his foot. "Let's take a look inside and see what makes sense."

CHAPTER 12

Najarian's phone rang and she stayed back to answer it as Alicia led us into the house via the rear door and continued through an aisle that sliced through ceiling-high walls of old newspapers and magazines.

A stripe of grubby gray linoleum sectioned the products of dead trees. A broth of must and mold tempered by a strange yeasty heaviness made its way through my mask.

Milo's big shoe tapped the floor. "Did we clear it or did you find it this way?"

Alicia said, "It's just like we found it, L.T. There's something similar up front so I guess she wanted two ways in and out."

The passageway continued a couple of yards before coming up against a perpendicular wall of paper detritus then hooked right and continued into a tiny dim space.

About a third of an already stingy kitchen. Dim because two small windows were so far past maintenance that their panes were brown.

A crime lab tech kneeling to inspect the interior of a refrigerator dimensioned for a college dorm stopped and said, "Cool but not super cold, probably just needs Freon. But no weird stuff seems to be growing anywhere. So far."

Alicia said, "Anything interesting in the fridge, Mark?"

"If you think juice, milk, stale bread, eggs that are stinking pretty bad is interesting. Who could live like this? Gross."

Mark stood and his glove slapped a chipped tile counter topping flimsy wood cabinets with warped doors. Both probably original to the house. No stove, just a toaster oven and a microwave, along with an old black plastic Mr. Coffee, a month's worth of paper plates and plastic utensils.

"People," he said.

The aisle continued to a ten-by-ten room where another tech worked. The floor was filthy rose-pink carpet, the walls grayed past whatever their original color was. Another pair of dusty windows ambered the meager contents: single bed, pecan-finish nightstand, dresser. The dresser drawers were open, revealing unidentifiable wadded-up clothing. A closet door advertised empty space.

Rolled in a corner was a navy blue futon bound by crime scene tape.

Alicia said, "Anything, Lucy?"

"Plenty of latents but so far they're all the same. So likely the deceased."

"Even on the futon?"

"No prints at all on that. We'll take it back, along with the mattress. But so far this is yielding nothing creepy. Unlike you-know-where."

Next stop: you-know-where.

The bathroom, tiled mustard yellow from floor to ceiling, was blocked by crime scene tape and splotched by purplish stains. Luminol had pulled up splotches of blood on the yellow linoleum floor and the sink, a huge wash of it inside the bathtub. The tub's drain cap had been removed.

Alicia said, "The trap's boxed for removal. Mark had to go underneath the house. Lots of rat shit and what he says is raccoon shit."

Lucy said, "Mark hunts, he knows his critters."

Milo said, "Is this the only john?"

Alicia said, "Unless one of the guys has uncovered another up front. Limited floor plan, huh? Imagine how much she could've crammed into a palace."

She walked a couple of feet up the aisle and pointed to a spot where the boxes ended midway to the ceiling. "This gap is from where I found the ten thousand. Where it found me."

We followed her toward the front of the house. Now the aisle was different. Wider, the linoleum cleaner, as if it hadn't been exposed in a long time.

Milo said, "We cleared this area?"

"Moe and Sean did in order to fit in," she said. "Mostly Moe, I knew all that gym time would come in handy. Everything that got moved is also in those boxes outside but there was nothing sexy that I saw."

Two suited figures worked fifteen feet away at the end of the hall. Windows were blocked by towers of junk, and light came by way of four battery-op fixtures. One figure stood on the floor, inspecting waist-high material. The other was perched on a step stool probing upper layers of tightly packed flotsam.

The one on the ladder, so muscle-bound his body strained the forensic suit, said, "Do I get a bonus, L.T.?"

The other, taller, lanky, said, "You deserve it, man. You were like a turbine, I was feeling kind of extraneous."

To Milo: "You should've seen him, Loot. Moving stuff around like a forklift."

He lowered his mask on a long, freckled face. Rusty strands of hair had escaped his hood. Detective Sean Binchy, cheerful as ever. Except when not. A few years ago, I'd saved his life. It had taken some time but we'd resolved that.

"Doc," he said, "this is right up *your* alley."

The bulky man got off the ladder, came over, and unmasked, exposing a pink baby face.

Milo said, "Getting a workout, Moses?"

Detective Moe Reed flexed arms as thick as thighs. "Nah, not even a warm-up."

Milo said, "I'm assuming you haven't found anything interesting."

"Just historical insight, Loot," said Sean. "Looking at all these newspaper headlines from way back. Turns out everything they said back then was wrong."

Moe said, "Back then and now."

I said, "What's the earliest date you've found?"

"Twenty years or so, give or take. But it's not just the *Times,* it's the *Daily News,* the *Evening Outlook,* and tons of throwaway papers and magazines. Plus subscription stuff and *unbelievable* amounts of junk brochures. Cruises, real estate brokers, what have you."

I said, "Martha Matthias was widowed twice, the first time when she was a newlywed and young. Her second husband died twenty-two years ago. I can see that being traumatic. Maybe that's what started her hoarding."

All four detectives stared at me.

Milo said, "Only you would think that way. Thank God. Okay, guys, I'll stick around and help. Thanks for coming, Alex, I'll walk you out."

We'd made it to the curb when Cheryl Najarian ran out, waving her hands. "We found more."

Milo said, "Money?"

"Whole new level, Lieutenant, Alicia's counting."

We returned to the backyard, where Alicia stood near the stack of boxes examining hundred-dollar bills that filled a rumpled manila envelope. Four other envelopes sat atop the stack.

Milo said, "The guys just found it?"

Najarian said, "Nope, my girl Lucy did. In the mattress."

"In," he said.

"A slit was cut and all this was slipped into it. Maybe it helped her sleep at night—sorry, don't want to be mean but this whole thing is wack lunacy." She shook her head.

Alicia said, "Ten thou in the first. If they're all like that, we're talking fifty K."

They all were.

Milo said, "Fifty grand inside a mattress. Guess whoever killed her wasn't privy to that."

Alicia said, "If I had a daughter with issues, I wouldn't exactly discuss finances."

Milo turned to Najarian. "How's this measuring up against dope dough?"

"Pretty well, actually." She smiled. "Maybe I should get an armed escort back to Hertzberg."

"It can be arranged."

"No, just kidding. Let's film everything and I'll narrate like with the first batch. Then I'll get going and make sure everything's registered to a T."

Once she'd left with the money, Milo said, "Sixty grand plus that small amount—which was probably petty cash for groceries and the like. But no idea how much was actually taken. If anything was."

I said, "If no will shows up, it'll go to probate along with the house. Unless another relative shows up, the daughter's claim should go smoothly."

Alicia said, "Butcher Mommy in the tub and profit? If we can prove it."

Milo said, "We *need* to find her."

CHAPTER 13

We waited until Sean and Moe had covered most of the remaining hoard. With only a few feet to go, no more money, no personal documents.

Cheryl Najarian said, "So what's the decision about all the junk?"

Milo said, "Changed my mind, sorry. I know it's a big hassle taking it all back but I can't see handing some defense attorney an opening about concealed evidence."

"That's a big jump forward, Lieutenant."

"What is?"

"From here to a trial."

"Optimism, Cheryl. I've been told it's healthy. For how long do you have the moving van?"

"It's a one-day minimum."

"You've got suits for those two?"

"We do."

"Then let them earn their keep. Have them pack up everything and take it back. No need to do anything right now, just store it."

"Makes sense," said Najarian. Not even close to meaning it.

Back on the sidewalk, Milo walked up to the pair of movers.

"No more boredom, guys."

"Huh?"

"Get those boxes ready."

Both men moved their lips. No sound followed but no confusion about intention.

At my Seville, he said, "No Social Security on Lynne Matthias, no welfare or disability payments, which you'd expect if she's impaired. You know what I'm thinking."

"Homeless."

"Just what I need."

A while back we'd worked on multiple murders that took us into the sad, addled world of the homeless. I'd been injured. He'd suffered more than me due to guilt.

I said, "There are other possibilities. Marriage or an out-of-state name change. Out-of-the-country, for that matter."

"Expat returns to chop off Mommy's arms. Any insights?"

I hesitated.

"What, Alex?"

"The mutilation was precise with no evidence left behind. I'd expect more gore and disorganization from someone seriously impaired."

"So who, then—don't answer that. I can't deal with the entire world as my suspect pool. And speaking of impairment, let's segue to my *other* open case. Could you try to find out if Darren Alberts really is grokked out?"

I drove home and phoned Dr. Lee Falkenburg at her office in Beverly Hills. Lee's a longtime friend and one of L.A.'s top neuropsychologists. Recently, I'd leaned on her for a favor that had strained professional boundaries.

She said, "Uh-oh."

"This is nothing like before, Lee. I know you evaluated Darren Alberts and wanted to find out if he's seriously impaired. It was court-ordered, so no confidentiality."

"They found something else he did?"

"His name came up."

"In a murder?" said Lee. "Because that's what your cop buddy does."

"It's not even close to that."

"But . . ."

"His name came up tangentially."

"Whatever that means," she said. "Well, yes. I can see Alberts doing all kinds of bad things. From the case file and his history he's a grade-A psychopath. How long ago did this tangential thing come up?"

"Couple of months ago."

"Then no way, Alex. All of us—Arnie Rodriguez, Bill Higgins, and myself—agreed that Alberts's dementia began at least four years ago, possibly earlier. Per symptoms charted by his internist and a consulting neurologist, both of whom I happen to know are smart and upright. Both suggested at the time that Alberts get evaluated but he said no way. The psychiatrist the D.A. sent to evaluate him felt he could be scamming to stay out of jail but I'd expect that. Anyway, around two years ago, end-stage dementia set in and it progressed pretty rapidly. Bowel and bladder incontinence, trouble swallowing, failure to wake up for days at a time, loss of speech, involuntary movements, excessive salivation. For the past year, he's been vegetative, Alex."

"Got it, thanks."

"Nasty man," said Lee. "I don't believe in karma, but in this case, it's hard to escape."

CHAPTER 14

Telling the truth is easy. Lying means shifting stories like a runway model speed-changing outfits. The most successful scams are often simple. Darren Alberts had been a master of simplicity.

Years ago, the story had been big so I knew the basics. I logged on to fill in the details.

After working as a short-order cook, a landscaper, a commercial fisherman, and the proprietor of several failed restaurants, Alberts enrolled in a non-accredited San Francisco law school at age fifty, graduated at the bottom of his class, and took four attempts to pass the state bar. Unable to find a job at a firm, he moved down to L.A. and started a practice as a slip-and-fall attorney, specializing in indigent, often uninsured clients.

That had earned him a comfortable income, but L.A. is a third-world nation with huge gaps between the haves and the have-nots and Alberts yearned to be at the top of the haves column.

It didn't take a math major to figure out that forty percent of mega-payouts would kick him up to a whole new level.

The key was to choose your target.

◆

The defendants Alberts focused on were large corporations. His clients were the working poor, often unaware they were parties to class-action suits.

After several false starts, Alberts's first big victory occurred when an Illinois-based manufacturer of chemical fertilizer forked over tens of millions of dollars in reparation for soil contamination in California's Central Valley that had allegedly led to cancer, birth defects, and other misfortunes. Allegedly because the case had never seen the inside of a courtroom.

That victory turbocharged Alberts's status on multiple levels.

Professional advancement as a major courtroom player earned him membership in something called the Trial Lawyer Hall of Fame. The money allowed him to distribute political campaign funds and gain access to the corridors of power.

Most gratifying in a town that trucks in fantasy and appearance, he achieved red-carpet status when *Dark Clouds,* a movie based on the plodding work of one of Alberts's investigators in the fertilizer case—a nondescript paralegal named Alice Pryzcik who'd since died—was supersized into a heroine-in-jeopardy action flick.

In the film, Alberts's character came across rumpled, avuncular, and altruistic. In reality, he'd switched long ago to contact lenses, Hermès shoes, Bijan suits, and a head shaved weekly to distract from pattern baldness.

The actress who played Alice Pryzcik—anything but nondescript—won a Golden Globe, was nominated for an Oscar, and developed a six-month penchant for eco-lectures. Darren Alberts got to go to all the parties.

Meanwhile, he'd traded his first wife for a newer model and his comfortable home in Encino for an estate in San Marino. The Playboy Mansion became a familiar haunt. There, Alberts had been known to cavort in Hefner's lagoon.

Subsequent legal triumphs included suing for a host of other toxic events and manufacturing defects. Ten years after the fertilizer case,

Alberts had won well past a hundred million dollars in damages and an even newer third wife.

Tiana Crown, a former *Playboy* model thirty years Alberts's junior, had met him at the lagoon. Her association with a "legal rock-star" husband snagged her a screen agent. The agent snagged her an audition for a proposed "reality" show featuring women with similar backgrounds, tentatively titled *Centerfold Contessas*.

Part of the pitch was the promise that hubby Darren would show up from time to time and, despite behaving "dignified and lawyerly," be outsmarted by Tiana.

Prospects for the show and everything else in the Albertses' life screeched to a halt seven years ago when a federal prosecutor named Kevin Van Osler revealed that after a joint investigation by his office, the D.A., LAPD, and the IRS, the attorney faced multiple felony charges, including, but not limited to, grand theft, perjury, fraud, and money laundering.

Once that story hit, the media "discovered" that over the past ten years Alberts had been sued a hundred sixty-eight times for ripping off clients but had avoided disciplinary action because of his chummy relations with the state bar. Including sitting on several committees. Among them ethics and oversight.

The legal documents ran to thousands of pages but Alberts's technique could be summed up in a sentence.

He'd systematically shortchanged or stiffed hundreds of clients, holding on to far more than the promised forty percent contingency. Borrowing from Ponzi-type schemes, he'd mollified some complainants by paying them from the proceeds of other people's lawsuits.

When that logjammed, attempts to collect were met with stalls, legalistic filings to delay, or outright silence.

It might've gone on unchecked but Kevin Van Osler had come across a filing by a Fresno attorney suing Alberts and gotten curious. The son of two judges and a cousin of the governor, Van Osler viewed his job as the anteroom to a political career, and nothing primes a political career better than a high-level case with heroic overtones.

Faced with the charges, Darren Alberts took the obvious route: declaring bankruptcy. Van Osler's army of federal agents and LAPD detectives set about searching for Alberts's assets and discovered that the San Marino estate, a house on Carbon Beach in Malibu, and a chalet in Aspen were mortgaged to the hilt.

A fleet of luxury cars turned out to be leased with payments due. Including a three-million-dollar Bugatti whose total mileage of one hundred thirty-five came from filmed drives to and from the offices of the *Contessa* producers.

Designer clothing reaped chump change at resale, furniture in all three houses consisted of cheap copies of signature pieces, and the Albertses' art collection heralded in the show's pilot episode was all cheesy reproduction.

No bank accounts or Wall Street investments surfaced. Tiana's jewelry was confiscated, revealing a few serious pieces but mostly costume junk. That was reputed to enrage the Contessa, who framed herself as another of Darren Alberts's victims and filed for divorce.

Van Osler, chastened by failure to produce headline fodder, continued to press the criminal case against Alberts. Years of delaying motions were no longer necessary when Alberts was judged mentally unfit to stand trial.

Just as he'd avoided the courtroom as a plaintiff, the master thief had slipped by as a defendant.

Sole defendant. I searched for other indictees but no charges seemed to have been leveled against anyone but the boss. Meaning either that Alberts had concealed the thefts from his employees or that they'd been incentivized by the government to turn against the boss.

Ratting on a grade-A psychopath could be dangerous, so maybe Michael Heck had been onto something.

I jotted down a timetable.

Kevin Van Osler had filed charges seven years ago, meaning he'd begun investigating earlier. Eight or more years ago.

Michael Heck had left Alberts's firm five years ago. Sticking around for two years during the initial prosecution.

Heck had claimed ignorance of the scam but his position—managing expenses—made me wonder. Perhaps he'd been vulnerable because he *was* dirty and had stayed on as Van Osler's plant.

During some of that time, Darren Alberts had been cognitively intact, not showing signs of dementia until a year after Heck quit.

More than able to plot revenge.

What better way to discredit a potential witness than by setting up a phony murder scenario?

But the timeline didn't work.

If Alberts had tried to silence Heck, he'd have done it years ago. Sometimes revenge is a dish best eaten cold but Alberts was well past the point of cooking up anything.

I ran an image search on him.

Smallish, inevitably smiling man nearing seventy. Spray-tanned, shaved pate as shiny as his yellow Bijan tie.

In every shot, he was flanked by movie stars, producers, directors, and elected officials. In most of them, he stood dwarfed by Tiana, tall, blond, busty, skin ironed smooth as a hotel bedsheet.

In every shot, Alberts came across looking his age but energetic and vital.

Now he was "vegetative."

The legal system had failed to stem Alberts's felonies but his own brain had finally voiced an opinion.

I don't believe in karma but in this case it's hard to escape.

CHAPTER 15

I got a cup of coffee and texted Milo: *Sophie unlikely related to Heck's work for Alberts.*

He called me moments later.

I said, "Got my text."

"Haven't checked. I'm calling because we I.D.ed Sophie's girlfriends through her phone. Nothing juicy in her call-dump but it's something. Any chance you can work late?"

That evening at nine, I pulled up to a four-story apartment building in Mar Vista. One of those cloudy nights where stars blur and the sky takes on the sheen of velour.

Nine p.m. had given me the chance for dinner with Robin. She'd been fine returning to her studio to work on rebinding an old Gibson Advanced Jumbo guitar. Late hour for Blanche, who'd sighed ambivalently, so I'd carried her over to the studio, kissed them both, and left.

I got there before Milo, was studying the building when he pulled up in the white Porsche 928 he shares with Rick Silverman. Once derided by Porsche-heads because it's front-engine, the model's now desirable and pricey. That means full-time garaging and limited use as a leisure-time driver. For two guys with rare leisure time.

"Going luxe?"

"Quality of life, every little bit counts. Or so I've been told . . . nice place."

Hacienda Linda was different from the other complexes on the block. Instead of space-hogging, hard-edged gray cement and glass cubes, this was cream-colored stucco with a Spanish tile roof, greenery in front, and wrought-iron balconies. Full security glass doors and a card-entry subterranean parking lot. The glass showcased a security guard behind a desk in the lobby.

As we headed to the entrance, I said, "You got the text."

"Darren's broccoli, thanks for checking. We'll be talking to Ashley Herrera and Maria Diffenbach. Heck didn't have it quite right. Ashley's not a flight attendant, she helps run Southwest's LAX office. I guess Maria Diffenbach could be classified as industry if you include bookkeeper for a promotion company."

"Whose place is it?"

"Maria's, Ashley lives in El Segundo. Neither of them has ever been in trouble and that's all I know so far."

He rang the bell. The security guard looked up but didn't budge. After Milo's second attempt, the guy waited another fifteen seconds before hoisting himself up and trudging over. By the time he got to the door, Milo's badge was flashing at eye level.

That set the guard's mouth twitching. He opened the door quickly and said, "Oh, hey, guys."

Thirty or so, with a name tag that read *L. Lemon,* he was soft-bodied and puffy-faced with an unfortunate sprig of fuzz the color of wet sand sprouting from a discouraged chin.

Milo said, "L stand for Lou?"

"Lee. So, hey, what's up?"

We walked past him to the elevator.

He said, "You know where you're going?" in a voice strained by desperation.

Milo muttered, "Depends if we're talking philosophy or geography."

"Pardon?" said the guard.

"Better than parole," said Milo as the elevator doors slid open soundlessly.

We rose up to 4. Maria Diffenbach's apartment number put her toward the rear of a pale-pink hallway carpeted in deep-brown plush printed with whiskey-colored O-shapes that resembled smoke rings.

Milo had texted her during the rise up and by the time we got there, a woman stood framed in the open doorway, backed by another woman.

She said, "Lieutenant? Maria. This is Ashley."

"Milo Sturgis, Alex Delaware."

"Come in, guys."

We followed her long stride into a subtly lit living room that smelled of lemon oil and some sort of designer perfume.

Maria Diffenbach joined Ashley Herrera, folding herself onto a taupe sectional with the ease of a professional dancer. Milo and I took two facing easy chairs on the other side of a five-foot-square marble coffee table. The walls were white, the floors bleached pine. Art consisted of three oversized abstractions. The place was open-layout but shutters blocked every window.

Ashley Herrera said, "So now Heck's back on the street."

"Crazy," said Maria Diffenbach.

Both women were around forty, tall, trim, and brunette with tight faces under identical bob hairdos. Herrera wore a black top over black leggings and orange running shoes, Diffenbach a black top over gray leggings and peacock-blue running shoes. No facial resemblance but the gestalt was twin-like.

Diffenbach smiled. "No, we're not sisters, it's just one of those weird things, that's how we met."

"At the gym," said Herrera. "People kept telling me my doppelgänger had just been there and I finally saw her." She turned serious. "The gym's also where we met Sophie. The three of us speed-ellipticaled."

Diffenbach said, "When Ashley told me what you told her I

couldn't believe it. We thought it was settled with his arrest. That made sense."

Milo said, "Heck being guilty."

"It's always like that, right? Some sicko ex who can't deal? My *thankfully* former husband stalked me for eight months before he found someone else to annoy. I actually bought a gun. A Glock like you guys use."

Ashley Herrera leaned forward. "Lieutenant, was there some sort of procedural screwup that forced you to let him go?"

"No," said Milo. "We're no longer looking at Mr. Heck as a suspect. Is there some reason you suspected him other than his being Sophie's ex?"

"Did Sophie tell us he was scary? No, but she did say he wasn't very happy when she dumped him."

Milo said, "Why'd she dump him?"

Maria Diffenbach said, "She kept hoping he'd turn interesting but he didn't."

"She found him boring."

"To say the least," said Herrera. "Sounded like he had the fascination level of drying paint. Sure, on the surface, he looked okay. Had a job, cute enough, and decent in the . . . physical department. But after a while it turned stale." She tapped her temple.

"Guys like that, all ego, bye-bye brain cells," said Diffenbach. "Sophie was a smart woman. She needed more than muscles and a BMW."

I said, "How'd Heck express his unhappiness with the breakup?"

Herrera said, "Sophie didn't go into details. I'm assuming he said things to her."

"But no stalking or harassment."

"Not as far as I know. You hear different, Mar?"

Diffenbach shook her head. "Can I ask you guys what was . . . done to Sophie? Because aren't there differences in how people you know as opposed to strangers . . . do it?"

"Getting up close and personal," said Herrera. "Strangulation, stabbing."

"Or that terrible thing, overkill," said Diffenbach. "All the paper said was Sophie was murdered and they didn't cover it extensively, just one paragraph in the beginning and after that, crickets. Same with the internet until Heck was arrested and even then there wasn't much. A suspect's been arrested, along with his name blah blah blah."

"Same old story," said Herrera. "Sophie wasn't famous enough to matter. Just a normal, great person."

Diffenbach said, "We—actually me—called your station and tried to get details but the person I spoke to was really closemouthed. I told them I was a friend and would be happy to talk to a detective and they took my number. But no one ever got back to me."

Milo's jaw tightened. "Sorry about that."

"So was it like that? Something terrible up close and personal?"

Milo said, "Sorry, we need to keep all that close to the vest."

"Close to the vest," said Herrera. "Haven't heard *that* in a long time. My dad used to say it. He *wore* vests. Part of his three-piece suits, he was a banker. We'd bug him about stuff and he'd puff out his vest with his thumbs and say, 'Nope, need to keep it close to the vest.'"

She blushed. "Sorry, that was irrelevant and inane."

Diffenbach put her arm around Herrera's shoulder. "No it wasn't, it was charming and life could use some charming, Lord knows there's so much freakin' *ugly* out there."

She began to cry softly, dabbed her eyes with her sleeve before Milo could produce one of the tissues he carries around.

Herrera studied her friend as if waiting for a cue. Her own eyes glossed but they stayed dry. She frowned, as if displeased by her limited grief.

I said, "Were there any other men in Sophie's life?"

"Not that we know of," said Herrera. "After Heck, Sophie decided to concentrate on Sophie."

"How so?"

"More time in the gym, reading, taking hikes. She talked about learning to sew. About going to France, the Loire Valley. She'd even thought about switching from her condo to a house with a yard so she could get into gardening."

Diffenbach said, "Between her marriage and losers like Heck, she decided to refocus."

Milo said, "There were problems in her marriage?"

"Just the fact that it ended," said Herrera. "Her husband—Bradley—was a great guy. She told us she really loved him. Then he got killed and it shattered her world."

"Freakin' drunk going the wrong way," said Diffenbach. "You live your life and some bastard ends it. At least the drunk died, too."

Herrera said, "Sophie said Bradley *was* interesting. Smart. Firefighter and EMT."

"No way Heck could live up to that," said Diffenbach. "He was, what, a paralegal?"

Milo said, "He manages a law office."

"Whatever," said Herrera. "It's not rocket science."

Diffenbach shifted uncomfortably. Thinking of her own job keeping the books?

Herrera said, "She needed more than someone she worked out with at the gym."

Irony in short supply tonight.

Milo said, "Same gym you guys use?"

Ashley Herrera waved a dismissive hand. "We're members at Platinum Bodies in Brentwood. Sophie joined after we did, after leaving that dump where she met *him.*"

"Which dump is that?" said Milo.

"Some place on Pico, couldn't tell you the name. She left because it was super loud and smelly with all the weight lifting and the grunting. You know. Guys trying to prove something."

"Sophie didn't want bulges, she wanted to be toned," said Maria Diffenbach. "She took *care* of herself. It's not *fair.*"

She began crying again.

Ashley Herrera said, "I need to hydrate," and hurried off to a well-appointed kitchen.

This time Milo was quick enough with one of his tissues and Maria Diffenbach had put it to good use by the time Herrera returned with four bottles of Dasani water. Three full, one half consumed.

She uncapped a bottle for her friend and put the other two in front of us. We watched as both women drank greedily.

Ashley Herrera finished hers and looked over. "You guys really should. A stressful job depletes cells."

We obliged with a few sips.

"There you go."

Milo said, "Is there anything else you can tell us that might help?"

Twin head shakes.

"Did Sophie meet anyone else at the dump gym?"

Ashley Herrera said, "You think there was another jerk before Heck?"

Milo said, "Just trying to get a feel for Sophie's life."

"It was a good life. And no, she never mentioned any other jerks."

"Can you think of anyone else who might've wished her harm?"

Herrera said, "No. So maybe it was one of those crazy stranger things." Looking at us, hoping to be contradicted.

When she wasn't, she said, "Absolutely crazy."

"Insane," said Diffenbach. She stood and patted a flat tummy. "Fluids in, fluids out, excuse me."

As she trotted off, Herrera touched her own abdomen. "Thank God she's got two johns. I'll see you guys to the door."

CHAPTER
16

As we stepped off the lift and into the lobby, Lee Lemon got to his feet and flashed bad teeth. "Get what you needed?"

Milo said, "It was big-time fun."

That creased Lemon's forehead.

Milo said, "Don't work too hard," and we left the building.

Back at the Porsche, he said, "Another whole bunch of nothing."

I said, "The gym on Pico might be worth checking out."

"Sophie met a jerk she never told them about?"

"Someone she threw over for Heck could've harbored resentment toward both of them. If there was someone, it had to end quickly, because Heck had only been gone for a couple of months. What if he suspected she was still in contact with Heck?"

"Some paranoid asshole strangling *her* and framing *him*? That's big-time crazy."

I smiled.

He said, "What the hell," and phoned Moe Reed. "Hey, kid, not too late I hope . . . great. I'm calling on the other case, Barlow."

He repeated the women's description of the gym on Pico. "Anything come to mind? . . . That many? Huh. How 'bout one relatively close enough to Sophie Barlow's place . . . say a coupla miles in either direction . . . okay, that's a little more manageable. If you have time tomorrow to help me make the rounds . . . terrific. If we need to break the ice, you can always deadlift a personal trainer."

Clicking off, he said, "Superman says five possibles, we'll check 'em out. Okay, homeward bound. Thanks for taking the time, Alex."

He walked me to the Seville. "That crack about paint drying made me think of Robin working with that whatchamacallit she puts on the instruments with those cotton pads. The shiny stuff."

"Spirit varnish?"

"Yeah. Slow process, right?"

"Definitely."

"But she's not bored."

"Never."

"Like you say, it's all about context."

As I got into the Seville, he said, "What I'm getting at is I'm not bored, either."

"Good for you."

"You think? What keeps me wide-eyed is fear of failure."

I drove home thinking about two failures in progress. First Sophie Barlow. Nothing to say about that so I shifted to Martha Matthias because Milo had a suspect for her murder.

As I'd told him, a schizophrenic would lack the mental organization to do what had been done to the former detective. But the only evidence of major mental illness in the stiff-gaited woman was Hawkins's description. So maybe Lynne Matthias—if that's who she was—suffered from some sort of neurological disorder that impaired her walk but was capable of planning and carrying out calculated viciousness.

Or she was an addict displaying damage caused by years of drug abuse. Maybe homeless as Milo had wondered and dreaded.

If so, opiates were the likely culprit, rendering users passive while stoned but amoral and manipulative when hungry for the needle.

Still, either way, the lack of public records—arrest, incarceration, public assistance, rehab—was puzzling.

Then a possibility came to me.

A public or private mental health center would bill for services but a place staffed by volunteers might not. The same went for charitable shelters. Flophouses that asked no questions if you had the cash.

In terms of the penal system, drug busts had been de-emphasized for years and for the most part the cops ignored simple usage.

If Lynne Matthias's life did consist of financing the next score and she'd discovered Martha's hidden fortune, it wasn't hard to imagine an explosion of violence.

But then, why the arms?

Because it had been about money but also more? The kind of rage seeded by intimacy?

Mother and daughter. Each withdrawing from reality in her own way.

A shared pathology that had eventually boiled over?

Martha Matthias had once been a bravely pioneering detective, confronting society's roughest edges for decades, only to replace a productive life with amassing towers of junk that shrank the dimensions of her world.

Tucking herself, like a skittish rodent, into a dim corner of a fetid, cellulose nest.

I'd suggested stress as the trigger. But that had been textbook psych that explained nothing.

And yes, obsessive-compulsive behavior *is* rooted in the reduction of anxiety. But anxiety doesn't cause most people to totally disengage. Quite the opposite: Humans are social animals and our instinct is to reach out for support.

If I had to bet, I'd say something in Martha's past, or her genes—or both—had led her to wall herself in. But in the end, it likely wouldn't matter. Whatever the reason, she'd begun an insidious process that had trapped her.

Because isolation feeds on itself in a uniquely malignant way.

People subjected to prolonged sensory deprivation inevitably hallucinate and grow delusional. Our brains crave stimulation and once we remove the richness of the external world, the neurons keep firing, leading us into an alternative universe of buzzing confusion, perceptual warps, weird what-ifs, and, ultimately, paranoia.

So no way Martha Matthias would've allowed a stranger into her home. But a daughter who'd bought into the process?

Welcome to the futon in the corner, honey.

I pictured two troubled women sharing hermetic escape. Then something—an errant word or glance, a shift in vocal tone, or most likely an argument about yet another handout of dope money—turns an asylum into a charnel house.

Rats in crowded cages end up eating each other alive. Convicts murder their cellmates.

No reason the same thing couldn't happen in a self-imposed prison.

By the time I got home, Robin was sleeping but when I slipped in beside her she made a soft, purring noise, reached out a hand, and laid it on mine. Her skin was warm, her pulse slow and steady.

We lay there that way for a while.

My world expanded. I slept well.

CHAPTER 17

Friday, I had custody consults from ten a.m. to two p.m. When the door closed on my final patient, I checked messages. Mostly junk and one call-me-back from Milo at noon.

I reached him at his cell.

He said, "Busy day?"

"Just finished. What's up?"

"Coupla things happened today that dovetailed in a weird way. This morning I get a call from Michael Heck. Seems he's been thinking about who might want to frame him and came up with a guy Sophie dated before him. Who she met at the gym. Which he named—Steam Iron—meaning Moses and I can stop canvassing sweatboxes. Interestingly, that one was next on our list."

"Jealous ex?"

"He thinks so."

"Thinks?"

"He and Sophie never talked about it but the guy threw him dirty looks when they happened to cross paths. I know I asked Heck to let me know if he had any ideas but now I'm wondering you-know-what."

"Is he being conveniently helpful to cast suspicion away from himself?"

He said, "And if that's the case, why? He's been cleared and will probably make a bundle in the civil suit."

"So maybe he's not innocent," I said. "Hired someone to do Sophie and it's making him nervous."

"Exactly."

"I'm assuming Bel Geddes doesn't know he called you."

"You're assuming right," he said. "He made a point of letting me know that."

"Trying to ingratiate himself?"

"Almost to the point of kissing up, Alex. Lieutenant this, Lieutenant that. Or maybe I'm just too damn cynical and the guy's sterile-clean and being a solid citizen."

"Who'd he direct you to?"

"Fellow named Frank Winchell. Moses ducked into the gym. The woman at the desk must've admired his muscles 'cause she gave up that Winchell was Black and a dentist. We rooted around and found a Francis Allan Winchell, male Black, forty-three, no priors, not even a parking ticket. Lives in Brentwood near his job as a dental hygienist at a practice on Twenty-Sixth Street. Where he is currently scraping and flossing for the next hour. I figured to catch him when he leaves. You up for some highly paid consultant work?"

When I stopped laughing, I said, "Sure."

He was at the house twenty minutes later, marched to the fridge without comment, slapped together a cold steak sandwich and finished it by the time we got down to the Impala.

The drive to Brentwood took longer than it should've due to a lane closure on Sunset with no apparent purpose followed by a queue of glossy vehicles picking up students at an exclusive girls' school.

Milo checked his Timex. "Still plenty of time, Winchell doesn't finish for twenty-eight minutes."

"How'd you find out his schedule?"

"I lied about being a patient and wanting a cleaning appointment with him. Apparently at Dr. Loring's office closing time means closing time."

Twenty-two minutes later, we'd pulled up to a profoundly charmless two-story building faced with liver-colored brick. Cater-corner to the Brentwood Country Mart where movie stars pretended to want privacy.

The lack of style and generous outdoor parking in back screamed construction during the blithe seventies. Being situated this close to the mart made the property prime L.A. dirt. Aesthetics wouldn't matter but the parking lot would when the time came for the inevitable teardown.

A silver Audi that Milo had identified as Winchell's was parked at the back. Milo slipped the Impala next to it.

"Four minutes to go, if he's punctual."

Eight minutes later a tall, broad-shouldered man in an aqua uniform exited the building and headed toward us carrying a cellphone.

Milo said, "Here we go."

Frank Winchell had close-cropped hair, a neat goatee, and an easy walk.

Milo was ready for him, smiling and flashing the badge and saying, "Mr. Winchell, Lieutenant Sturgis and this is Alex Delaware. Don't be alarmed but if we could talk to you for a second about Sophie Barlow that would be great."

Winchell stopped, wide-eyed. His torso stiffened. "Sophie? What about?"

"You haven't heard."

"Heard what— Oh, Lord, cops. You're going to tell me something horrendous."

"Afraid so, sir. She was murdered."

Winchell's eyes rounded and his lips parted on perfect teeth. "You're kidding—no, of course you're not." A hand rose to the side of his face. "Oh my God, when?"

"Several weeks ago."

"Several weeks ago," said Winchell. "Meaning it's unsolved so you're flailing around talking to everyone."

"We're trying to learn what we can about Sophie."

"Sophie murd . . . I—well I don't know what you think *I* can tell you." Winchell's eyes swept the lot. "I'm not comfortable talking to cops out here. All I need is for someone to see it and the rumor mill kicks in."

"Got it," said Milo. "Where would you like to talk?"

"I don't know—this is freaking me out. Last time I had anything to do with cops was in college. Walking to my dorm, bunch of you converge on me flashing guns and put me down on the sidewalk. Supposedly I resembled a mugging suspect. When I was in high school and had the nerve to drive while overly pigmented, I got stopped all the time for nothing."

His head jerked back. Two women had left the building and were headed toward the lot. "Oh shit." Sidling past us to his Audi, he remoted the driver's door open and bent low, using us for cover. "I'm not trying anything, just let me sit inside till they're gone."

The women headed to separate Mercedeses and drove away.

Winchell rolled down his window and said, "Those were my bosses, Dr. Loring and Dr. Chan. Last thing I need is *them* wondering."

Talking rapidly, licking his lips. "Now you probably think I'm all nervous because I've got something to hide but I don't. It's just . . ."

"We get it, sir," said Milo.

"Do you? Well, anyway, there's nothing I can tell you about Sophie. And come to think of it, why'd you even *come* here? Did someone tell you something about me? If they did, it's bullshit."

Talking louder and faster.

Milo said, "We're just trying to educate ourselves, sir. Do you want to have the conversation here?"

"I don't want *any* conversation," said Winchell. "But I also don't want you harassing me because you think I held back. I mean you say you get it, but what does that *mean*?"

"It means, sir, that we're not out to hassle you in any way. Or to put you in a tough situation. So if you'd prefer, I'll give you my card, you call me, and we can arrange a sit-down."

"And if I don't want a sit-down?"

"You're under no obligation."

"But you'll suspect me," said Winchell. "And maybe get more aggressive, like marching into the waiting room and making a big thing of it."

"That won't happen, sir. Scout's honor."

"That," said Winchell, "means nothing to me unless you *were* a scout."

"Eagle."

"Where?" said Winchell.

"Small town in Indiana."

"That so."

"It is."

"Well, I earned my Eagle badges in St. Louis, Missouri. Collected twenty-six of them, which is five more than I needed."

Milo said, "I squeaked by. Scored my twenty-first at the last moment."

"Maybe you should've paced yourself better," said Winchell.

"No doubt. Here's my card."

Winchell took it. "Homicide. Ugly ugly word. Hard to believe Sophie—what exactly happened to her?"

"You do want to get into it here?"

"I'd like to know—no, no—okay, no sense stretching it out. You want to speak to me, drive out of the lot, turn right, and go up a block. If there are no busybodies around, park and we'll talk. If there are, keep going until there aren't."

"Sounds like a plan."

"Be prepared," said Frank Winchell. "Any Eagle knows that."

CHAPTER 18

As we tailed Winchell's Audi, Milo said, "A little edgy but to me he seemed genuinely surprised about Sophie."

"To me, as well."

"So that's probably why."

"Why what?"

"The edginess," he said. "Walking while overly pigmented."

The street around the corner was residential with permit-only parking that left lots of curb-space available. Like most daytime streets on the West Side, devoid of people, the sole fauna a few randy squirrels.

Milo placed the car across from a well-tended two-story Spanish Revival with no vehicles in the driveway. We were out and waiting when the silver Audi zoomed in and short-stopped behind us.

The three of us convened under a pepper tree.

Frank Winchell said, "Okay, what do you think I can tell you about Sophie?"

Milo said, "Can you think of anyone who'd want to kill her?"

"Of course not. She was a good person. Plus we didn't date for that long and it's been months since I've seen her. Who directed you to me, anyway?"

"Sorry, can't get into that."

"Yeah, right," said Winchell. "Probably the dude she dated after me. Some lawyer type, something."

"Why would you think that?"

"Because it's logical," said Winchell. "I met Sophie at the gym—helped spot her on some forty-pound bench presses—" Smiling. "Later, I saw him do the same thing. Am I right?"

Milo said, "How long did you and Sophie date?"

"Two months or so, maybe fifteen dates. And we're not talking hot, heavy, and exclusive. After I spotted her, she started talking to me. Good-looking girl and she seemed nice. Next time we saw each other at the gym, we went out for tea—I don't drink. She was easy to be with. That's why when you ask who would hurt her, it's crazy, she's the last person someone would hurt."

I said, "Tea and then . . ."

"More tea," said Winchell. "Then eventually something to eat. Did it lead to something? Yes it did but not always. Sometimes we just talked and went our separates."

He sighed. "Neither of us deluded ourselves we had a big romantic thing going."

Milo said, "Purely physical."

"No, no," said Winchell. "That makes it sound tacky. Sophie and I liked each other, we could converse."

"You've been to Sophie's place."

"Sure. Oh. She was killed there?"

"Afraid so."

"Right in her own place," said Winchell. "That's . . ." His voice broke. He swiped at his eyes. "Yes, I was there. Months ago. But I didn't kill her. Are we through?"

Milo said, "Almost. Why'd the two of you stop dating?"

"Oh man. Why? Was it some big emotional thing? Not even close. I had some vacation time and asked her to come with me for a week in Maui. She said she couldn't so I went by myself and met someone there. Who turned out also to be from L.A. Who I'm still seeing. When I got back, I told Sophie and she did this little pouty thing."

He demonstrated. "But then she laughed and gave me a cheek peck and said congratulations."

"Good sport," said Milo.

"No," said Winchell. "Sophie didn't need to be any kind of sport, because it honestly didn't bother her. We had fun but it wasn't hearts and flowers between us. And it didn't take her long to find someone, next time I saw her at the gym she was with the lawyer dude. She called him Mike. Standing around while he overhead-pressed. About half of what I press. Then sure enough, he's spotting her for her forties and afterward they're leaving together. Then she stopped coming to the gym and so did he. What I'd like to know is why the bastard tried to snitch me out."

Milo said, "Don't assume anything, sir. And please don't act on any assumptions."

"Like I'd actually do that," said Winchell, "and risk having to deal with you guys again. Anyway, that first time, when I saw her leaving with him, I gave her a wink and she winked back. Letting me know we were still cool. 'Cause she *was* cool. No reason for anyone to hurt her unless *he's* some kind of psycho."

"The last time you saw her was . . ."

"Like a week after I saw her with him at the gym and no, we didn't call or text. Her leaving the gym made sense. She shouldn't have been there in the first place, it's for serious lifting not girlie stuff but she probably went there to meet dudes."

"Why do you say that?"

"Because it worked," said Frank Winchell. "She met me, then *him*. You ask me, it's *him* you should be looking at, because his thing with her was more recent. And let's face it, lawyers are halfway to criminal, anyway."

Milo smiled. "Anything else, Mr. Winchell?"

"Not unless you want my advice on rubber-tipping and flossing. Sorry, I shouldn't be a wiseass, this is serious."

He laced his hands together. Twisted them palms-out, then loosened his fingers and let them drop. "Worse than serious. It's horrendous."

Milo said, "Thank you, sir. If you think of anything else, get in touch."

"Of course," said Frank Winchell. "Sophie didn't deserve this. Especially with what she went through in Oklahoma."

"What's that?"

"Losing her husband in a car crash. She talked about loving him crazy, said she'd never feel that way about anyone. Did that threaten me? Not even close, like I said, it wasn't Romeo and Juliet."

Winchell took two steps toward the Audi and stopped. "What was that last badge you squeaked in?"

Milo said, "Cooking."

"What'd you make?"

"Beef stew."

Winchell laughed. "Me too, everyone said it was the easiest. Throw stuff in a pot and heat it up."

He looked at me. "You also a scout?"

I said, "Did a few years in the Cubs."

"Why'd you quit?"

Because my raging alcoholic father cut it short. Like most everything I enjoyed.

I said, "Time constraints."

"Whatever that means," said Frank Winchell, raising his eyebrows. Nodding at Milo, he left and drove away quickly.

Milo said, "What do you think?"

"If Sophie picked up other guys at the gym, one of them could've reacted more strongly than he did."

"I meant *about* him."

"No new suspicions. And how would he have access to Mike Heck's DNA?"

"The same way any suspect would. Follow Heck and Sophie to Heck's place, watch Heck dump his trash, and retrieve the butts.

And his being an ex might mean Sophie would let him in to her place."

"The same could apply to any ex."

"True. And there's nothing in his background—no domestics, no restraining orders—to suggest he's got temper issues."

I pulled out my phone, plugged in Winchell's name, found his Instagram pages. Recent photos—lots of them—showed him with a pretty Asian woman named Randi. The earliest shot featured the two of them having dinner backed by a brilliant Maui sunset.

I showed the screen to Milo. "Backs up his story and they say they're still together."

He scrolled, returned the phone, smiled. "You thinking of a career switch to defense attorney?"

"Hey," I said, "he was an Eagle Scout."

"Speaking of which, what's the real reason you quit the Cubs?"

I told him.

He said, "Oh . . . okay, onward."

Back in the car, I said, "Did you really make beef stew?"

"Hell yeah, and it was tasty. My brothers demolished it. What I didn't tell my scoutmaster was that I burned Mom's Dutch oven in the process."

"Assuming you've learned from the experience, one day you can fix it for Robin and me."

"And Blanche," he said. "If someone French is happy, I know I've aced it. Sure, why not, our place. Once things settle down."

He pulled away from the curb.

I said, "I've been thinking about Martha's daughter. Maybe one of the detectives Martha worked with knows something about her."

"I've been trying to find out who she paired up with," he said, "but it's a long time ago and no luck, so far. Only old homicide guy I found is dead."

"Maybe she didn't pair up with anyone."

"Going solo? Yeah, it happens when you don't fit the mold."

"When was her last assignment?"

"She packed it in around six years ago."

"Maybe one of the fraud D's can help."

"Maybe," he said, switching to a police band and pretending to listen to random calls.

A mile later, he turned it off. "Why not? Nothing else is working."

CHAPTER 19

Saturday, he phoned at eleven-twenty a.m. Weekends off isn't a concept for homicide D's.

"Good idea you gave me, Mr. Wizard. Took a while but I finally managed to find someone Martha worked with who's still alive. Not a fraud guy, a homicide D well before my time named Hans Lieder. Eighty-three, lives in Coeur d'Alene, sounds sharp. He was shocked to hear about Martha but had no first-impression suspicions."

"As in the daughter probably did it."

"As in. He met the daughter once, didn't remember her name. His impression was she was mentally slow. But Martha didn't share anything about her personal life and yes, she did work alone. The only reason he found out she had a daughter was one day after shift, Martha's car broke down. She was supposed to pick the girl up from some kind of special school and she asked Lieder to drive her. He said she clearly wasn't overjoyed at having to ask. The school was somewhere in Venice, near the canals. More like a house than an institution. Ring any bells?"

"No, but I can try to find out."

"I couldn't find anything that fit the bill but sure, give it a go. Anyway, Lieder lived in Huntington Beach so it was on his way home. He waited while Martha went in, she brought the girl out, Lieder described her as quiet, maybe a little sad-looking. He dropped them off and drove home."

"Did he go inside Martha's house?"

"Nope, and when I told him how Martha was living he was stunned. Said she'd been a sharp detective, extremely detail-oriented."

That wasn't at odds with compulsive tendencies. Quite the opposite.

I said, "Did Lieder have any idea why she transferred out of Homicide?"

"Nope, that was another surprise for him, it happened after he retired. Then he said come to think about it he'd noticed things about Martha. Holding on to memos and other crap she didn't need, stuffing her desk drawers full. Also, she liked to line stuff up on her desk—pens, pads, whatever. If someone moved anything, she'd get annoyed and put it right back. So I guess there were signs."

"How old was the daughter when Lieder saw her?"

"Early teens but she seemed younger mentally."

"If she was developmentally disabled and had no other issues, violence would theoretically be unlikely."

"Theoretically. But?"

"She could've had serious behavioral problems that Lieder didn't see. Let me make some calls and see what I can learn about the school. Reputation, philosophy, the types of students they took."

"Assuming it's still there," he said. "Sure. Thanks."

But his tone said, *Not gonna make a difference.*

I paged through a mental Rolodex, looking for people I knew who specialized in developmental disabilities, and came up with a list of three names. The first two didn't answer the phone. Irwin Baumgarten, MSW, did.

He said, "Alex, it's been a while. You still doing that thrilling police stuff?"

"I am, hence my call."

"Oh no, I swear I've been law-abiding."

When he stopped chuckling, he said, "What can I do for you?"

"I'm looking for information on a school for DD kids. Venice, a house near the canals. But a while back."

Irwin said, "Has to be the Kadar Institute. Run by a couple of Hungarian immigrants, both physicians. Bela and Edith were old when they started, very nice people. They died and the school closed down. I rotated through for a couple of weeks when I was doing a practicum. Which shows you the kind of ancient history we're talking about."

"Good place?"

"I thought so. The atmosphere was nice—structured but humanistic. Terrific student-teacher ratio, meaning expensive."

"No one took over from the Kadars."

"Definitely not. My new gig's working for United Way and I know all the current places. Why all the curiosity?"

"The mother of a possible student has been murdered."

"An alumnus with antisocial tendencies? I suppose it's possible, Alex, but the Kadars had a pretty narrow focus so I'm sure they screened for severe behavioral issues."

"What focus was that?"

"Raising the academic level of medium to mildly slow kids so they could be productive members of society. The kids that I saw were a quiet, compliant bunch. Occasionally there'd be tears—frustration, that kind of thing. But nothing beyond that."

Consistent with Hans Lieder's brief observation.

"Still," said Irwin, "you know."

"People change."

"That they do," said Irwin. "That they definitely do. But killing your own mother? Whew, I hope not."

"Thanks for the information, Irwin."

"Sure."

"If I was looking for a place that handles DD adults nowadays, where would I go? Residential but with an open-door policy."

"That," said Irwin, "would depend on how broad a geographic area you want to tap."

The disheveled woman had been seen on foot. I gave him Martha's address. "Say a two-mile radius from there."

"I have no idea where that is—hold on, I'll use Google Maps . . . okay, here we go. You're talking West L.A. . . . pretty close to the Westside police station. Is that the crime scene?"

"It is."

"That could be annoying to your cop pal, no? His home turf getting violated."

"He's got other things on his mind."

"Oh sure, don't mean to be flippant . . . okay, two miles . . . let me check my book . . . looks like four places would fit the bill. Want the addresses now or should I email them to you?"

"I'm listening."

"Old school," said Irwin. "Speaking of which, how's your car?"

"Third engine."

"No planned obsolescence for you. Okay, ready?"

CHAPTER 20

I used my title and got quick cooperation from the Vanguard Developmental Center in Culver City. But no resident named Matthias, Lynne or otherwise, was listed and the place turned out to specialize in patients with senile dementia.

My second call went to Safe Place: A Residential Treatment Facility in West L.A. A little under a mile south of Martha Matthias's home.

When I told the receptionist who I was looking for, he went silent.

Then: "Hold on, I'll transfer you to my boss."

Three clicks later a woman said, "This is Pam Buttons. I'm at home but they told me a doctor was calling. We've been looking for Lynne. Is she hospitalized?"

"Her whereabouts are unknown."

Silence.

"Who did you say you were?"

I began to explain.

"Police psychologist?" she said. "Well that beats all. I reported Lynne missing to the police the day after she didn't come home. And that was a week ago. She told us she was going to her mom but when she did, she always came back the following morning. I phoned her mom and no one answered. So I tried to file a missing persons with the cops and they told me adults are free to come and go but apply online and they'd look into it. I heard nothing for two days so I called again, got voicemail, and no one has gotten back to me. I tried to explain this adult has the cognitive functioning of a twelve-year-old but basically I got brushed off. What's going on now?"

"Who'd you speak to at the police?"

"Hold on, I wrote it down, someone named . . . Pocan." She spelled it. "He was *not* helpful. Now why's a psychologist calling me out of the blue?"

"It's best I don't get into it. A detective will contact you promptly. Lieutenant Milo Sturgis."

"Sure. For what *that's* worth."

Milo said, "Harvey Pocan, total waste of space. So she's been gone since a coupla days after Martha's murder. Doesn't mean she couldn't have left before, also. Like sneaking out late, when the dog barked. Thanks for the sleuthing. I will now call Ms. Buttons."

Five minutes later, he was back on the line. "Man, my ears are burning. Not that I blame her. I asked if we could come down to Safe Place, talk to other residents, but she said no way, too disruptive and besides it's her day off. I looked it up, found an image. A house just like that Kadar place you told me about, I can see why Martha would go for it. Anyway, Ms. Buttons surprised me by volunteering to come to the station to talk about Lynne."

I said, "Nothing to hide."

"Or she wants us to think so."

"When's the love-fest scheduled?"

"Two hours. I asked if you could be there and she said, 'Sure. For what *that's* worth.' "

"Same thing she said about you."

"Ah. So we'll share the joy."

CHAPTER 21

Two hours gave me plenty of time to learn about Pamela Lee Buttons. A robust social media presence made the process easy.

Her photos showed her as late thirties, tall, with an outdoor tan and long blond hair. Former college volleyball player at the University of Colorado, into parasailing, rock climbing, skydiving, bungee jumping, Bikram Yoga. And crocheting. Her training was in management, not clinical work, her most advanced degree, a master's in public administration. She had taken the job at Safe Place a year ago, moving from Denver where she'd worked in HR at an orthopedic hospital.

The woman who marched up to us at the entrance to the station hadn't changed but for darkened hair cut short. Pam Buttons reached Milo's six-three in flat shoes. Unlike Katherine Santos, no slouch. Quite the opposite.

She said, "You've got to be the psychologist."

I said, "Good guess."

"My ex was one. That same look in the eyes. Okay, let's do this. Is Pocan going to be involved?"

Milo said, "Don't see any pigs soaring overhead."

Pamela Buttons hazarded a half smile. "I just might like you."

A glance in my direction said, *You? Not so sure.*

Milo gave her the choice of stairs or elevator.

She said, "One flight? Stairs, unless one of you is cardiac-insufficient."

Out in the second-floor corridor, she walked ahead of us despite not knowing her destination.

Milo said, "Here, ma'am," as she passed the door to one of the smaller interview rooms, causing her to backtrack.

He'd set the space up with three chairs arranged around a small square table. Center of the room, not pushed into a corner like when he wanted to crowd a suspect. Atop the table were energy bars and bottled water.

She wrinkled her nose. "Not exactly fresh in here. This where you pressure people and make them sweat?"

Milo said, "When necessary. Have a seat, please."

Pam Buttons inspected the lone chair as if checking for mold and finally settled, facing us. Touching one of the energy bars with a fingertip, she smiled. "My brand. You investigated me?"

"That's us, thorough," said Milo. "Nope, lucky break. First of all, I want to apologize for the response you got from Detective Pocan."

"Forget it," said Pam Buttons. "There's deadweight in every organization. Fortunately that doesn't include David, our receptionist. We've got her listed as Lynne Gutierrez, not Matthias, but when David heard 'Lynne' he notified me. I knew her mother's name is Matthias and put it together immediately."

Milo scrawled in his pad.

Pam Buttons said, "I'm assuming Gutierrez is her father."

"Was. Her mother's first husband," said Milo. "Deceased."

I flashed back to Martha's marital history. Remarried with no time to spare after Pablo Gutierrez's death. Maybe an affair, maybe wanting someone to help her care for a child with special needs.

Maybe both.

Pam Buttons said, "Whatever. Now can you please tell me what's going on?"

"Lynne's mother was murdered."

Pam Buttons's hand flew to her mouth. "Oh my God, *that* I wasn't expecting. I've been worried Lynne was a victim of something. Which is why I agreed to come here. Also, my dad is a retired deputy sheriff. When I told him about getting nowhere with you guys, he said don't push it anymore but on the off chance someone does call be cooperative."

"Appreciate your dad," said Milo. "So what can you tell us about Lynne?"

"You don't seriously think she could've done it."

"We don't know enough to think anything, Ms. Buttons, but we want to talk to her. What's she like?"

Pam Buttons thought for a moment. "Quiet, no problems. Our approach is problem prevention so we try to select residents unlikely to pose any serious issues. And Lynne's been there for—I guess decades, and has never caused a disturbance. Safe Place is her home. She has her own room and keeps it beautifully."

"Well behaved."

"Always. That's the rule when it comes to our residents, not the exception. We're not a clinic, we don't administer any kind of medication or formal treatment. We're a home for otherwise well-adjusted delayed individuals without alternatives."

I said, "People with no family."

"No family or a family unable to take care of them. They get nutritious meals plus ample snacks, TV, content-protected internet, and, if they want, classes. Crafts, exercise, music. I teach crocheting."

Injecting some lilt into her voice as she recited. A walking brochure.

I said, "The residents are free to come and go as they please."

"Exactly, they're residents, not inmates. For their security, the doors are locked from the outside but callers ring in and are evaluated. Or they can text."

"The residents have cellphones."

"Those whose families fund cellphones do."

"Did that include Lynne?"

"No," she said. "I learned that when I tried to locate her."

Milo said, "They don't find being out by themselves scary?"

"Residents who are anxious don't leave. Others take guided outings with relatives."

"Lynne was relaxed enough to go solo."

"She came and went successfully so I'd assume so." Buttons fooled with her hair.

"Did she have any friends?"

"Not that I saw."

"A love interest?"

"None that I've seen. Look, I'm not going to lie. I've only been there a year and I have my hands full running the place, you won't believe the organizational mess I inherited. From someone like Pocan, actually. But we don't have that many residents—eighteen at last count—so I do have opportunity to observe and Lynne was *not* problematic in any way. That's why I can't believe she'd harm anyone, let alone her mother. That's just a crazy notion."

I said, "She's been there for decades."

"Most of the residents have. That should indicate the caliber of the services we provide."

Milo said, "Despite issues caused by your predecessor."

"Those," said Pamela Buttons, "were organizational. Even he was okay when it came to providing service. The problem was . . . but that's not your concern."

"Where does the funding come from?"

"Inheritance and trust funds, private insurance, and whatever supplements Medicare and Medicaid and other agencies provide. Okay, I'll tell you the problem I had to deal with: inadequate billing for services rendered. Invoices were never sent and deadlines passed. I've just gotten on top of it."

"Who owns the place?"

"We're a nonprofit corporation set up by three charitable family trusts fifty-five years ago. The Steins, the DuBuques, and the Landermans. Wealthy families with DD children wanting to help the less fortunate. They've funded all kinds of things—cultural, artistic, medical. Our endowment is a drop in their bucket."

I said, "Is there anyone on your staff who could tell us more about Lynne?"

"I guess David. In addition to handling front desk, he's our exercise coach and music teacher and popular with the residents."

"Including Lynne?"

"I'd have no reason to exclude her from that appraisal."

I have no clue but don't feel like saying so.

Milo said, "What's David's last name, please."

"David Le Gallee."

He had her spell it. "Thanks. So how much contact did you have with Lynne's mother?"

"I've never met her, only spoke to her once. It was shortly after I arrived. The state had cut back on payments and while the trusts were solvent, lower interest rates cut into our income. So the families' copays rose. Nothing extreme, a couple of percentages, and I had the fun job of notifying everyone. When I tried to email Ms. Matthias, there was no address in the file, so I called."

Sighing, as if use of the telephone required self-sacrifice. "I informed her, she said she'd send a check for a year's worth of the overage. Which she did."

I said, "Brief conversation."

"She didn't come across as someone who liked to talk. Kind of icy, actually. Which I guess fits with her never visiting."

"That's not typical."

"Some residents have no living family but those with relatives often do receive visits. But it didn't seem to be a problem for Lynne. At least from what I saw. Maybe because she could visit her mom whenever she wanted."

"No complaints about being alone."

"No complaints about anything. And I don't believe it was just because of her speech limitations."

"She had difficulty talking?"

"She slurs pretty bad, is hard to understand. Maybe that's why she doesn't try to talk much. Or she just doesn't like it. Her mother wasn't exactly chatty."

Milo said, "That sounds below a twelve-year-old's developmental level."

"Not necessarily," said Pamela Buttons. "People can have problems in one area but be okay in others. She can read a bit, do simple arithmetic. But you probably *should* speak with David. Want me to text him?"

Milo said, "Please."

She worked her phone keyboard, put it down on the table. "I can't believe you'd suspect Lynne in a murder. When did it happen?"

He fudged. "Right around the time Lynne left."

"Well, that doesn't mean a thing. If anything, she might have also been victimized."

Her phone rang and she snatched it up, grateful for the interruption. "David? Thanks for getting back. I'm with the cops . . . yup, Lynne . . . no, they haven't, but it's complicated. I figured if anyone could tell them about her, you could. Can I hand you over to them? Thanks."

Milo took her phone and put it on speaker.

"Mr. Le Gallee? Lieutenant Sturgis."

One of those voices that manages to be buoyant even when faced with a gray day said, "David. No word on Lynne?"

"Would it be possible to talk in person?"

Pam Buttons scowled and shook her head.

David Le Gallee said, "I guess . . . sure. I'm off in forty-five minutes. If you can meet me in front of Safe, we can do it."

"Perfect. Thank you, sir."

Milo returned the phone to Buttons.

She said, "Can you find another place to talk to David? We like to keep things calm for the residents."

"Ma'am, we're not talking about a SWAT team charging in, guns blazing. Just chatting with Mr. Le Gallee out front. At some point, if we do need to enter, all we'd do is take a quick look at Lynne's room. If you'd allow us."

Pam Buttons said nothing.

Milo said, "Okay, we'll table that for the time being."

"A quick look will be unnecessary, Lieutenant. I already checked Lynne's room after she was gone for two days and trust me you won't learn anything. Like I said, she keeps it nice. And organized, which seeing how much stuff she has is pretty impressive."

I said, "She's a collector."

"Quite a collector. Dolls, toys, ribbons, hair clips, costume jewelry. And lots of old magazines—teenage stuff, mostly. I'm sure she's had them for years. In stacks up to here."

She leveled her arm three feet off the ground. "But neatly arranged and she keeps a little whisk broom to make sure dust doesn't settle."

I said, "Any diaries?"

"Nope," said Buttons. "That's what I was hoping for. A diary, some sort of personal note that could help me locate her, and believe me, I wanted to. I mean, this has been crazy-stressful. I even went so far as to contact Culver City PD. Guess what they said?"

"Not their jurisdiction."

She aimed a finger-gun at me. "Bingo. Anything else?"

Milo said, "No, ma'am. Thanks."

"Let's hope," she said and stood.

CHAPTER 22

Pam Buttons raced down the stairs ahead of us. When we got to the station door, she sighed and said, "Margarita time," and speed-walked north on Butler.

We returned to Milo's office, where he looked up Lynne Gutierrez, found several women with the name, winnowed the list to the right one, saved and printed and stashed everything in his attaché case.

"Time for Mr. Le Gallee, hopefully he'll know more."

We exited the station, crossed the street to staff lot, got in the Im pala, and drove to a place we couldn't enter.

Safe Place occupied a corner lot in a quiet residential neighborhood. No signage on or near the two-story Spanish house painted generic beige. The stucco was impeccable, the front door arched and hand-hewn, the entry presaged by a low wrought-iron fence and gate at the sidewalk followed by a lush green lawn. A row of healthy succulents lined up like toy soldiers against the house's frontage.

The kind of place three wealthy families would've approved of fifty years ago. Grandfathered in back when zoning was more plastic. Still, keeping up appearances continued to matter. When you're housing people easy to stigmatize, it pays to be discreet.

We arrived on time, had been sitting in the car for five minutes with no sign of David Le Gallee.

Milo texted. *We're here.*

Ping. *Right out.*

Cupping the nape of his neck with both hands, Milo craned forward, set off audible crackles, and winced. He hooked a thumb at the house. "Ms. Buttons clearly doesn't want me in there."

"You could call her dad and have him recommend it."

He laughed. "Something tells me he'd groan. Unfortunately, at this point the strings are hers to pull. With the little I've got so far, no grounds for any type of warrant, suspect or victim. Think she's hiding something or just being protective?"

I said, "Hard to say. I did find her description of Lynne's room interesting."

"Stacks of magazines," he said. "Like mother, like daughter, until maybe the relationship took a bad turn? So far Lynne's the only person ever seen entering Martha's house and she's been conveniently gone since soon after Mama got cut up. So despite Buttons claiming she's pure as milk, I'm sniffing *eau de suspect*—okay, here he is."

The arched door had opened and a man stepped out. Spotting us, he waved and came forward.

David Le Gallee was forty or so and compact. Five-six, one fifty, with a head shaved clean and an angular face so free of extra flesh it looked carved out of modeling clay. He wore tiny oblong eyeglasses, a black mock-turtle, jeans, and white tennis shoes.

We were out of the car before he reached us. Milo made the introductions.

Le Gallee said, "Police and a psychologist, yes, Pam filled me in."

"She warned you, huh?"

Le Gallee laughed. "She's like that, detail-oriented. Which is great for us, she inherited a mess and turned it around. Did an incredible job. Lynne being gone has really gotten to her. To all of us. It's the first time I can recall anything like this happening and I've been here eight years."

I said, "During that time, did you ever meet Lynne's mom?"

"Never. Which isn't common but it does happen."

We looked at him.

He said, "Sorry, don't mean to be vague. The sad truth is, sometimes Safe serves as a repository."

I said, "Families abandoning children who don't fit the mold."

"Adult children, we don't deal with anyone under twenty-five. But it's best not to judge. Getting old and having to worry about your own health plus a dependent adult can be a nightmare. Most of our residents are here because their parents have grown infirm or have died. Twenty-five's the minimum age but some are considerably older when they come here. In many cases, it's siblings who set up the move. Some stay in touch, others don't."

I said, "Martha Matthias never visited."

"I'm sure she had her reasons," said Le Gallee. "Maybe the fact that Lynne could visit her satisfied both of them."

"There were no problems due to Lynne's visits."

"Just the opposite, Doctor. Lynne left happy and returned the same way. That's why the thought of her harming her mother is totally preposterous. She's the last person to be violent."

"No behavioral issues."

"None. We screen for that."

Milo said, "How long has Lynne been living here?"

"I can't answer that, Lieutenant. Not because I don't want to but part of the mess Pam walked into was a whole bunch of missing records."

"How'd that happen?"

"The former director was well meaning but totally disorganized and kept putting off the conversion from paper to computer. Finally it started three years ago, with techs we brought in working backward from the most recent records. But when they got to something like six, seven years ago, everything was gone. I wouldn't put it down to anything suspicious, just carelessness."

"Who's this genius?"

"A guy named Barbour Spears. He moved to Maryland and got a job with the federal government."

Milo said, "Is that a punch line?"

Le Gallee laughed. "Wish it was, but nope, he got hired by some sort of oversight committee."

I said, "You have no idea at all when Lynne arrived?"

"What I can tell you," said Le Gallee, "is she was well established by the time I got here eight years ago. All the current residents were."

"No one new has come in?"

Le Gallee shifted his feet. "I know it sounds strange but did Pam tell you how this place started?"

"Three wealthy families funded it."

"Three wealthy families with developmentally disabled kids, all of whom ended up dying at places that turned out to be less than great. So they got together and established Safe Place."

I said, "The mandate's always been the children of the affluent?"

David Le Gallee removed his glasses, peered through the lenses, and restored them to the bridge of an avian nose. "We're not supposed to talk about that. But yes, with exceptions made for the occasional police and fire family, we're here for long-term, affluent residents. From what I understand the exception's because Mr. DuBuque's grandfather was a fire captain."

"The exceptions are your charity cases?"

"When pension money is available, it's tapped."

Milo said, "You know what Lynne's mother did, right."

"Pam said she was some sort of cop."

"Did Lynne ever talk about that?"

"Oh, never," said Le Gallee. "Lynne doesn't talk much, period, due to her speech impediment. She doesn't lisp or stutter, she's just extremely indistinct. Once you get used to her, you can get the gist, but she's shy to begin with so there's not a lot of conversation."

I said, "How does she make her needs known?"

"Her needs are pretty simple, Doctor, and they're taken care of in advance. When she does want something that hasn't been provided, she points. And smiles. She smiles a lot. I don't want to make like she's mute, not at all. But prolonged conversations are out of the question. She's a very sweet woman."

"Did she talk about her mother at all?"

"Just that she was going to visit her—she called her Mama," said Le Gallee. "And she'd give that smile. It was obvious that seeing Mama was something she looked forward to. There's simply no way Lynne's capable of harming anyone, let *alone* her mother."

"It's nearly a mile from here to her mother's house. No safety concerns about her walking by herself?"

"Typically," said Le Gallee, "residents who do want to leave are accompanied in the beginning and once they can clearly demonstrate they're okay, they go it alone. Honestly, it doesn't happen often, for the most part residents don't want to leave."

"Lynne was the exception."

"I believe Lynne and one other person have taken outings. Neither of them are severely disabled. She can read a few words, do simple addition, is okay with personal grooming."

"She was described as having a stiff walk."

"Well, that's true. She's knock-kneed and has developed arthritis."

"Pam described her as a neat-freak," said Milo.

"Oh, definitely," said David Le Gallee. "I was in the air force for thirteen years, servicing fighter jets. I like neat."

I said, "Pam also said she's a collector."

"Not in the sense of constantly acquiring. Whatever she has was assembled well before I got here."

Milo said, "She holds on to the same stuff."

"Exactly. Like a little museum. She plays with her things. Setting them up, arranging them. Taking care of them. She has a little whisk broom, you'd be challenged to find a speck of dust on her treasures."

"Meticulous."

"Oh yes."

"Did she do any crafts?"

"No, she was happy to be with her treasures. Lynne was—is a

happy woman, in general. A lot more content than some so-called normals I've known. I tell my own kids that—I've got two. Appreciate what you've got and make the most of it. Speaking of which, I need to pick my kids up from their mother's in a few. Anything else?"

Milo said, "Nothing right now, thanks for your time."

Le Gallee's face tightened. "This is a terrible situation. We're not naïve, we know what it means when someone vanishes and time goes on. It's an overall safe neighborhood. But things happen."

I said, "Did she ever walk at night?"

"No, never. Of course not."

Meaning the dog had been alerted to someone else.

Milo said, "Thanks, sir. Anything else?"

"I hope to God I'm wrong but I'm not feeling great about this." He threw up his hands, said, "Good luck," and walked to a lime-green Prius.

As he pulled away, Milo copied down the tag.

I said, "He twangs your antennae?"

"Everyone who's too nice does."

We sat in the car while he did a first-line check.

In the eyes of the criminal justice system, David Le Gallee didn't exist.

Milo said, "First Winchell, now him. Too damn many solid citizens." He hooked a thumb at Safe Place. "What do you think? Bizarre, no?"

I said, "I'm sure there are others like it."

"Repositories for the rich we never hear about."

"And a few regular folk from police and fire."

"Ergo Martha . . . wonder why she couldn't handle one kid."

"Couldn't," I said, "or didn't want to."

"Ditching her daughter so she could live her best life and create a hoarder's palace?" He shook his head. "You never know about people."

I said, "Martha transferred out of a successful career in Homicide.

That says her stress level had been high for a while. She welcomed Lynne for brief visits, maybe all she could take."

"Happy-time sleepovers with Mom," he said. "*If* Buttons and Le Gallee are being straight with us and not keeping it safe for Safe Place. You notice that even while reciting the party line, he wasn't crazy about Lynne walking by herself. What do you think of the policy?"

"I wouldn't have authorized it."

"I think it's downright nuts. Like an unfenced pool, right? All it takes is once."

I said, "Despite her problems, Lynne's a legal adult, so if she insisted, there'd be no way to stop her."

"Why'd you ask about her doing crafts?"

"Crafts involve tools."

"Oh. Like a jigsaw. Man, the way your mind works."

"On the other hand, Le Gallee said she'd developed arthritis. If that included her arms, it's doubtful she could've pulled off dismemberment."

"Too stiff to saw? Maybe, but if we find her with a bloody blade, so much for that excuse." He grunted. "Le Gallee was right about one thing. One way or the other, this ain't gonna turn out well."

Nearing Olympic Boulevard, he began changing lanes serially without apparent purpose. I closed my eyes and spent the time thinking. Ended up with serious doubts about Lynne Gutierrez as a viable suspect.

I was about to tell him that when his phone pinged.

He said, "Mind checking it out?"

Text from Basia Lopatinski. Final report. I read it out loud. Not much new.

Martha Matthias's cause of death had been manual strangulation, her dismemberment postmortem and cleanly accomplished by a serrated instrument. The blood recovered from the bathroom was all hers. DNA from the futon featured a small amount of her and multiple samples consistent with a female offspring.

He said, "So we've verified the sleepovers. Now all I've got to do is find Lynne."

I said, "The more I think about it the less I see her as a murderer. We were led in that direction by Hawkins's description of a mentally ill woman lurching down the street. But a developmentally delayed woman everyone describes as gentle choking her mother out then cleanly severing both her arms just doesn't fit. Let alone wrapping the corpse in plastic and managing to haul it to a deep-freeze in the garage."

"If not her, who?"

"A psychopath with serious body strength and at least a rudimentary knowledge of anatomy. That doesn't mean a doctor or a butcher. I'm sure there are plenty of charming YouTube instructional videos on quick and easy amputation."

"Still," he said, "she just happens to disappear right after the murder?"

I said nothing.

He said, "You see her as a victim like Buttons did?"

"Unfortunately for her, I do."

"Mother and daughter," he said. "You know I'm an atheist when it comes to coincidence."

I said, "Daughter may have been murdered because she could direct you to Mother."

"The bad guy is someone Lynne knows. She blabbed about Mama's cash-stash and led him to it."

"Could be. But how would she meet anyone?"

"On a walk to Mama's," he said. "And that means she might not be a victim but has lammed with him. I know Buttons and Le Gallee say she's harmless and you agree. But I'm not giving up the comfort of cynicism yet."

Another stretch of silence.

He switched a couple more lanes and said, "Whatever the case, the same damn conclusion: *Gotta* find her."

CHAPTER 23

It took until Thursday at nine a.m. for him to phone me.

"Alex." He managed with one word to transmit weariness. I'd assumed no news was bad news, so no surprise when he said, "Found her."

I said, "Not alive."

"I wish. Poor thing's body showed up at a landfill out in Irwindale, a backhoe driver saw a foot sticking out from a mountain of the garbage. Private outfit, fortunately they're super organized and stuff gets arranged in grids. So they were able to backtrack to the garbage truck that brought her. That particular load was collected from any of a dozen dumpsters, all in alleys downtown. Whether or not downtown's where she was killed or just an interim dump site, no idea. But Central has the case. Either way, it's unlikely we're gonna get a more precise fix."

"She was recently found?"

"Nope, she was brought into the crypt a week ago, logged as a Jane Doe, and assigned to a pathologist who hadn't looked at her yet. Then Basia, God bless her, noticed the sex and the approximate age, ran DNA, and got a match to the futon. Lots of decomp, without that it woulda taken dental records. I just called Safe Place and they have the records but it's moot. Spoke to Le Gallee who came across pretty broken up."

I said, "A week ago is so soon after she left Safe Place."

"Maybe even the same day. Some shredded pieces of industrial-sized garbage bag were wrapped around her. Basia says body gases probably inflated it and it burst. Unfortunately the bag's common and no trace evidence was on it."

"Oh Lord," I said. "A foot? She was also dismembered?"

"No, everything was intact. Relatively speaking. And she was fully clothed, except for one shoe that fell off and exposed the foot. COD was blunt-force trauma to the back of the skull. Three blows with something heavy and round like a baseball bat. The Central D handling it is a guy named Hector Villalobos. I've got a meet with him at noon. You're invited."

"I've got an appointment until twelve fifteen, can be there late."

"Better than never. It's right near you. That fusion place up at the top of the Glen."

"Convenient."

"Intended as such for you."

Domo Mario is a nouveau-Japanese-nouveau-Italian restaurant on the east side of the high-end strip mall perched atop Beverly Glen just south of Mulholland.

Crudo coexisting with sashimi. Could world peace be far off?

Working a custody consult had distracted me from the horror of Lynne Gutierrez's death but by the time I got in the Seville for the drive, images of a gentle, slow woman ending up in a trash pile hit me hard. I'd had nothing but dry toast and coffee at seven but my appetite was dead.

Discovery of Lynne's body hadn't discouraged Milo nor a man of his approximate girth feasting on an array of bounty from the ocean. Two sets of chopsticks clicked rapidly. What looked like iced tea was half gone from a pair of twenty-ounce glasses.

Hector Villalobos was fifty or so, with spiky white hair, the facial features of an unsuccessful prizefighter, and a bull-neck. Black suit, white shirt, gold tie, impeccable manicure. Central Division was Skid Row and sometimes worse. A smart person did what it took to feel clean.

Milo introduced us and Villalobos stood, smiled, and offered a rib-steak-sized hand. Despite the oversized paw and massive shoulders his height was a surprise. Five-eight, tops.

He said, "Pleased to meet you, Doctor," in the voice of a much younger man. "I've heard about you."

I smiled.

"Some people call you a wizard," said Villalobos. "There are a few who don't trust shrinks but that's their problem. There's also some cussing because Milo's got dibs."

Milo said, "Well earned, Hector."

"How?"

"Deep, abiding friendship."

Villalobos laughed. "Guess homemade tamales wouldn't do the trick. My mother's are killer, Doctor."

Milo said, "Forget it, he's beyond temptation."

"Well, if you change your mind. So. Crazy cases. Plus your other one. Planting DNA? C'mon, that's TV bull-crap."

"First time for me, Hector."

"Hopefully the last."

Milo said, "Amen. I'll get the waiter."

I said, "Don't bother, had a big breakfast."

"See what I mean, Hector? Earthly pleasures don't distract him. That's why he looks like he does and we don't."

Villalobos ran a finger around the interior of his collar. His eyes were soft brown and acute. "In high school I weighed one forty. My wife claims she still loves me but then she tries to get me on all kinds of diets."

He eyed his plate. Twenty or so bits of raw and cooked fish. "This I can tell her about, no butter, no eggs."

Milo said, "What're you drinking, Alex?"

"Coffee would be great."

He beckoned for the waiter, put the order in, specifying, "Black." When the man left, he turned to Villalobos. "Why don't you fill him in on Lynne, Hector."

Villalobos said, "Milo gave you the basics so I won't repeat. Only thing that's new is we've narrowed the number of potential dumpsters from thirteen to nine but they cover a wide area—Olympic all the way to Sixth and Spring to Broadway. No cameras so far—businesses don't care what happens to their trash. But we haven't finished looking. We being me."

I said, "You're doing it solo?"

"I, me, and myself. Low-priority case according to my boss. He actually tried to palm it off on Robbery-Homicide and they turned it down."

"Why?"

"They don't need a reason," said Villalobos. "His attitude is we're not even sure if it was a Central murder, she could've been killed anywhere. The real reason? A body out in the Irwindale dump is a low-probability close and the department's all about stats. And so far, can't argue with that. Doing the camera thing is worse than surveillance—I'm going cross-eyed—but at least I can take bathroom breaks. And the truth is, Doctor, even if I find something it could just be a dark figure in a hoodie tossing a big bag in at night."

He chopsticked a sliver of salmon, dipped it into some kind of sauce, and ate. "Any thoughts are appreciated."

I said, "The weapon was cylindrical. Any wood fragments in her hair?"

"Nope, we're thinking a metal bat or something along those lines." Villalobos winced. "Where are the nice, small-caliber gunshot wounds when you want them? I mean, how many blunt forces do we get?"

Milo said, "Not many."

"I see bums beating the crap out of each other on Skid Row regularly but it's rarely fatal. The last homicidal BFI that I had was five years ago—bum-against-bum thing, the victim got sucker-punched, fell, and hit a wall. No whodunit, the puncher hung around next to the punchee sipping Night Train."

Both of them ate.

Villalobos said, "I've got a question for you, Doc. Hard to imagine the same bad guy not doing both victims. So why dismember one and not the other? And why use strangulation on one and blunt force on the other?"

Milo said, "Top of that, it's not a typical dismemberment. No attempt to hide identity, no sexual overtones."

I said, "All I can do is speculate but it's possible the victims meant different things to the killer."

Villalobos said, "Explain."

"Martha was likely the primary target. She was murdered first, the killer took time with her and got up close and personal. We know how long it takes to strangle someone. At the scene Dr. Lopatinski suggested the arms meant something to him. I agree but no way to know exactly what. Afterward he posed them in a bizarre imitation of normalcy, wrapped her up carefully, and deposited her in the deep-freeze. Then he left her to be discovered. Proud of his work. Lynne, on the other hand, he dispatched quickly and tried to conceal. Her murder feels more like tying up loose ends. Maybe because she could lead you to him."

He curled his arms and held his hands palms up, as if hefting something. "In terms of the bad guy, he'd have to lift and lock, get the body to the rim, and boom. Not that the poor thing weighed much. In life, I mean. What was left of her came in at ninety-six but medical records from that place she was stashed put her at one thirteen. Still, even dealing with that much deadweight can be tougher than people think and this creep did it twice. Way my back is, I'd be hello chiropractor. So we're talking some degree of strength."

Milo said, "Mike Heck works out seriously but I can't see any way to tie him in to Martha, let alone Lynne. The guy we spoke to at Safe Place isn't overly buffed but he looks in shape and he was in the service."

"Which branch?"

"Air force mechanic."

"Heavy equipment," said Villalobos. "I was a Navy SEAL, but now? Definitely spinal adjustment time."

"Impressed, Hector."

"Don't be. I was thrilled when they accepted me, went in all gung-ho. Then eighteen months in, we were doing deep-sea training and I developed chronic ear infections." He shrugged. "Got discharged honorably and decided to pamper myself with a nice cushy job in Homicide."

My coffee arrived.

Villalobos pulled out his pad and turned to Milo. "What's Mr. Airforce's full name?"

"David Le Gallee."

He spelled it and Villalobos copied.

"He bother you at all?"

"Not so far," said Milo. "But he knew Lynne's routine and was aware of Martha."

"So we can hope. Okay, I'll check him out. Doctor, what do you think of the place itself?"

I said, "Haven't been inside."

"I mean the whole setup. Letting someone like that walk by herself, even in a decent neighborhood. C'mon."

"It wouldn't have been my policy."

Villalobos said, "The bleeding hearts think they're being kind but they usually end up making a mess. Like the whole homeless thing—sorry, let's stay on topic."

Milo said, "Working Skid Row, you're entitled, Hector."

Villalobos smiled at me. "Listen to him, getting all therapeutic. Obviously, you've been a good influence, Doc. Okay, back to basics. Assuming Martha was the primary, we're thinking it was about her money?"

Milo said, "Can't see money not being a factor. We found a huge stash but it took time. So for all we know, there was more that was easier to snag and he made off with a serious haul. That level of success, there'd be plenty of motive to tie up loose ends."

Villalobos wrote something.

I said, "Brutally murdering two family members in short succession with one dismembered feels like a whole lot more than just robbery."

Villalobos said, "The money plus something else? Like what?"

"Some sort of grudge against Martha. She did put away bad people."

"So take a look at any murderers she busted who might be back on the street."

"Or their relatives."

Milo said, "I'll do it."

I said, "Don't want to complicate things but despite everything I just said, it's possible Lynne was the starting point. He learned about the money from her, stalked her when she walked to Martha's, then returned and began educating himself about Martha's routine. If Genevieve Winslow's dog means anything, the murder began with his showing up during the early-morning hours. But he could've positioned himself in Martha's backyard and overpowered her when she emerged later."

Milo said, "Maybe he got her when she was carrying something out to the deep-freeze and got an idea."

Villalobos said, "Oh man. Bad, bad dude. Then he goes for Lynne a couple days later."

"The next time she walked to Martha's," I said.

Milo said, "Sounds like someone who worked at Safe Place."

Villalobos slapped his pad. "Mr. Airforce. Definitely going to educate myself about him."

Milo said, "I checked and no criminal record."

"So he changed his name. Bad Dude 101."

"You have a point," said Milo. "Someone like Le Gallee, Lynne would've trusted to give her a ride to Mama's. Once she's in his vehicle, she's finished. He takes her somewhere and beats her to death."

Villalobos said, "Head wound. Wherever he did it, there's gonna be lots of blood. But one question, Doc. If he knew he was gonna do both of them, why not pull it off when they were both at Martha's?"

I said, "One victim at a time was easier."

Two sets of chopsticks tilted like tiny lances.

"Efficient," said Milo.

"Dirty word," said Villalobos. "Hey, this food is pretty darn good."

CHAPTER 24

Just as both detectives cleaned their plates the waiter showed up, grinning. "Dessert, guys? We've got some great ones."

Villalobos said, "Better not."

Milo shook his head.

The waiter said, "We've got a mochi special and it's on the house."

"Well," said Villalobos, "can't be rude."

We left the restaurant and walked to where their Impalas sat side by side. Milo's an unsettling greenish bronze, Villalobos's black.

Villalobos said, "Had that mochi stuff before—Little Tokyo's in my beat. Chewy but once I got used to it I liked it."

Milo said, "Interesting."

"Ha. That's what we used to call homely dates. Okay, I'll get the warrant for Safe Place, go through whatever possessions poor Lynne had, and check out the staff for maniacs. We'll keep each other posted."

"Sounds like a plan, Hector."

"It's something." Villalobos shook his hand, then mine. "Nice to meet you, Doctor. And don't forget: tamales."

Winking, he got in his car and was off.

I said, "One guy on a whodunit."

Milo said, "Solid guy, I checked. But yeah, it stinks."

"The curse of statistics."

"It keeps getting worse, Alex. Used to be solve-probability wasn't an official factor on our end, just the D.A.'s. Now everything's about looking good. *Optimally efficacious* is how some pencil pusher they sent from Parker called it."

"The joy of algorithms."

"One day they'll have actuaries in every station, figuring out the daily odds."

I said, "New career opportunity: law enforcement bookie."

He cracked up. Turned serious. "A friendly Safe Place staffer is looking better and better. I kinda liked Le Gallee. You feel different?"

I shook my head.

He said, "Still, you never know about people . . . before we sayonara, anything else come to mind?"

I said, "How broad was the canvass of Martha's neighborhood?"

"Four blocks in all directions."

"You might want to expand a bit, see if anyone spotted a vehicle that didn't belong."

"He parked and walked."

"That would fit with Winslow's barking dog. And with wanting to avoid a tag I.D."

He chewed his cheek, brushed hair off a pockmarked forehead. "I'll take care of it myself. Get some fresh air and it's not like anything else is happening."

I said, "Did Villalobos mention going public before I got here?"

"He wanted to do it right away but got nixed by his captain. High risk of too many bad tips with no manpower to handle them."

"You're kidding."

"Wish I was." He opened his driver's door. "I put off seeing what I could find on Martha's homicide cases because it felt unlikely. What Hector would call TV stuff. No fresh air on that one, but let's see."

He patted my shoulder, said, "Have a nice rest-of-the-day," got into the car, and started the engine.

I motioned for him to roll down his window.

He complied, black, shaggy eyebrows arcing.

"Just thought of something. Two methods could mean two killers."

His lips pursed then he gnawed the lower one. Running his hand over his face like washing without water, he said, "I deeply appreciate your fertile mind, kiddo, but my head hurts."

CHAPTER

25

In the beginning, I shielded Robin from the work I did with Milo. It created tension and I learned that overprotectiveness can come across patronizing. Worse, insulting.

More important, serious blank spaces in a relationship don't work.

Anyone who meets Robin finds her charming but at her core she's a sensitive introvert who's chosen to spend her life with inanimate materials. I've seen her eyes mist up when coming across roadkill.

Horror doesn't play well with a mind like that. But things needed to change so we worked out a system of sorts. When cases begin, I offer the basics. After that, she sets the pace.

So far, what Robin knew about Sophie Barlow and Martha Matthias were the basics plus. Two women strangled, no mention of dismembering, though I had told her about the deep-freeze and the hoarding palace.

Before I'd left for the meeting with Milo and Villalobos, I'd placed a note on the kitchen table letting her know "Big Guy" had called me away. When I got back home, I was pretty sure she'd be curious.

She was in the kitchen, hair pinned up, wearing her go-to black overalls over a red T-shirt, drinking orange juice, nibbling on a cookie, and reading *Acoustic Guitar.*

Curled at her feet, Blanche snored like a steam compressor. Dogs sleep easily and extensively but not deeply, and my footsteps brought her upright and shaking off canine dreams. She waddled forward for a neck rub and a mutual smile-fest.

Robin put the magazine down. "Hi, handsome. Progress?"

"Not sure how to categorize it." I told her about the discovery of Lynne Gutierrez's body, left out the dumpster, the landfill, and the shattered skull.

She said, "Oh no. Where was she found?"

"Irwindale."

"All the way out there? Near the racetrack?"

I hesitated.

"Alex?"

Sitting down, I recited the ugly details.

As she listened, she bit her lip, tugged at her hair, played with her hands. When I finished, she said, "Repugnant. The poor, poor thing, so vulnerable. You're figuring the same person did it."

I said, "Hard to see it otherwise."

"Was she strangled like her mom?"

"Hit over the head."

She grimaced.

I picked up her hand. Her skin was cool and tight, her fingers unyielding.

She said, "Admire your ability to deal with it."

Standing suddenly, she kissed me hard on the lips and announced, "Back to work." Without looking back, she headed for the service porch door that leads to the garden and her studio at the far end.

Blanche remained in place for a second, debating her options. Then she left, too.

I washed Robin's glass. Brushed away cookie crumbs and tossed them in the trash.

It wasn't like her not to clear. She's organized and neat, snips loose ends reflexively. Good quality when you work with power tools.

Shaken by what I'd just told her.

An imperfect system.

My stomach was growling so I downed two glasses of juice and demolished three cookies. If my blood sugar skyrocketed, I wasn't feeling it. Just a cold, hollow sadness at the fate of three women. A trio of cases that, so far, had defied comprehension.

Time for escape into my basic shrink philosophy: When life tosses you lemons, get lost in the problems of other people.

I walked to my office where obligation awaited: a court report summarizing work I'd done on a particularly malignant child custody case. One of those dreary parental jihads where you know the kids will suffer and there's not a thing you can do to prevent it.

I wrote for two oblivious hours. Read, re-read, revised, saved, and printed the hard copy that would go to the judge and enter the official case file. Futility formalized.

Seconds after closing the file, my mind snapped back to the murders.

Sophie.

Martha, Lynne.

When you begin thinking of people you've never met by their first names, you're committed.

Two unrelated strangulations within a week of each other. Followed by a blunt-force trauma.

Something itched the back of my brain but I couldn't put it into focus.

Then it hit me: the math.

Strangulation's a common cause of death in murders depicted on screens of all sizes. Both fictional homicides and the real-life savagery that gets true-crime bloggers salivating.

But it's incredibly rare.

I keep yearly FBI homicide reports on file, pulled up the most recent annual summary not expecting the facts to change.

They hadn't.

Strangulation and asphyxiation combined amounted to less than one and a half percent of murders nationally.

Blunt-force killings were a bit more prevalent but still uncommon: around four percent.

Guns, knives, fists, and feet—in that order—cause the bulk of the deaths people inflict on one another. Mostly guns and like most homicide detectives, that's what Milo customarily deals with. Yet during a brief interval, he'd picked up three outliers.

He and Villalobos had talked about the rarity of blunt-force homicides but they hadn't wondered about the total picture. Neither had I, until now.

Because we were all caught up in the details.

Hello, trees; go away, forest.

But what if?

I sat at my desk for a long time but failed to come up with anything that could tie in the death of an office manager in her thirties strangled at her kitchen table and that of an elderly former homicide D choked out in the hoarder's palace she'd created.

Toss in planted DNA at Sophie's crime scene and postmortem mutilation in Martha's case and the differences grew.

Toss in the brutalization of that same detective's mentally impaired daughter and they ballooned.

But.

The math.

It took another hour of headache-inducing concentration before the giant, fuzzy question mark in my head began to take on sharp angles. Bad headache, as if my brain could take only so much.

I self-medicated with caffeine and that reduced the throbbing to an oddly comforting two-two beat.

Then I phoned Milo.

CHAPTER 26

Voicemail at his desk phone and his cell. I left call-me-backs at both and hung up.

The two-two pulsation going strong.

Not a musical earworm but the rhythmic equivalent. That brought back memories of the cheesy phony rumbas and sambas I'd played earning my way through college. Gigging on guitar with a wedding/bar mitzvah band of middle-aged alcoholics and druggies. Bones, Thumper, a bassist who called himself Rigor-Tony. Others whose nicknames I didn't recall.

My tag had been bestowed the first time I showed up: Egghead.

The beat grew stronger, began to hurt again. Maybe real music could quiet it down. Unlatching the case of my old Martin, I strummed, finger-picked, flat-picked, concentrated on note-for-note renditions of challenging songs, and when that didn't work, I tried to distract myself with improvisation.

Useless.

What I'd wondered about wouldn't leave my brain.

Likely a question Milo, with his resources, could eventually answer. But he wasn't answering.

I tried several search engines.

Total failure. Took a run up the Glen and back, returned home sweating with a clear head and snatched up my phone. Still nothing from Milo. I took a shower and as I was toweling off, he responded.

"Hey." Sounding distant. "It's been tough finding Martha's old cases. The few bad guys I have found are dead. We must've inspired Villalobos because he hustled right over to Safe Place. He's still there, taking pictures of Lynne's room, but it's not looking promising. Nothing weird there, and Le Gallee and all the other employees are alibied for the day Lynne left to visit Martha. Small staff, most of them women who've been there forever. A few rich ladies volunteer from time to time. Hector described the atmosphere as four-star bleeding heart, everyone's torn up about Lynne. Any additional thoughts or did I guess right and you wanted an update?"

I said, "What if Sophie and Martha's cases are related?"

Silence.

"Where's this coming from, Alex?"

"You know the statistics on strangulation murders. What's the probability of two unrelated strangulations turning up one right after the other?"

"What connection could there be?"

"Michael Heck."

"Back to him? *He* killed both of them? All *three* of them?"

"I'm not saying that but he could be the common factor. He gave you a possible motive for the planted DNA. Someone thinking he'd ratted out Darren Alberts was out for revenge. Martha transferred from Homicide to Fraud ten years ago. The investigation into Alberts began soon after. What if she worked on it?"

"She retired soon after, couldn'ta been on it long."

"You said she was an effective detective. Maybe long enough to do some serious damage to someone."

"Lotsa maybes, Alex. And Alberts is in no shape to get payback. Your own contact confirmed he's green salad."

"Doesn't have to be him," I said. "Someone else at the firm."

"Someone else who waits seven years to get payback on a snitch and a cop?"

"Okay," I said. "Just passing it along."

"Passing it along." His laughter was harsh. "That's kinda like, hey, there's a drunken, three-legged elephant staggering up Pico. But don't look."

CHAPTER 27

I didn't hear from him the rest of the day so I figured he'd ignored my theory.

The following day, I had back-to-back evaluations from nine to six, switched my phone off as I always do and stashed it in a bottom desk drawer.

Five minutes after I saw the last patient out, Robin and I were on our way to a mom-and-pop Italian place on the southern edge of Westwood. By eight o'clock, we were home, by nine still naked and relaxed, by nine thirty showered and ready for some quiet time.

Still nothing from Milo. Then I remembered and retrieved my phone.

Two attempts, an hour ago and twenty minutes later.

I pushed the little red button.

He said, "You don't like me anymore?"

"Patients all day, turned the phone off and forgot."

"I'm hurt," he said. "Anyway, you got me thinking so I rooted around on Alberts."

He'd had no luck retrieving any official paper on the case. Backtracking local press coverage revealed that Kevin Van Osler, the politically motivated federal prosecutor who'd spearheaded the probe, had turned corporate litigator at a New York firm. A year later, he was dead. Heart attack at an Oyster Bay country club.

Unable to find mention of any other attorneys on the case, he'd tried Deputy D.A. John Nguyen. Reaching John at home and annoying him.

"No idea and don't ask me to look for it."

"Just an initial stab, John?"

"The only stabs I'm into are when you bring me corpses."

"John—"

"We are swamped, man. The case is ancient history and got beaucoup press coverage. Go find some alleged reporter."

"The Times *guy's in Thailand and not answering emails and the rest of it was wire service with no bylines and online rehash."*

"Then I guess you're S.O.L. Let's face it, the entire premise sounds freakin' flimsy. The daughter was likely some homeless deal and if Villalobos gets anywhere it'll be because some homeless blabs."

"You don't think mother and daughter could be linked."

"Because they both got done? West L.A. and Irwindale? Totally different methods? Plus the daughter had IQ issues? I know you think Delaware's a genius and granted he's been right about stuff, but stick with the here and now. Do your due diligence and if that doesn't turn up anything and you're struggling to breathe, maybe I'll find you an oxygen tank."

I said, "That's cranky even for John."

"I think I interrupted a date. Timing's everything, right?"

Ignoring Nguyen, he'd persisted, chewing up most of the evening trying to find anyone who'd worked the Alberts case. A series of calls to former colleagues finally got him a name but no details. A White Collar Crimes detective named Angela Batchelder.

"Retired, lives near Spokane. Right off she tells me, 'Sure, Martha was part of the team, sorry to hear about her.' Do I have to say it? Yes, I do, self-abasement's good for the soul. *You. Were. Right.*"

"What was the team?"

"Three D's from us and a bunch of FBI agents specializing in money crimes. Martha was on it for a year. Batchelder said Martha had been a real bulldog, extremely detail-oriented—compulsive, she called her. Working long hours, compiling the thickest file. Knowing what we know now, that makes sense. What would Freud call it—adapting your hang-ups to the job?"

"Sublimation. But Freud had an answer for everything."

"Well," he said, "doesn't sound like Martha was sublime. Just the opposite, according to Batchelder. Hyped up, almost manic. To the point where she and the others were wondering about her. Then suddenly, she surprises everyone and packs it in. No face-to-face, she put notes on everyone's desk. Wanna guess what I'm thinking?"

I said, "Some sort of payoff."

"Unfortunately, yeah. Don't wanna see her as corrupt, Alex, but one day she's digging up dirt on Alberts like a hyperactive gopher and the next she's gone? But even with that, why would someone want to kill her and cut off her arms years later?"

"Could be someone with their own mental health issues," I said. "Last year, I read a case in a psych journal. IRS clerk in Cleveland, had problems with co-workers, quit and went on disability. Eleven years later, she walks into the office and shoots four people. People who see themselves as aggrieved can stew and seethe. If their lives turn out okay, they may be able to put it aside. If not, the anger festers. It's the root of most workplace homicides."

"So all I need to do is to find someone in Alberts's firm whose life has totally dead-ended and who hears voices telling him to wreak vengeance. Problem with that, Alex, is Batchelder couldn't tell me who else worked in the firm because for all the dough Alberts took in, it was a one-man operation. No other lawyers, just him and a bunch of paras and secretaries and Alberts was the sole defendant. So why would they be aggrieved?"

"None of them were subpoenaed?"

"Not that she was aware of but she said the Feds mighta done that."

"And kept it to themselves?"

"That's how it was throughout the entire investigation."

"The in-crowd and the out-crowd."

"She said Van Osler favored the Feds, basically gave her stuff to file, made her feel like a clerk, the whole assignment was a giant pain in the ass. In fact that was her guess as to why Martha retired."

"Makes sense," I said. "So maybe I'm off base."

"Stop. It's too late in the day for heresy. Can you give me more about what kind of personality would do what was done to Martha? And Lynne. Because despite Nguyen's bile-based sermon, a connection is obvious."

I said, "Someone who amplified whatever injury he suffered due to delusional thinking. It could've been as simple as losing a job and then having difficulty finding another one due to personality issues and substance abuse."

"Paranoid doper nutcase with crap job skills."

"Given the precision of Martha's murder, a paranoid schizophrenic is unlikely. But psychopaths always blame others and that can lead to delusions of persecution."

"So how do I find this gem of a human being?"

"You could try Mike Heck, see if he remembers anyone."

"Actually, I couldn't. Captain and all the brass hats are well aware of the lovely Ms. Bel Geddes and the certainty of a civil suit. I am *enjoined* from further contact with Heck."

"How about one of the FBI agents?"

"Batchelder recalled a couple of their names but I haven't been able to locate them. Makes sense if they're retired. Cops who leave the job usually want to be forgotten. Only reason I got lucky with Batchelder is she and her husband breed show horses and have a website. I did bring up the possibility that someone's after everyone who worked Alberts. She said she lives on two hundred fifty acres with an ex-SWAT hubby, coupla Neapolitan Mastiffs, and an arsenal. Her exact words were 'Let 'em try.' "

I said, "Contacting the FBI's out of the question?"

"I'll try it but they'll probably stonewall me on principle and tell me to file a Freedom of Information request. There's got to be a quicker way in but so far I haven't come up with it—hey, you know what, I'm gonna send Alicia out to the facility where Alberts is housed, see if he's actually that far gone. No offense to your friend."

I said, "I've always found her reliable but go for it."

"Yeah, yeah, probably a waste of time. But when the going gets tough, the tough turn to creative futility."

CHAPTER 28

The following day, my schedule was open and I kept my phone nearby.

Robin had gone to her studio but she was back minutes later.

I said, "Everything okay?"

"It's a gorgeous day and I'm feeling the lazies. You up for playing hooky?"

"Tempt away, Jezebel. What do you want to do?"

"See some gorgeous."

Fifty minutes later we were forty miles east in San Marino, strolling the grounds of Huntington Gardens.

It's a one-of-a-kind place, the former estate of a playboy insurance heir, combining two-hundred-plus acres of world-class botanical specimens with a couple of serious art museums and a massive scholar's library that Robin uses when she's researching antique instruments.

We spent the day filling our senses with a crazy quilt of fragrant roses, the serenity of the Japanese Garden and the Chinese Garden, a collection of cacti that could've come from another planet. After an early dinner at a seafood place on Huntington Drive, we were back home by six forty-five and tending to Blanche.

Robin said, "That was lovely, babe . . . I want to check a bridge repair on that Stromberg. Darn thing popped the first time."

"Sure."

"When I finish, we can watch something dumb."

"You bet."

She kissed me and left. Moments later, Milo called.

"What's up?"

"Alicia verified that Alberts is totally out of it. I finally connected with one of the FBI guys but he said he knew nothing. Then the second turned out to be an honorable gentleman named Walter Karski. Happy to talk but couldn't do it right then because he and his wife were babysitting grandkids. We agreed to meet tomorrow, he lives in Ventura. You busy making the big bucks or can you spare some time for altruism?"

"What time tomorrow?"

"Eleven."

"My morning appointments end at eleven thirty."

He said, "That would get us there twelve thirtyish but beggars, choosers, and all that. I'll ask Karski if we can push it up. If you don't hear from me, we're on."

I set the timer for tomorrow's coffee, had just finished when Robin returned. "Good news, the bridge is stable. How about a bath before we rot our brains?"

"Love it when you get sybaritic."

"Love it when you use professor words."

At eleven thirty a.m. Milo rolled up in front of the house and idled the Impala, revving a few times with an itchy foot. The moment my door closed, he U-turned, coasted back down to the Glen going north, continued into the Valley, and picked up the 101 North at the Van Nuys on-ramp.

An hour of driving stretched to eighty-five minutes due to a lane closure just past Tarzana. Two miles of orange cones shunting traffic to the right in order to protect a road crew.

No crew in sight. A sign proclaimed *Your Tax Dollars At Work!*

Milo said, "Salt in the wounds."

Once free of the snarl, he compensated by pushing the car to eighty-eight. Cops aren't immune to CHP tickets but he pretends they are.

When it became clear that we'd still be late, he phoned Walter Karski.

A cheerful voice said, "Whenever you're here."

The house was a white-clapboard bungalow in the hills overlooking the Beaux-Arts masterpiece that houses Ventura city hall and beyond that, Main Street, the primary artery of the city's Old Town. This high up, the bonus was a thin blue line of ocean hovering above rooftops.

Small house, beautifully kept. A path of herringbone brick led to a door painted aqua. The siding was immaculate, the lawn pristine even where a robust crepe myrtle shaded the grass. Running along the front was a lush border of impatiens and daisies.

I said, "Cheerful."

Milo said, "Maybe it'll rub off."

He lifted a door-knocker shaped like a dolphin and let it drop. Seconds later the door opened on a tall, thin, bald man with a bushy white beard, wearing a white polo shirt, baggy blue linen pants, and huarache sandals.

"Milo? Walt Karski. And you must be the doctor."

"Alex Delaware."

Quick, firm handshake. "My daughter's a psychologist, works at Sloan Kettering in New York with cancer patients."

Milo said, "He did that, too."

"Did you?"

I said, "Pediatric oncology."

Walt Karski flinched. "Rebecca says it's tough work but rewarding, but I can't imagine kids. Come on in."

He stepped back and we entered an open-plan layout with windows on three sides. Living room, dining area, a white-on-white kitchen that looked new. A door to the left led to a hallway backed by a rear window framing an eyeful of green.

The furniture was rattan with brown hibiscus-patterned pillows and a circular glass table. On the walls were soft-focus seascapes and photos of Karski, a plump blonde his age, a couple in their twenties with two small children, and a young woman in doctoral graduation regalia. Dark-blue hood, same as the one I'd worn years ago.

Sometimes retired people display career mementos. No indication how Walter Karski had spent his working days.

He settled facing us, crossed long, tan legs, and placed his hands on his knees. "So here we are. I always wondered if someone would get curious."

Milo said, "About the Alberts case."

"About tons of money spent to boost a rich kid's career. You know about Van Osler's connections?"

"Governor's cousin."

"Plus his parents are big-money Northern Cal types, the guy grew up in Atherton," said Karski. "He gave speeches to us about justice but you could tell he didn't mean it. That politician look, you know? We all figured the plan was to confiscate a whole bunch of money in order for him to look heroic so he could run for something. But wouldn't you know it, Alberts was broke."

I said, "Cancel the whiz-bang press conference."

Karski smiled. "Exactly, whimper, no bang. Van Osler moved to New York and went white-shoe corporate and the rest of us civil servants got reassigned. Haven't heard from him since."

Milo said, "He dropped dead at a country-club dance."

Karski blinked. "Did he. Yeah, he always had that flushed look. And now here I am talking about him and the good old days. Never figured it would be due to a homicide, let alone Martha's. Fill me in however much you feel you can."

Milo gave him the basics. When he got to Lynne Gutierrez, Karski's eyes widened.

"The daughter, too?"

"Afraid so. A few days later."

"Wow."

Milo continued. When he got to Martha's dismemberment, Karski's face compressed.

"My God, that sounds psychopathic weird—am I wrong, Doctor? Can't see how any of it would relate to a ten-year-old fraud investigation."

Milo said, "Not on the surface but there was another murder shortly before Martha and both have connections to Alberts."

"Another. Good Lord." Karski slumped. Reacting like a civilian. Aka a normal person. Retirement can be like that. I never hardened when I worked the cancer ward but I was able to focus and keep my feelings secondary. Years later I visited and found myself fighting tears.

When Milo finished filling Karski in on Sophie Barlow, he uncrossed his legs and stroked his beard.

"So the connection is this gal once had a thing with Heck but she wasn't at all involved with Alberts."

"Not that we've found, so far."

Karski said, "Crazy . . . listen, I'm not going to tell you how to do your job but on the surface it sounds kind of tenuous."

"It does, Walt, but you follow the breadcrumbs you get tossed. And what are the odds of two strangulation homicides popping up within weeks of each other?"

"Never worked any homicides directly, just some organized-crime money stuff related to hits," said Karski. "You're going to give me a number, huh?"

Milo cited the statistics.

Karski whistled. "See what you mean. What about the blunt force to the daughter?"

"More common but still less frequent than guns or blades."

"Three atypicals. So what's your working hypothesis on all this?"

"Wish we had one. That's why we're here."

"Don't know how I can help but I'll try. Can I get you guys something to drink?"

"We're fine."

"I'm thirsty from gardening, hold on."

Karski strode to the kitchen, took a pitcher of orange juice out of the fridge, and brought it over with three glasses festooned with Disney characters.

"Sure I can't pour you? Freshly squeezed from my Valencia out back."

"In that case, sure."

"Here you go . . . I grew up back east and I know I'm sounding like a total rube, but the ability to go out and pick fresh fruit still awes me."

We drank.

I said, "Delicious."

Karski beamed and sat back. "So how can I help you?"

Milo said, "Let's start with what you remember about Martha."

"What I remember . . . okay, didn't hang out with her but she impressed me as a really hard worker. Little busy bee. When she wasn't interviewing POIs, she was at her desk, writing, filing, never looking up. Then she'd straighten the desk. Take her time doing it before leaving without a word. Neat as a pin."

I said, "Not very social."

"Not in the least," said Karski. "But to be fair there wasn't much socializing going on, period. We weren't exactly a team."

I said, "People working in the same room but not together."

"Precisely, Doctor. We were on one side of the room, you guys on the other. And not by accident, Van Osler set out to divide us from the get-go. Wanting control, you know?"

I said, "Where was the workspace?"

"Rented warehouse east of downtown. Van Osler brought in a construction crew to build a corner suite for himself. With windows. Besides that, there was one interview room and the rest was a big open space with no view of anything but walls. Our guys called it The Wasteland."

"Control. The politician thing."

"Exactly, Doctor. What else motivates those losers but control?" said Karski. "Do I sound bitter? Maybe I do but that's after working in D.C. for years." He shook his head. "If only we could elect people who don't want the job."

Milo said, "Martha was all about work."

"That's what I observed. Petite little thing, she gave off this hummingbird energy."

I said, "Did she hang out with anyone on her side of the room?"

"Hmm," said Karski. "You know, Doc, now that I think about it, I don't think so. The others were guys and they'd go out together but if they included her, I never saw it. Not that she seemed to mind. Just threw herself into her work, did that desk-straightening thing, and went home."

"What aspect of the investigation did she work on?"

"Couldn't tell you," said Karski. "Which shows you how pathetic the whole thing was. We were given assignments by His Majesty and that's what we stuck to. The Bureau was clear we shouldn't make waves."

Milo said, "What kind of assignments?"

"Ours was going through the numbers. We were all trained in forensic accounting."

Milo said, "You said Martha interviewed POIs. So our guys worked the offender angle."

"Your guys seemed to be doing some sort of fieldwork, because they were in the office a lot less than us. Come in, talk on the phone, leave. Sometimes they'd return, sometimes not."

"But Martha spent more time in The Wasteland."

"That she did," said Karski. "From what I saw she mostly did desk work but occasionally I'd see her take someone into the interview room. So maybe the others trawled the POIs and handed the catch over to her."

I said, "Given her homicide experience, that would make sense."

"Maybe." Karski edged forward. "As I'm talking about this my ignorance is starting to hurt. I mean here was a supposedly big-deal investigation and none of us really had an overall picture."

I said, "Like the atom bomb. Built in Chicago, D.C., Manhattan, Lawrence Livermore, and other places. So no one would know too much."

Karski laughed. "Excellent analogy, Doc, because this thing sure bombed."

Milo said, "The people Martha interviewed. Any idea who they were?"

"I assumed employees of the firm. And Alberts's wife, she came in looking miserable. They all did. But turns out Alberts was a one-man scam machine, no one else worked the fraud so no one got charged."

Milo showed him a photo of Michael Heck.

Karski said, "Who's that?"

"Heck."

"Yeah, he was there. I remember him because he came in with a lawyer which made me wonder, Does this guy know he's been a bad boy? But like I said no one materialized as a suspect except Alberts."

"Who was the lawyer?"

"Some female. Cute, looked too young to be practicing but she had that lawyer look about her—scanning the room, accusatory looks. You know, lawyer bullshit."

Milo scrolled his phone but I was already there with mine, showed him a photo of Bettina Bel Geddes.

Karksi said, "Yup, that's her. Back then, she was blond. Platinum, you know? The Marilyn thing. Come to think about it, maybe a wig. Though why a young chick would need a wig, I have no idea."

He returned the phone.

Milo said, "She's still his lawyer."

"Long-lasting relationship?" said Karski. "So maybe more than just business?"

"Could be. Was Heck the only one who came in with representation?"

"From what I saw, Milo, but I couldn't swear to it. So now you've got him connected to both your victims but with a rock-solid alibi for at least one. Going to question him about Martha?"

"Maybe."

"Only maybe?"

"He's got assertive legal representation."

"Cutie Pie needs to allow it."

"She does, indeed."

"Still," said Karski, "even with all this I can't see any obvious reason for Heck to harbor a grudge against Martha. It's not like she arrested him. More likely she cleared him, because, like I said, all of them were cleared. Even the doctors and the therapists Alberts used. That's because his cases weren't bullshit slip and falls, they were actually righteous. The problem was he didn't disburse funds to his clients."

I said, "Where did the money go?"

Karski grinned. "Finally, something I know." He began ticking fingers. "First off was gambling—massive bets, six figures on sports, both online and casinos. Vegas blackjack and high-stakes poker. Then there were private planes to *get* to Vegas. And back. And Aspen, wherever. NetJets alone cost him nearly a mil a year. He also piled up art, furniture, clothes, cars. A lot of which turned out to be overpriced crap, just goes to show you *can* cheat a cheater. He had three huge houses but all were mortgaged to the hilt. But the *biggest* hit Alberts took was on bad investments in the stock market. High-risk short selling, commodities, futures. It was like a primer on how to lose a fortune fast. My guys are getting backaches sitting at our desks all day expecting a big payoff and there's goose-egg to recover. So the tents got folded overnight. Meanwhile, Alberts stalls his way out of prison with some sort of diminished-capacity bullshit. Haven't heard he's ever come up for trial, so I guess that's still working."

Recounting the details had flushed Karski's face. He looked younger, more fit, perched on his chair with muscular tension that said ready to pounce.

Milo said, "Turns out he really is impaired, Walt. Pretty much vegetative."

"That so?" said Karski. "Well, at least he told the truth once."

His posture slackened as he drained a glass of juice, poured another. "The whole thing was about headlines, pure and simple. Want something to eat?"

"No, thanks. Anything else come to mind."

"Sorry, no. Wish I could help more and feel free to follow up with questions but I can't think of anything."

"Thanks."

"I guess I should be thanking you," said Karski. "First time I've felt useful in a while. The whole retirement thing, you know?"

The door opened and the woman in the photos entered, carrying shopping bags. OshKosh B'gosh, Gap Kids. Thinner than in the image on the wall, her hair longer, allowed to gray.

Karski got to his feet and they shared a lip-peck.

He took the bags and deposited them on the kitchen counter. "Judy Grobel, aka my far better half. Hon, this is Milo and that's Dr. Delaware."

Judy Grobel shook our hands with the same quick firmness as her husband. "Psychologist." She grinned. "No doubt Walt told you about our Rebecca."

"He did."

Karski returned. "Productive shopping for the munchkins?"

"Very. Our oldest, Mark, lives nearby in Goleta, he's in tech, had the good graces to get married and produce grandbabies."

Karski said, "Rebecca will get there."

Judy Grobel crossed her fingers. Slate-blue eyes lowered to the table. "Enjoy the juice? Walt's pride and joy, he raised the tree from a puppy."

We smiled.

Milo said, "Delicious. We were just leaving."

She looked at her husband. "Productive session?"

Karski said, "If only."

"Got it," said Judy Grobel. To us: "We hated the whole thing—Walter working Alberts. He because he knew it was a joke and me because I had to live with him. Shortly after, we both retired from the Bureau."

Karski said, "She worked national security."

Grobel said, "Not as hotshot as it sounds. I liaised with TSA, basically visited airports trying to ensure the stupid was kept to a low level."

"She's selling herself short."

She kissed his cheek. "I'd offer this guy to you on loan but I generally like his company."

Both of them walked us to the door and continued outside the house.

Walt Karski said, "Good luck."

Judy Grobel said, "That always helps."

CHAPTER 29

We drove down to Main Street, found a space in front of a small antiques mall, and parked.

I said, "Karski thinks he told us nothing but he's wrong. Bettina goes way back with Heck."

"How about that?" He worked his phone, found Bel Geddes's profile on her law firm's website.

"Got her degree nine years ago from Cal, so she was a rookie when she represented him on Alberts."

"Like Karski said, there could be more to their relationship than attorney-client. And that got me thinking. The woman at the alibi hotel with Heck was never identified because Heck said she was married and he refused to name her. And given how things unfolded, there was no reason to push it."

"You think it could be Bel Geddes? What got you to that?"

"You told me all the video revealed was a blond head, which is exactly how Karski described her ten years ago.

"L.A.'s not short on blondes."

"True, but Heck's chivalry was puzzling, given that he was facing a murder charge. What if he endured two days in jail knowing he had a rock-solid alibi because Bel Geddes told him to."

"Why would she do that, Alex? And why the hell would he listen to her?"

"If she was the woman at the hotel, both of them knew Heck could be exonerated immediately. False arrest, PTSD, what better setup for a massive civil arrest suit? Hang in there for a couple of days, Mike, and you'll never need to work again. Neither of us will."

He swiveled in the driver's seat and stared. "The way your mind works."

"Not likely?"

"Damn likely," he said. "With enough payoff I can easily see Heck chancing it."

"I know the lawsuit's been hanging over you. Prove Bel Geddes colluded to obstruct a criminal investigation and your problem's over."

"*That* problem's over," he said. "Assuming she's *the* blonde. Which is still a big if, Alex. Meanwhile, I've got three whodunit murders and Heck's been confirmed as a link between Martha and Sophie. Screw his alibi, I'm back to he coulda hired someone."

Walt Karski had raised a good point: *What's the motive?* I kept that to myself and said, "As long as the lawsuit's an issue, your access to him is nil."

He went through a series of face-contorting grimaces. Wider repertoire of tortured muscles than I'd ever seen.

Sighing, he pulled out his phone and put it on speaker.

"Alicia? New development."

When he was through, she said, "Crazy, L.T. Wouldn't that be something."

"You into anything urgent right now?"

"I wish. Total stall on Martha, the same for Villalobos on Lynne. And he's been working it well—good guy. Not one of his downtown sources had a thing to say, same for the cameras. Hate to say it, L.T., but the air's starting to feel frosty."

"Let's see if we can warm it up, kid. Dig up whatever you can regarding Bel Geddes being at the hotel. We've got no grounds to subpoena her cellphone but if you can pull any video that captures her face, we will. Lacking anything inside the hotel, expand to the parking lot. They resist, push 'em. Also, find out what Bel Geddes drives and see if it shows up in the lot."

"Can I get Sean or Moe on it, too? You know about video ADD. I want to make sure nothing's missed."

"Sure," said Milo. "If you can get both of them, even better."

"On it, L.T."

"Gracias."

He was speeding the 101 past Newhall when Alicia called back. He handed the phone to me.

She said, "Oh, hi, Doc."

Milo said, "Doc and *moi.* I'm being a law-abiding driver."

"Good for you, L.T. Okay, all I've gotten from the hotel interior so far is one view of Heck and the woman going on the elevator and another coming off. Makes sense because the room key log says they stayed in there the whole time. Unfortunately, both are shot from above and don't clarify a thing."

Before showing the images to Milo, I studied them. The camera was positioned high enough to turn the top of Michael Heck's head into a small dark disk. Same for the platinum cap of a black-clad female form stepping into the elevator ahead of him. Heck's free hand on the pop-up handle of a wheelie bag. Same sequence upon exit.

Alicia said, "Looks like a wig to me. Which I guess makes sense if she's stepping out on her husband and is being paranoid. Or she just gets off on the mystery-woman thing. I sent Bel Geddes's photo to a desk clerk who'd been on duty that day but it meant nothing to her."

Milo said, "Does the height fit?"

"Hard to say from this angle but she doesn't look huge, so I guess. The hotel's still looking for files with parking lot shots, they've had some technical issues with the cameras. DMV lists two rides for Bel Geddes. A two-year-old red Porsche 911 and a brand-new white Range Rover. We've been good little detectives, maybe one of those will show up."

"Thanks, kiddo."

"Hey, I'm motivated, L.T. We nail her for obstruction, wouldn't that be something? Even better, we somehow tie both of them in to Martha? That happens, *I'll* be thanking *you.* As in forever."

"Thank Alex, he thought of it."

"Did he? The way your mind works, Doc."

No conversation for the remainder of the freeway ride. Same for the trip up the Glen to Mulholland and the descent toward the L.A. portion of the snaky road.

As we neared the unmarked turnoff leading up to my house, Milo looked at his watch. "Nearly an hour since she called in . . . I know it takes time to find more video . . . her and Hector . . . maybe *something's* happening."

Pulling his phone from his pocket, he gave it the longing look of a reformed drunk contemplating a bottle. Muttered, "Bugging her's not gonna change anything," stashed it back in his pocket, and dropped me off uttering a rapid, "Thanks for your time," before roaring away.

CHAPTER 30

Things changed just before ten p.m. Robin was reading in the living room and I was playing guitar.

When the phone rang, I took it into my office.

Milo said, "Blessed are those who listen to shrinks. Neither of ol' Bettina's vehicles showed up in the lot but guess what: We nailed her at the passenger door to Heck's BMW waiting for him to open it for her. He's fumbling for his keys, she's tapping her foot, like what's taking you so long, moron. He drops the keys and she uses the time to pull off a blond wig and shake out a whole bunch of red hair. Then she has the good graces to turn and inadvertently face a nearby camera and it's clearly her. Hold on, I'll send it to you."

Moments later I was looking at Bettina Bel Geddes's face.

I said, "Annoyed."

"Alicia called it the 'I'm-thinking-of-dumping-you look.'"

I laughed. "Maybe eventually but not with a huge lawsuit pending. But so much for that. Congratulations."

He said, "Let's see what the people in power want to do."

The following morning I was in his office at nine as he called Deputy D.A. John Nguyen who said, "No shit she's screwed. Awesome, she annoyed me from the git-go, my head's filling with criminal charges. A litany, as the journos call it."

Milo said, "If you don't mind, John, I'd like to deal with the civil suit first."

"Why?"

"We can't have access to either of them as long as it's pending."

"Damocles' Sword?" said Nguyen. "Shit. Hate to admit it but you're right. Okay, I'll call someone over at you-know-where. Don't hold your breath, they lay down snail-trails."

You-know-where was the city attorney's office, a place Nguyen and other D.A.'s regarded as junior college.

The chief deputy there told Nguyen, "Yeah, I've been picking up rumors a shitshow might be imminent due to your screwup."

"Obviously not a screwup," said Nguyen. "I'd think you'd be grateful given your chronic manpower issues."

"Person-power. Yeah, I guess this could be helpful."

"What are you going to do about it?"

"Link you up to my best person."

That turned out to be a thirty-something Stanford grad named Rachel Stone, the daughter of two Century City entertainment lawyers. Slender, pretty, decked out in Prada, easy contender for the role of Bettina Bel Geddes's brunette sister.

Bel Geddes's quiet, thoughtful, poised sister. She shook each of our hands then settled across from us in a city attorney meeting room, proceeded to listen without uttering a word until Milo, Alicia, and Nguyen had all finished.

"Interesting," she said. Several seconds of nothing ensued as Stone's wide, brown eyes studied each of our faces. Ending with me.

"You've got nothing to say, Doctor? Even though you originated the hypothesis?"

I said, "They've covered everything."

More silence.

Nguyen said, "You don't think it means anything?"

Rachel Stone said, "I think it means everything in terms of minimizing or even obviating the risk of a lawsuit. Bel Geddes was clearly knowledgeable about Heck's alibi and chose to conceal that knowledge, which puts her on dangerous ground in so many ways. The problem is, she hasn't filed a lawsuit or taken any other steps yet indicating she's planning to exploit the deception. So currently, I don't see any charges we could bring."

Nguyen said, "What about withholding evidence?"

"Of what?" said Stone. "Sleeping with a client?"

"You're kidding."

"Over in your place they file charges prior to a crime?"

A vein in Nguyen's neck throbbed.

"No charges yet is fine with me," said Milo.

Nguyen stared at him.

"What I'm saying, guys, is I'm totally comfortable showing her what we have and heading her off at the pass. It'll knock off the lawsuit and prevent her from obstructing when I want to question Heck. Who is back in my sights as a murder suspect."

"Why is that, Lieutenant?" said Rachel Stone.

"Because he's the only link we've found to two of our murder victims—Sophie Barlow and Martha Matthias. Three, if we consider Lynne Gutierrez as tied to Matthias. Plus *his* role in the deception shows the kind of guy he is, meaning he could have premeditatedly set up an alibi while hiring someone to do the actual killing. Getting rid of a bogus false-arrest money grab will give us grounds to dig deeper."

"That all sounds pretty theoretical."

"That's my point, Ms. Stone. If I can get access to Heck's phone records and his financials, I might be able to turn it from theoretical to empirical."

Rachel Stone placed smooth, manicured hands flat on the table.

John Nguyen said, "I concur totally."

Stone said, "An ounce of prevention."

Nods all around.

Stone said, "What if Mr. Heck casts Bettina aside and gets himself another lawyer who bears no liability in the case. What stops him from continuing to stonewall you?"

Using Bel Geddes's first name. Maybe they went to the same parties.

Milo said, "That's also theoretical."

"Not quite, Lieutenant. I can imagine any competent lawyer attempting to block your subpoenas."

Nguyen said, "Block away, given Heck's lies on record, we'll get past it."

No reply.

Human beings have low tolerance for silence so therapists use it as a way to encourage self-revelation. Attorneys use it, too, the way they use everything: as a weapon, to confuse and intimidate.

Rachel Stone's motive for keeping us waiting was unclear. Whatever her reason, the air in the room seemed to empty of oxygen.

I said, "Is there something about Bel Geddes we should know?"

She blinked. "Why would I be aware of that?"

"Just wondering if you knew her outside the courtroom."

"I don't know her *in* the courtroom, Doctor. Why are you asking me this?"

"You called Heck mister but used her first name."

"Oh wow," said Stone. "I'm being analyzed?" Her laughter was brittle.

Our turn for collective silence.

"As a matter of fact," she said, "we have attended some of the same social functions, but no, we're not pals."

No one responded.

Stone laughed again. Uneasily. Her hands curled.

"Okay, this doesn't leave these four walls but she's got a reputation. I'm not going to tell you for what but let's just say putting her in her place wouldn't be disappointing."

Nguyen said, "Great. So we're on? You'll move on both of them?"

"Not so fast," said Stone. "We need to know exactly where we're headed. The way I see it, our options are binary. Which is a good thing, too many choices confound the situation."

She waited. No one bit.

Looking disappointed, she said, "Binary. A, we wait until Bel Geddes takes action and thus incriminates herself, then come down hard on her. B would be as you say, Lieutenant, we head her off at the pass. I will discuss this with Mr. Rimpau and get back to you, Deputy Nguyen."

Before Nguyen could reply, she stood and left the room.

Nguyen looked stunned. "Better check the bottoms of my shoes."

Alicia said, "Can you imagine her and Bel Geddes at the same shebang? The earth would shift on its axis."

Milo rubbed his face and shook his head. "It seemed like an obvious deal. What's the next step, John?"

"What do you think?" said Nguyen. "We wait. I know these guys. Afraid to get their hands bloody."

"Snail-trail."

"Exactly, Milo. It could get long and slimy."

It didn't.

Two days later, Stone called Nguyen and told him, "Feel free to head off at as many passes as you like."

"Which translates," he told Milo, "as it's your heap of shit, dude, we want nothing to do with it."

"Great, John."

"Depends how it turns out, Milo. Stone was right about one thing: If Heck's smart enough to get himself another lawyer, you'll still be up a creek."

"Better than nothing, John. How do you want me to go about it?"

"Up to you," said Nguyen.

"My heap of shit, you want nothing to do with it."

"I will deny that if queried."

CHAPTER 31

Full assembly in the station's big interview room. Milo at the board, the rest of us facing him.

Everyone was aware of the situation but he reviewed it anyway.

Sean Binchy put his palms together prayerfully.

Moe Reed said, "These two need to go down hard. What's the plan of attack, L.T.?"

Milo turned to me.

I said, "We've done some background on Bel Geddes. She's a successful attorney, extremely bright, got fast-tracked to partner at a top-notch firm two years ago at age thirty-one. Interestingly, almost all her work has been in contracts and business litigation, including some entertainment cases. With the exception of Michael Heck. He's the only criminal case she's ever handled, which tells you their relationship has some substance to it."

"Ah, true love," said Alicia. "As opposed to her husband, maybe. Speaking of which, what's his story?"

Milo said, "Bedford Drive cosmetic surgeon named Straub. They got hitched three years ago. No kids, coupla big careers, no joint vacations on Instagram."

"Not-so-true love, L.T.? That would give Heck an opportunity. Is he an old flame she reconnected with?"

"All we know so far is she repped him on Alberts and is doing the same thing now."

Moe said, "Any criminal liability for him on Alberts?"

"Not that we know of."

Alicia said, "Seven years between the cases, plenty of fun in between."

Milo said, "She also does some entertainment law. I can see her imagining a megabucks suit *and* a film deal."

Alicia said, "Hey, that's exactly what happened with Alberts when everyone thought he was a hero. *Kaching, kaching.*"

Binchy said, "She may be smart but she slipped up in that parking lot. Careful enough to wear a wig but she misses the camera."

Alicia smiled. "The wig might just be a bit of kink, Sean."

Binchy blushed.

Milo said, "Legal work's all about preparation and Bel Geddes convincing Heck to endure brief jailing in order to file a false-arrest suit constitutes serious planning. However, we don't know if it actually says anything about Heck's involvement in any of the murders—"

"Heck," said Binchy, "he could've handed his own DNA over to a hired bad guy. Get away with murder and make a bundle."

Nods from Alicia and Moe.

Milo said, "If the stars align, it'll go down that way and subpoenas will go a long way in proving it. But we can't eliminate that Heck had nothing to do with the murder and when he was arrested he and Bel Geddes saw an opportunity to profit."

"No offense, Loot," said Sean, "but that sounds kind of iffy."

"With millions of dollars in damages at stake?"

"Hmm."

I said, "Whatever the specifics, Milo and I noticed something during the meeting we had with both of them. It was subtle but Heck seemed to be moving away from Bel Geddes emotionally. Asserting his independence—just a bit, nothing dramatic. But the fact that it happened at all might turn out to be relevant."

Alicia said, "Opportunity to get a wedge in between them."

"Maybe he just got tired of being dominated," said Reed. "The video, she's always out in front of him, does that toe-tap thing while he's looking for his keys."

Alicia said, "Yeah, he's total whipped cream."

Sean said, "So now we've got an opportunity to divide and conquer."

I said, "Exactly. Which is why I think they need to be approached separately. And I'd start with Bel Geddes. Confront her when she's alone and do it without warning."

"No opportunity to prepare."

Reed said, "Okay, how exactly do we go about that?"

Milo said, "Glad you asked."

CHAPTER

32

It began with surveillance.

Sean and Moe kept a watch at Michael Heck's West L.A. apartment while Milo and Alicia took Bettina Bel Geddes's Tudor house on the 600 block of Trenton Drive on the western edge of the Beverly Hills Flats.

I saw patients and read the detectives' daily reports.

For the first three days, both subjects went to work, came home, and stayed there. On the fourth day, Michael Heck stuck to that routine but Bettina Bel Geddes and her husband took the red Porsche to an Italian restaurant on Little Santa Monica Boulevard. Ernest Straub, M.D., was fortyish, tall, slim, and gray-haired, favored unstructured suits over T-shirts and wildly colored running shoes.

Alicia and Bel Geddes had never met so she ventured inside the restaurant while Milo stayed in the Porsche 928.

Alicia emerged moments later and got back in the passenger seat. "Both of them are busy on their phones. Wouldn't it be something if she was calling Heck with Hubby right there? Not that he's being the least bit attentive."

"Modern romance," said Milo.

Ten minutes later, Bel Geddes exited, shifted a few feet to the west of the restaurant in front of a now-dark boutique, and pulled out her phone.

Milo and Alicia waited to see if Straub would join her and when he didn't, they converged on her.

"Evening, Bettina."

She clicked off, eyes flashing. "What the fu—"

Then her eyes shifted to the photo in Milo's palm. The hotel parking lot, full view of her face as she stood next to Heck.

Anger shifted to confusion. Then terror.

She looked over at the restaurant, blinking rapidly, lips quivering. "I don't understand."

"Don't you?" said Milo. "We need to talk, Bettina."

"I—" Another glance at the photo. "Put that away! Away—*please.*"

"No prob, if you agree to chat, Bettina."

"Sure, sure, fine, whatever but now . . . I . . . later. Put it *away*!"

Milo slipped the image back in his pocket. "Not too much later, Bettina."

"Fine. Tomorrow."

"Tonight would be better."

"How can I—I'm with—how *can* I?"

"Finish your dinner with Dr. Straub, then go home and tell him you want to take a walk."

"I—he . . . I . . . fine. When?"

"Whenever you're ready. We'll be able to see you."

"You've been watching me—I can't believe—this is fu— . . . crazy."

"*Bon appétit,* Bettina."

"As if. I'm going to vomit."

But she didn't, drawing herself up on stiletto heels, fluffing her hair, reentering the restaurant and appearing thirty-two minutes later with Straub.

Neither of them talking.

Alicia said, "*This* guy walks in front of *her*. But love the shoes."

Milo said, "Maybe the reason she digs Heck."

"Nut for every bolt, huh—okay, the valet just drove up with their Porsche."

She caressed the edge of a leather seat. "Speaking of which, very nice, L.T. Appreciate the ride-along."

"Perk of the job, kid."

They followed the couple back to Trenton Drive, watched them park in the driveway and enter their house. Ten minutes passed. Fifteen, twenty.

Alicia said, "Like Doc said, she's a big one for prep. Maybe she's calmed down and is calling her own mouthpiece."

Milo texted Bel Geddes.

Happy to knock on your door.

Seconds later, Bettina Bel Geddes hurried outside, ponytailed, clench-fisted, wearing black velour sweats and pink Nikes.

Fifteen feet to the south, Milo flashed his brights.

She ran over, breathing hard. Milo and Alicia stepped out.

"I had to *change,* okay? *You're* the one who *wanted* this whole—I can't exactly run in *heels,* can I?"

The passage of time had restored some of the attorney-edge to Bel Geddes's voice. But it wasn't a durable change and her volume faltered, dropping to a near-whisper at the tail end.

Milo said, "Let's talk, Bettina."

"Not here for God's sake, the next block, I don't want anyone seeing me with you."

Alicia said, "We're not contagious."

"*Please!* This is bad *enough.*" Bel Geddes's voice broke.

Milo's notes said, *Det. Bogomil and I allowed suspect Bel Geddes to distance herself from her residence.*

The three of them walked quickly to Walden Drive. Milo stopped on a quiet, tree-shrouded corner and said, "Here."

Bettina Bel Geddes looked around and stood there, tapping a foot. Not impatience, this time. Fear.

People in poor neighborhoods often take to the streets after dark, escaping cramped, poorly ventilated quarters. The higher-priced spreads in L.A. become ghost towns, and Walden was no exception.

Bel Geddes said, "Okay. What's this about?" Aiming for tough talk but falling well short.

"You saw the photo, Bettina."

"Fine, I'm sleeping with another man. My husband's not exactly a saint."

Milo said, "Not any man, Bettina."

"So he's a client."

"That's irrelevant to us. Though it is kinda unprofessional. What does matter is the date of your mini-vacation in La Jolla."

"Meaning?"

"You're going to make me explain it? No prob. Check out the time stamp."

Bel Geddes turned away.

Milo said, "Okay, I'll spell it out. You were with Heck during the time his alibi for Sophie Barlow was solidified. So when he was arrested, you both knew immediately that he could weasel out of any charges. Despite that, you let him sit in jail. Beyond that, you *advised* him to sit in jail so you could claim PTSD and file a false-arrest suit."

"You don't know that."

"You're denying it?"

"Why wouldn't I?"

"Because you're at risk for an obstruction charge and the more problems you pose, the likelier a compound indictment is. That's straight from the D.A.'s office."

Bettina Bel Geddes chewed her lip but said nothing.

Milo said, "Heck's also going to be charged for obstruction but in his case it goes way beyond that. Now that we know he colluded on a planned fraudulent lawsuit—"

"You can't prove that."

"Now that we know what the two of you were up to, Heck's credibility is gone and we're putting him back on the suspect list for Sophie Barlow. High on the list. And who knows, you may end up there, too."

Her head snapped back. "That's absurd."

"At the very least, all of this is going to come out in court documents, Bettina. You're a pro, so you'll do as good a job as anyone on damage control. But you won't be able to avoid public exposure. Assuming you're not involved with Sophie Barlow's murder."

"What? How can you even think that? I never met the woman, had no reason—this is big-time fucked *up,* why are you *doing* this?"

"To get to the truth, Bettina."

She clamped her hands on her hips. "More like to prevent your own incompetence and negligence from coming to light."

"Are you really going to play it that way, Bettina? No prob."

He turned away and headed back toward Trenton, Alicia at his side.

Ten steps later, Bettina Bel Geddes said, "Wait."

The detectives remained in place, keeping their backs to her.

The lawyer said, "I may be able to help you."

CHAPTER 33

The meeting was called for eight a.m.

No faux-sophisticated club; a smallish interview room down the hall from Milo's office.

He rarely used the space because the lighting was harsh and nothing rescued the air from chronic staleness.

The furnishings were a small, scarred metal table and four unfriendly folding chairs. On one side, Milo and me. On the other, Bettina Bel Geddes and a nervous-looking Michael Heck. They'd arrived thirteen minutes late. His head was down. Her posture was exaggeratedly erect.

Postur*ing.*

She pointed to me. "What's he doing here?"

Milo said, "Consulting."

That seemed to kick up Heck's anxiety. A faint sheen of sweat had veneered his face. His hands were fisted tight, his eyes jumpy.

He said, "I don't—"

Bel Geddes quieted him with a throat clear.

Milo said, "Good morning, folks. Here's the deal, Mike."

◆

As he spoke, Heck shifted his body away from Bel Geddes. Subtly, less than an inch each time. By the time Milo was finished, over a foot gapped their chairs.

She noticed it and frowned. He avoided looking at her.

She said, "All right. I'm going to respond to all that—"

Heck said, "No, *I'm* going to respond because this comes down on me."

"Michael, we—"

Heck waved her off. "Here's the real deal, Lieutenant. I had nothing to do with any murders. Not Sophie's, not that lady's, no one's. Ever. I'm not that person. Just a guy caught up in a . . . Did I screw up by going to jail for two days? You bet, it wasn't fun."

"Michael!" Bel Geddes's arm landed on his sleeve. He shook it off.

"And for that I'm sorry, Lieutenant, but you need to know it wasn't my idea in the first place. And I'm still the one who suffered. For real. Even for two days, that shithole is hell on earth, I'm not even going to describe some of—"

He wrung his hands. "Like a bad dream but yeah, I own it, my bad, I shouldn't have agreed to it but she thought it was a *great* idea."

Bel Geddes talked fast and loud. "Oh no you don't, mister! You do not do that. No, you do *not.* Whatever ensued was the product of a genuine attorney-client weighing of the relevant—"

"Cut the bullshit, Bettina. You thought of it and you convinced me."

"I was looking out for you! For your welfare. Because until things were clarified you were going to have to spend at least some—"

"Bullshit, Bettina. You could've stopped it cold but you didn't want your husband to find out what you were doing. *Then* you thought of the money shit and you went straight for it like a—"

"Shut up, moron!"

"Oh, so now I'm the moron." Heck laughed.

Bel Geddes sprang to her feet, red-nailed hands curled into talons.

"You stupid, lacking-in-judgment son of a bitch! You should be thanking me, not trying to screw me."

Michael Heck said, "Screwing's already been taken care of."

She moved toward him. Heck's hands came up protectively.

Milo's arm got between them. *"Stop it. Now."*

Bettina Bel Geddes stood there, red-faced, panting, rocking laterally like a boxer seeking an opening.

"Sit down, Bettina."

Bel Geddes remained on her feet.

Milo said, "If you're gonna disrupt, leave. It's Mike we're interested in talking to."

That widened four eyes.

Bettina Bel Geddes said, "You know what? I'm out of here." To Heck: "You are now officially on your own, moron."

Heck licked his lips. "Okay, sorry, let's back it up, Bett—"

"Uh-uh, you crossed the line, Brain-Death."

She stomped out, slammed the door.

Michael Heck seemed to deflate. "Maybe I should leave, too."

"Not your choice," said Milo, "once we book you for all sorts of things."

Heck's face lost color. "Book me? C'mon, man, I've got no more guiltiness than I did before—okay, what can I do?"

"Bettina claimed she could help us, Mike. We assumed she meant you could help us."

"Well," said Heck. "It's not like it's . . . *CSI* or anything. Maybe it's nothing. I can't say for sure."

Milo smiled. "Would you like something to drink? There's a bigger room we can use. With coffee—or tea if that's your thing. Or water or Coke."

Heck scratched an arm, did the same with the other. "Sure. Let's get out of here. I'll take coffee."

"Got some pastries, too."

Heck touched his gut. "No way, I'd heave."

"You never know, Mike. Sometimes the truth heals."

CHAPTER

34

The big room. The size of the room caused Heck to stop outside the threshold. The setup made him hesitate longer.

The long table pushed to the wall. Leaving a triangle of three chairs in open space. No barrier between our two and his.

My suggestions.

Milo said, "Ditch the table to make him feel vulnerable, I like it. Wonder why we don't do it more."

Once inside, Heck sat and accepted a cup of coffee but didn't drink it. With nowhere to put it, he passed it from hand to hand, finally set it on the floor.

Milo said, "Tummy still off?"

Heck grimaced. "I'll be okay."

Milo said, "Don't want you to kick it over," retrieved the cup, and brought it back to the urn. "You change your mind, Mike, you know where it is."

He sat back down, stretched, smiled.

Heck licked his lips. Rubbed his arm and tapped his feet and waited for Milo to speak.

He didn't.

I said, "So how long have you known Bettina, Mike?"

Heck's eyes shot to mine. "Like eight years. Met her right before the thing, so when I needed a lawyer I went to her."

"The thing being the Alberts investigation."

"Yes, sir."

"Where'd you and Bettina meet?"

"Tinder," said Heck.

Milo said, "Tinder," and scrawled in his notepad.

Heck said, "Is that relevant?"

"We never know what is and what isn't, Mike."

I said, "Tinder."

Dividing his attention between us made Heck frown. "It was just for . . . you know. Her thing more than mine."

"She's a big fan of Tinder."

"Oh yeah, she's been sleeping around for years. Before and after getting married. She says he does the same thing but I don't know, that's just what she says."

I said, "You and Bettina were sleeping together before the Alberts investigation so when you thought you needed a lawyer, you turned to her."

"Actually," said Heck, "she thought I needed a lawyer and volunteered."

"You figured you were okay without a lawyer."

"Because I knew I did nothing. But she said don't be careless so I said okay. She wasn't charging me anyway. I just had to take her to nice places."

"Hotels."

"Hotels, restaurants, we went a lot to Ojai, Santa Barbara. I'm not sure it didn't end up costing me more than a regular lawyer."

"You were never charged for anything she did on Alberts."

"Not 'cause of her. I was innocent. Everyone was."

"Everyone except Alberts."

"Exactly. He ran a one-man show."

"So," I said, "Bettina and you go back a way."

"Nothing steady, here and there."

"Did you meet Sophie Barlow on Tinder?"

"No, no, nothing like that. Her it was the gym. She shouldn't have been there."

"At the gym."

"At that gym. I'm not being a sexist, some girls can handle it but it wasn't for her."

"Not strong enough."

"Not hardly," said Heck. "She would've been better with machines, light weights, yoga classes."

"This gym was . . ."

"Hard-core free weights. It even got to a point where I said enough."

"Sophie went there because . . ."

"She read a Yelp rating or something. She looked kind of lost. Wearing these dance-type leotards that showed off her body. Very slim but no muscles."

I said, "You got a good look at her body and decided to meet her."

"It wasn't that," said Heck. "I wanted to help her."

I kept silent.

"Okay, sure, she's good-looking, why not? But let me go on record again: I didn't kill her, there'd be no reason."

I said, "What's a good reason for killing someone?"

"I—that's not what I'm saying, sir. There's no good reason, never, not ever. But Sophie and I, we got along great, there were no fights, it didn't get complicated, no nothing. We just decided to end it. Actually, she did."

"Why?"

"She said it was just wanting to be friends," said Heck. "I figured it was another guy. Which is fine, plenty of fish in all the seas. So I made it easy for her."

"You made it easy for Sophie by . . ."

"By letting her do her thing. Talk about what she wanted. Women love that, talking it out."

He sat up straighter. "I just thought of something. If there *was* another guy, you should be looking at him. Because obviously I'm innocent."

Milo wrote.

Heck, unsure how to interpret that, stared, frowned, looked for a hint on Milo's face. When he didn't get one, he sighed.

I said, "You and Sophie had the talk."

"Friendly talk," said Heck. "Like I said, plenty of other things going on."

His eyes shot to the right. Concealing something.

I said, "Things being . . ."

"Dates. Chicks."

"From Tinder."

Reluctant nod.

I said, "Including Bettina."

"Her when she decides to booty-call me." He shrugged. "What can I say, I like women and they seem to like me. And she can be pretty . . . you know."

"We don't."

"Passionate."

I said, "You like women and let them express their feelings."

"Well," said Heck, "I'd like to think it's more than that."

Milo said, "A regular Romeo."

"You're joking, sir, but basically that's true. I'm romantic to the core. Never touched a woman when she didn't want to be touched, no means no, okay? And what turns me on is turning them on, okay? So I sure wouldn't kill anyone. That's crazy. And obviously, I didn't because that whole DNA thing was obviously bogus and obviously someone was out to shaft me."

I said, "But initially you kept your alibi to yourself."

"*She* said keep your mouth shut, this is an opportunity. Jail scared the hell out of me but . . . what can I say? It was stupid."

Milo said, "Stupid and illegal."

"Listen . . . yeah, okay, I screwed up. Big-time. I admit it. But now

I'm being honest about it and I'm still the one spent time in that hellhole while *she* slept in her big bed in Beverly Hills."

I said, "Jail was tough."

"Oh man, what do you think?" said Heck. "They put me in a cell by myself but I'm still surrounded by gangbangers. One's in the cell across from me, laughing while he's jerking off and telling me it'll be me in there with him tonight. I mean, c'mon, man. It was hell. So yeah, I screwed up by listening to *her* but I more than paid my dues."

I said, "Let's talk about Martha Matthias."

"Who's that?"

"The detective who interviewed you on Alberts."

"Her? The old lady? Why?"

"Because she was murdered."

Heck jerked forward in his chair. "You think I had—oh, that's *insane.* Why would I have anything to do with that? Why the eff? C'mon, man. I met her twice."

"Tell us about that."

"Nothing to tell," said Heck. *"Nothing."*

I said, "If it was nothing, why twice?"

Heck sat back. "I can't talk about it."

"Why not, Mike?"

"Not my idea, theirs."

"Theirs—"

"The government."

I said, "You informed on Alberts."

Heck rubbed his brow and shook his head. "I can't."

Milo said, "Mike, that investigation's long over and the prosecutor's long dead."

"Dead? Oh no, now you're going to try—"

"Calm down, Mike. Natural causes."

Heck exhaled. "Okay . . . well, I still can't say anything. But I'm not going to deny, okay?"

"Deny what?"

He looked at me. "What *he* just said. Okay? That work for you?"

Milo said, "You served as an informant and gave Detective Matthias your findings."

"There were no findings, that was the thing," said Heck. "The first time we met was away from that place."

"What place?"

"Where they worked, downtown, looked like a warehouse they stuck desks in."

"Where did you and Detective Matthias meet?"

"Some restaurant—a Denny's, I think. In Culver City? Yeah, Culver City."

"How did that come about?"

"He—the asshole in charge—had told me to look for papers, notice whatever I could and I'd be safe from prosecution. I knew I'd done nothing but he came on strong and the whole thing freaked me out so I did it. So I met with her—the old lady—at Denny's and told her there was nothing. She pushed back, said there had to be something. No nonsense, like one of those teachers who give you a hard time? But I was being honest so I held my ground and she got up, paid the tab, and left."

"The second time was . . ."

"In her office. To finish off."

"Finish off what?"

"Whatever they had going. That was the deal. People would get ordered to come in, no choice where or when, just show up. They'd talk to her or some other cop and whatever got said would be written down. For some kind of report, I guess. But it was all total bullshit because no one had anything to say because no one *knew* anything. Except Darren. That was his thing. Keep everyone separated so no one learns anything from anyone."

The same technique Kevin Van Osler had used with his investigators. Devious minds finding common ground.

Milo said, "Divide and conquer."

Heck said, "Exactly. So there was nothing anyone could've known.

The whole deal—the scam—was the payment part. Everything else was legit. The cases, the legal work. Which is what I told her."

"Detective Matthias."

He shook his head. "I try to convince her, she gives me this look like she knows I'm lying. Not talking, just staring me down. Didn't bother me 'cause I knew I wasn't. I said feel free to check. She must've 'cause the next time I went in it was to sign off. Obviously it *had* to go that way because I was telling the *truth.* Which I'm obviously doing *now.*"

We said nothing. He began fidgeting. "Okay? Can *we* sign off?"

I said, "Why'd Van Osler choose you as an informant?"

"He said because of my job," said Heck. "Managing the office, writing out checks, I was in a position. But the checks I wrote out were for the staff and expenses, not payment to the clients. Darren kept that deal for himself, said he was changing lives, wanted to hand over the money in person and watch their faces."

"That never happened."

"Actually," said Heck, "it did a little. He paid out some of what he owed to some of them but never most of it and not to all of them. At least that's what she told me—Detective Matthias. When she was trying to make me feel like a liar. She said, Listen, we know what's going on, Mike, it's the Ponzi. And we also know that *you* had to know. Pressuring me. I didn't know squat. But she kept pressuring me anyway."

His mouth dropped open. "I just realized I told you something wrong. It wasn't two times I saw her, it was three. Forgot about the first, it was when she got me coming out of the office and did the badge thing. We walked a few blocks to her car and that's where she said what I just told you."

"We know that you know."

"Pressuring me. Then Osler does the same thing and I was feeling really hemmed in so I said what the hey, I'll see what I can find out. Which was nothing. I'm telling you I made a mistake about three days not two because I don't want you coming back on me saying hey, Mike, you lied, so we're looking at you again, dude."

I said, "The *second* time was . . ."

"Like I said, Denny's. Like a couple weeks later. That's where *I* told *her* I didn't find anything, she could say what she wanted but that was the situation and now I had a lawyer so go talk to her. Which she did."

"Martha talked to Bettina."

"She called her. Bettina told me, told me I'd screwed up by not asking her first."

"You were observed talking to Martha with Bettina."

"By who?"

Milo smiled.

"Okay, fine," said Heck. "Yeah, that's true but that was the *third* time, okay? Signing off, making it official. Detective Matthias takes me and Bettina into this little side room—like the one you just put me in first. I sit there keeping my mouth shut, Bettina makes this lawyer speech to Matthias."

"What'd she say?"

"This is the situation, stop bugging my client, that kind of thing. Tough talk, you know? And that was it. I signed some papers and left."

"How did Detective Matthias react to tough talk?"

"She listened all stony-faced, like she wasn't impressed, same way she'd treated me. Then she walked to the door, came back with papers, and I signed them. Not a word. Like we didn't exist. Bettina and I are outside the building, she's like, what was that? Is the bitch planning something else?"

"She called Detective Matthias the bitch."

"Yeah, but that's just the way Bettina—no, no, nah, I've got my issues with Bettina but she'd never hurt anyone. Not physically, anyway. She uses her mouth, that's all."

Another rightward eye-shift.

I said, "Not physically."

"Never. Anyway, we never heard nothing from Martha or anyone else and then Darren got indicted and I never got subpoenaed, no one did, so we figured that was it. Which it was. Which Bettina took the credit for."

"How so?"

"She's walking around nak— We were together, it was afterward, at the Ojai Valley Inn. She's prancing, she likes to prance. Proud of her body. Says crazy things like 'Look at the Post-Modern Venus' and does a bunch of dance moves naked."

"How'd she take credit?"

"She said, I read that bitch the riot act and she melted. Or something along those lines. Which was b.s. but why argue? Then she said, now you're going to take me to dinner tomorrow at Spago, white truffles are in season. *That* I remember clearly because that shit *costs,* man. And that's all I got to say."

Milo looked at me.

I said, "We're confused, Mike. Bettina said you could help us but so far you haven't."

Heck wiggled in his chair. Like a kid in the principal's office. Weird surprising movement.

He said, "Well, I don't know if it'll actually help—and I have to be off the record, okay?"

Milo moved his chair closer, his knees an inch from Heck. Stared into Heck's eyes and began talking in a low voice.

"Not okay, Mike. You're in no position to make demands."

"Listen—"

"No, you listen, Mike. This is a multiple murder investigation and you're a person of interest. Of strong interest—hold on, let me finish. Maybe you didn't strangle Sophie yourself but you could've hired someone to do it—"

"That's crazy! What's my motive?"

"Who knows, Mike, maybe the whole thing was a way to set up a huge civil lawsuit . . ."

"That's fucking—"

"People have murdered for a lot less . . . let me finish, Mike. Here's the deal: Until now we've lacked grounds to get hold of your phone and financial records but the scam you and Bettina tried to pull off gave us grounds. So before we do a deep dive into your life, if there's something you want to tell us that will help you, now would be the time."

Michael Heck stared at him. Small deer, large headlights. On bright.

His hands shook. His chin vibrated. He sank low and hung his head.

People in that situation usually make one of two choices: shut down completely or spill. Heck did neither.

Instead, he got up suddenly, retrieved the coffee and took a few sips while standing. Murmuring something.

Milo said, "What's that, Mike?"

"Tastes like shit—no offense."

"None taken, Mike. Though I am a little hurt."

Heck put the coffee down, trudged back to his chair, and sat.

"Here's the problem," he said. "What if what I think might help doesn't?"

Milo said, "Why don't you just tell us and we'll see."

"Sure, you'd like that, nothing to lose. But *I'd* be back to square one with you making my life miserable. For no reason."

"No matter what you tell us, Mike, we will be reviewing your phone communications and your cell-tower locations as well as your bank records. If something comes up that—"

"Nothing will come up," said Heck. "Just like before. Just like with Darren. But you screwing around in my life can still ruin my life. Once you got hold of something, it's public."

I said, "There's stuff you want to keep private."

"Hell, yeah, wouldn't you?"

Milo said, "Hard to say because we have no idea what you're talking about."

"You don't? C'mon. You're going to find Tinder, okay? A bunch of it. And . . . other stuff. Texts, videos—nothing creepy, just normal stuff but who wants that publicized? Mike likes brunettes with hairy—whatever."

"If you've got nothing to hide other than sexting and legal images, don't worry."

"So you say. But *she* told me once you had anything in your clutches it would be public domain."

Milo smiled. "Our clutches."

"Her words, not mine."

"Well, she told you wrong, Mike. Bona fide evidence can find its way into public documents if it leads to an arraignment but—"

"None of that's going to happen because I'm totally innocent."

"Then you have nothing to worry about and I have to say, Mike, given what I just told you about your legal vulnerability due to that attempted big-time fraud you and Bettina cooked—I wouldn't be concerned about hot dates and porn."

Heck stared at the ceiling. Then at the long table pushed up against the wall.

"This place sucks," he said. "Your coffee sucks. I could walk out right now."

"Yes, you could, Mike."

"But I'm *not* going to because I *do* want to help you. Especially now. 'Cause it's changed. When it was all about Sophie, I thought I kind of wanted to but wasn't sure. But now that you told me about Detective Matthias, I definitely want to. Because no way am I getting crucified for *that.*"

CHAPTER

35

Michael Heck took another trip to his coffee cup. He took a sip, put it down. “Still sucks and now it’s cold.”

When he returned, our legs were crossed and we looked relaxed.

He tried for that but it didn’t feel right and he placed both feet flat on the ground, hands on his knees. Looking past us. Pressing his hands against the sides of his face and compressing it to a rubbery mask.

“Okay,” he said, letting go. “I might possibly know who did it. And if you’re smart, you’ll get off my case and look at her.”

“Her?” said Milo. “Bettina?”

Heck cracked up. The opportunity for scorn relaxed him. “No-o-o, not Bettina. Like I said, she’s all mouth. Another her. His wife. Darren’s.”

We sat there, caught off guard and trying not to show it.

Milo said, “Really.”

“Yup,” said Mike Heck. “Here’s my thinking: Number one, she hated both of them. And me. Number two, trust me, she can be bat-shit crazy.”

Milo thumbed through his pad. “We’re talking about Tiana Crown.”

“That was her Playboy Mansion name. Her real name’s Rhonda.

Rhonda Cronin. I know that because I saw some forms Darren had me fill out for her. Don't ask me for what, I don't remember."

"Why does she hate all of you?"

"For different reasons," said Heck.

Smiling. Rejuvenated.

Milo said, "Love to hear them."

"No prob. She hates *me* because I finally dumped her. Also, originally, because she thought I ratted Darren out. Which I didn't because like I said I knew nothing."

I said, "She suspected you of being an informant. Which was true."

"Not if I didn't inform. And anyway, I convinced her that I didn't. So we started . . . you know." He jabbed a finger horizontally. "Again."

"Resuming an affair."

"Not an affair, just plain in and out. And not from Tinder. She was easy-peasy, met her in a bar, she's the one got me the job at the firm. We kept it going while I was working for Darren. She'd come into the office, tight clothes, big hair, you know, signaling. We'd go take a break for some afternoon delight."

Able to cross his legs now and lean back.

Milo said, "You and women."

"What can I say? It's always been that way. I was twelve the first time."

"Impressive, Mike."

"What can I say?" Heck repeated.

"So you and Tiana—"

"She was *ripe,* man. Because Darren couldn't satisfy her. Little blue pills didn't do it for her, she wanted reality. Which I provided."

"When did you end it?"

"Right around when I started seeing Sophie. Who was *normal* here." He tapped his temple.

I said, "Unlike Tiana."

"Sophie being normal showed me how weird it had went with Tiana. 'Cause it had been a while with Tiana, she left town."

"To go where?"

"Their place in Aspen, after the investigation started she went there. If she went other places, I don't know. But she was gone, even after they lost all the houses. Like for three years. Then she was back half a year ago and calling me. It started off okay but then it got weird. She was always into control but now she's kicking it up, you know?"

We said nothing.

Heck licked his lips and smiled. "You want the details, fine. She was always like let me get on top and hold your arms down. Which was fine. Now it's let me tie you up with neckties, which I did a few times and then I said no effing way. That pissed her off, but she didn't push it. So what does she do the next time? Pulls out effing *handcuffs.* Starts jangling them right after we're getting into it. Guess she had them under a pillow or something. I say uh-uh, no way, she's like you got to let me, Mike, it satisfies me. Making a big deal out of it. But I'm, nope, not happening. She's getting obnoxious. Finally I get off her and put on my clothes and book. Took the effing cuffs with me, also. Tossed them in a dumpster like a mile away."

Milo said, "A mile from where?"

"Some motel on Centinela. Big difference from how it used to be. We used to go to her place. Their place in San Marino. She got off on doing it in she and Darren's bed. Crazy big place, like twenty rooms."

Wider smile. Smug. "We tested out a whole bunch of the rooms."

I said, "You ended it and you think she hates you for that."

"I don't *think,* I *know.* She told me."

"When did that happen?"

"Few months ago. I was with Sophie in Palm Springs, the next day, I was with another girl in Pasadena. Then I'm by myself resting. *Needing* rest, you know? And *she* shows up at my place with champagne and Mollies, wants to party. I go to the door, I'm half asleep, made it a whole lot easier to say no. Told her you need to get yourself some wuss who likes being dominated and that ain't me. And she goes *ballistic.* Tells me I just proved myself as the king of the wusses because a real man would have the confidence to yield. Her word. *Yield.* Like I'm a car on the freeway or something. Then she tries to push her way in and she's strong, man. For a girl. But I shove her out and close the door. She pounds a bunch of times, hard. Finally gives up and leaves and that's the last I seen of her. So, yeah, she hates me, she said so."

I said, "You began sleeping with Tiana years ago but stopped recently."

"It's true whether or not you want to believe it," said Heck. "It wasn't a relationship. Never. Just off and on, sometimes she'd call, sometimes I'd call. And like I said there was a lot of time we had no contact after the investigation began. She probably wanted to steer clear of the whole thing."

"Was she in on the scam?"

"You know," he said, "I wish I could say she was but if I had to bet, I'd say no."

"Why's that?"

"Because there was no reason for Darren to plan with her, she's no genius. And she was super mad about how Darren had screwed up. Said all he had to do was take his contingency cut, it would've still been a shitload. But no, he got greedy. *Stupid* and greedy, she called him. Said if she'd known she'd have set him straight."

"Would she have been able to set him straight?"

"Who knows? Like I said, she was dominant and Darren liked the arm-candy. The whole Playboy Mansion thing. But he was pretty alpha, himself. Even though with clients he played Mr. Sensitive."

I said, "Your theory is Tiana hated you because you dumped her. And she hated Sophie because—"

"I was *with* Sophie and not her."

"Jealousy."

"And also," said Heck, "she probably wanted to get back at me. Kill two birds, you know—" He colored. "Sorry, wrong way to put it."

I said, "Did you tell Tiana about Sophie?"

Head shake. "No way. But she could've found out. It's not like I was hiding anything, you know? She could've watched me, you know? Going to Sophie's, taking her out. I was seeing Sophie pretty regular. More than the others."

Milo said, "How many others were there?"

"At that time?" said Heck. "Probably . . . five, six."

"Names."

"Oh, c'mon. Why?"

"To make sure they're okay."

"They are," said Heck. "I still see them. Except for Bettina, that's over. Obviously."

Milo said, "Names."

"I just told you they're all okay."

"We like to be thorough, Mike."

"Shit. Fine, but don't freak them out, okay?"

"We'll be gentle."

Heck blinked, kneaded one palm with the opposing hand. "Okay . . ." He reeled off a list of five women, first names only.

Milo said, "Last names, too. And contact information."

"I don't know their numbers by heart."

"We'll borrow your phone."

"Aw, c'mon," said Heck. "Like I said, there's all kinds of stuff— okay, fine, but you need to swear to keep it private."

"Mike," said Milo, "your dick pics interest us as much as drying paint."

"Hey," said Heck, "they're actually pretty— Fine, here's the phone. But I need it back before I leave."

Milo placed the phone in a jacket pocket. "We'll transfer it and get it back to you as soon as that's through."

"You're going to always have my data?"

Milo said, "If there's nothing murderous in your data, you have nothing to worry about."

"Geez," said Heck. "I'm trying to help and—"

I said, "Why'd Tiana hate Detective Matthias?"

"Got to be something Detective Matthias told her."

"Such as . . ."

"I don't know exactly, but I saw it."

"When?"

"The day I talked to her in her office. Tiana was in there before me. I was on time but she kept me waiting—Detective Matthias. I go ask one of you other guys, he says just go back and wait. A few minutes later, I'm sitting there and the door swings open, Tiana stomps out and slams it hard. Her face is totally red. And sweaty and tight, you know? Like someone stretched her skin. Also, her eyes are that crazy bright they always get when she's in a batshit crazy place. Same way she was when she showed up and I wouldn't let her in."

I said, "Tiana doesn't like being told no."

"Oh man," said Heck. "It's like a switch gets flipped. I'm just sitting there and she sees me, stops cold, points back to the door she just slammed, and goes like this."

He ran his hand across his throat.

CHAPTER

36

Milo's face was unreadable. I took that as a sign and kept my mouth shut.

Michael Heck said, "I mean that's hatred, right?"

Milo said, "Did Tiana tell you what upset her?"

"Not *upset* her, pissed her off to the *extreme,*" said Heck. "And no, she didn't say because I didn't ask her. Didn't want to know. I was just worried she wouldn't believe me that I wasn't a rat. But later she said she did and we were cool and we started hooking up again."

"You didn't discuss Detective Matthias."

"Why would we?" said Heck. "That was negative input and I just wanted the whole thing to be over."

"You had no curiosity why Tiana would resent Detective Matthias."

"You don't understand," said Heck. "Tiana's not someone you have a discussion with. She's scary, man. Carries a knife in her purse. This folding thing, like military. And she knows how to shoot—kept guns in the house. Hers and Darren's. Rifles, shotguns, pistols. Big safe full of them that she showed me."

Milo said, "Where does she go to shoot?"

"No idea, I just know what she showed me and told me. And like I told you, she's strong. I took her to the gym once—same one where

I met Sophie because she was bugging me to show her what I could do. She watches me, pats my butt, winks, goes over to the barbells, stretches, and starts deadlifting. She weighed probably one twenty. Totally toned. I watched her deadlift two fifty. Her muscles didn't even look that big but they *worked,* man. Guys were staring. She loved it. The attention. When I said something about it, she said, 'No big deal, used to be a tomboy before I grew boobs.' Then we left the gym and went to my place."

Milo's phone beeped a text. As he read, his eyebrows rose.

He said, "What does Tiana drive?"

"Nowadays? No idea. Back then she had an Aston Martin. Black convertible. She let me drive it, great car. When Darren got busted, she lost it along with everything else."

"No more big house."

"Nothing."

"Where does she live?"

"Last time I saw her, she took me to her new place. Grungy dive in Pico-Robertson. She held on to her clothes, though. Two-bedroom place, one just for her clothes."

"What was she driving at that time?"

"Never saw a vehicle. She called me to pick her up at Pink's, when I got there she said she left her money at home, could I pay for her chili dog so I did."

Heck's eyes brightened.

"Hey, maybe *that's* why she's been doing this crazy stuff. Hit rock bottom and wants to take it out on the world."

Milo kept him in the room for another twenty minutes posing different versions of the same questions. Detective 101. It produced nothing but growing fatigue on Heck's part and when Milo finally said, "Okay, we'll be in touch," Heck nodded glumly and got to his feet.

"So when can I get my phone back?"

Milo made a call. Moments later, a young, dark-haired detective named Carla Bonair entered stone-faced, gloved up, and carrying a paper bag.

Like a bull in rut, Heck tried to make eye contact with her but she ignored him as Milo gave her the phone.

She dropped it into the bag. "We keeping it or just doing a plug-in, Loo?"

"Plug-in. When can you get it back to this gentleman who's been very cooperative?"

Heck smiled at Bonair.

"If there are no glitches, right away."

"Great, thanks."

Heck said, "There's going to be some racy stuff on it."

Bonair said, "Password."

Heck told her.

She said, "Bye, Loo," and left.

Heck said, "Cute. Is she gay or something?"

CHAPTER 37

We walked Heck to the elevator, Milo studying his own phone.

More lack of interest made Heck antsy and when the door opened, he rushed inside. When it closed, we returned to Milo's office.

I said, "Villalobos spotted a car?"

He said, "How the hell—"

"Right after you got the text, you asked Heck what Tiana drove."

"Ah. Sure, it was obvious, how silly of me."

He shook his head. Sat down and rocked his desk chair, setting off a chorus of angry mice. "Yeah, that was from Alicia. One of the dumpsters Lynne Gutierrez's body coulda landed in showed—here, a picture's worth a zillion syllables."

He pulled up the phone photo and handed it to me.

Dark alley, aerial view of the rectangle created by the top of an open dumpster. Low-quality, nighttime shot blurring contours and graying colors.

The alley was narrow, the type of afterthought created decades ago when L.A. was adjusting to motor vehicles. The camera was aimed, as so many seem to be, downward from what looked like a story and a half.

Nothing for several seconds, then a dark SUV pulled up and came to a stop to the right of the dumpster. Two parallel rectangles, the vehicle parked inches from the bin, preventing any movement on the driver's side. The passenger side out of camera view.

Any movement toward the dumpster would be limited to front or rear. Rear would've offered a clear view. But no such luck, as a dark-clad figure, medium-sized and hooded, materialized close to the front bumper, obscuring much of the activity. The figure bent out of view momentarily then reappeared upright, holding something large and oblong in both arms.

Another bend, not as deep. The type you take when you're hefting and mustering strength.

Then: a single smooth movement heaving upward. The oblong teetered on the edge of the bin for an instant before rolling over and in.

The figure headed toward the driver's side, stepping completely out of view. Seconds later, the SUV was gone.

The time stamp fit the parameters of Lynne Gutierrez's abduction and murder. The size of the discarded package could easily be a body.

He said, "Exactly as Hector predicted."

I watched the sequence again, returned the phone to Milo. "Any idea what the vehicle is?"

Milo said, "From that angle, I don't even think a motorhead could tell but I'll ask. What it ain't is an Aston Martin, yeah, yeah, she lost everything. But I didn't spot anything feminine. I know Heck said she was strong but he could be snowing us to keep us away from some guy he hired. Or even him."

I said, "To my eye, the person's too small to be Heck. How tall is Tiana?"

"Guess we'll have to find out." But he made no move toward his keyboard.

I said, "You're not impressed with his theory."

"'Bout as much as I am by flat-earth morons. C'mon, Alex, what do guilty criminals always do?"

"Deny and distract."

"Guy's no genius but he could be thinking he's clever getting me to chase down someone else. So before I go running off on a tangent, I'm gonna earn a Ph.D. in Mike's Phone. *And* his financials. Which I've already put in subpoenas for. Which, you'll notice, I *didn't* tell him. Crafty, no?"

He cursed under his breath. "Playboy Mansion gal goes on a rampage because of stuff that happened years ago? Sophie I could maybe see—hell hath no fury. Though even that's a stretch, going to all that trouble with the cigarettes. But a woman sawing off Martha's arms, wrapping her body, and stashing it in a deep-freeze? Then abducting and bludgeoning her daughter? All because of one supposed meeting where she supposedly ran her finger across her throat? Yeah, I know, Heck made sure to let us know Tiana carries a knife. But that could be another diversion. And bottom line, he and Bel Geddes were planning a monster civil suit payoff, so he remains on the Scumbag List."

"Good point."

"But?" he said.

"No buts."

"Great. Hate that word. Even worse than I hate 'if.'"

He turned and typed, brought up the DMV database.

"Here we go, Tiana Rhea Crown, forty-three years old, blond, blue, five-eight, one thirty-three. Guess she can't be eliminated on size alone . . . drives a . . . five-year-old Toyota Camry, which is *not* what we just saw. But just to be professionally meticulous, let's see what NCIC has to say about her criminal past."

Click click. He sat back, smiling. "Not a word. Blameless as a yearling romping in the meadows. That sound like someone who could slaughter three innocent women?"

I said, "Where's her current address?"

"Why?"

"Maybe she'll have something interesting to say about Heck."

"Sure, why not. Yeah, good point . . . fine, once I get through Heck's damn data and can take over from Moe watching Heck, I'll send him out to interview her, maybe his muscles will help establish rapport."

He returned to the DMV data. His smile faded.

"What?"

"She still lists the house in San Marino as her address. Guess that could be nostalgia, denial, whatever. Or she just never bothered to update it."

"Or," I said, "she doesn't want to be found."

Putting into words what he'd thought of. He was rubbing his face when Carla Bonair came to the open door.

"Hey, Loo." She reached in and handed him a zip drive. "Mr. Heck's phone records."

"That was quick, thanks. Anything interesting?"

"Didn't study it," she said, rolling her eyes, "but couldn't avoid noticing some of it. Guy's got problems."

"Criminal problems?"

"Not that I spotted at first glance. But hormonal problems, for sure."

Milo loaded the zip drive and logged on. Frame after frame of porn filled the screen, a never-ending fleshy grid.

Bonair said, "Hope the captain doesn't walk in right now."

He laughed. He scrolled. Kept scrolling. "Jesus, how much does he have?"

"He could open his own porn site," said Bonair. "Those guys don't sue for copyright infringement, right? Or maybe they do. Not my world."

She smiled, saluted, and left.

Milo returned to his desktop, speeding through page after page of thumbnails. "Nothing personal or illegal, so far." He laughed. "Can you imagine if I'd asked Sean to do this?"

"Grounds for a harassment lawsuit."

"Thank God the kid's true and blue . . . okay, I'm gonna save these for later, and start examining the calls. No sense hanging around, Alex. Don't want to turn you into an innocent bystander."

CHAPTER

38

Three days later, he called at ten a.m. Perfect timing; I'd just finished with a patient.

"Villalobos did a great job finding that footage but it doesn't amount to much. He called it visual compost. He couldn't find anyone around there who noticed the SUV and no other cameras have picked it up anywhere else. A motorhead in Auto Theft named Meyers says it could be a Toyota Land Cruiser or a Land Rover but he'd never put it in writing. Next, Heck's phone. Porn, more porn, take-out grub, and calls to the six other women. I did phone interviews with the five besides Bel Geddes and got consistency: Mike's not too bright but he's available when you need him. No violence, no problems at all, but none of them see him as long-term relationship material. As one of them put it, 'He's eager to please and try finding that.'"

I said, "Middle-aged boy-toy."

"Oxymoron but you're permitted an occasional lapse. In terms of his finances, there's an Amex, a MasterCard, a checking account with a debit card, and a 401(k) co-contributed by his current employer. That one has eleven grand in various stock funds and he's never withdrawn a cent. He takes home six grand a month, pays three and a half in rent directly to the landlord, puts a grand into the 401(k) and the rest into the checking account. Pays bills with the debit card, except for his auto loan which he Amexes. He stays within his means, rarely pays penalties. Are you snoozing yet?"

I yawned.

He laughed. "Now the wake-up call. Given all that zero, I had nowhere to go but the unlikely Ms. Tiana. Most of her social media presence is old pictures of when she was a hottie hanging out at Hef's lagoon. Then I accessed her Instagram account and learned that she makes cute little birdhouses that she sells on Etsy and eBay. When she's not donating them to sick kids. She also says she donates her time."

"Woodworking. Tools."

"So much for my instincts. Problem is, can't find any current address for her. I had San Marino PD go over to check the mansion she and Alberts shared, just to make sure she's not squatting there. Family from Taiwan bought it years ago at auction and is living there happily."

I said, "Who does she donate her time to?"

"The birdhouses are for sick kids, so probably them. Or maybe it's b.s. showboating. But in case there's something to it, could you call Western Peds and ask if they know her?"

"No problem."

"You never are."

I trained clinically at Western Pediatric Hospital, got hired there as a new Ph.D., and was appointed to dual faculty positions: the psych department at the old university in West Adams and its med school. I still do some occasional supervision and teaching on campus but I hadn't been to the hospital for a while and hoped some of my contacts were still around.

My first bet was lucky.

Stacee Vasquez at the volunteer office said, "Hi, Dr. Delaware! Long time! We still remember you playing guitar for the kids."

We chitchatted a while then I told her what I wanted.

"Sure, let me look. What's that name again?"

"Tiana Crown. Or possibly Tiana Alberts."

"An alias, huh? Sounds juicy—that police work you do, huh . . . nope, nothing under either. She never volunteered here."

"One more thing, could you please check under Rhonda Cronin?"

"Is that a different person?"

"Same person, maybe another alias."

"Wow. Sure . . . nope, again. Which is good, we wouldn't want anyone the cops are after."

"Absolutely. Thanks, Stacee."

"Anytime, Dr. Delaware. We miss you. Come by and bring your guitar."

I spent the next hour trying people at a few child-welfare groups I'd worked with. No one had heard of Tiana Crown under any name. I was about to put it to rest when I thought of something.

After considering it for a moment, I phoned Milo.

He said, "How'd you get from sick kids to that—forget it, no need to explain. Sure, why not, can't hurt to try. I'm downtown with Hector going through some more video from a few blocks away. You mind making the call?"

"Sure, but if they don't want to talk to me—"

"Everyone wants to talk to you."

I phoned Safe Place, hoping to bypass Pam Buttons—too new, too defensive—and connected with David Le Gallee.

"Oh, hi, Doctor. There's progress on Lynne?"

"Wish there was. I'm calling because you mentioned people volunteering. Was a woman named Tiana Crown among them?"

"She sure was . . . oh no, you're not saying—no, that's crazy."

"Did she spend time with Lynne?"

"I'm sure she did. As well as with other residents. But it was always positive contact, Doctor, no way I can see that as relevant to . . . what happened."

I kept my voice smooth-lie-even. "I'm sure you're right but when cases bog down, and this one sure has, the detectives go back and dig through every possible detail. The last place Lynne was seen was Safe House, so they want to know who she associated with."

"The detectives do the digging, but you're the one calling."

I laughed. "To be honest, it's kind of low priority."

"Well, that's good, because the idea of someone here having anything to do with Lynne's disappearance is ridiculous."

"No doubt," I said. "Do you have the names of the other volunteers, Dave?"

"You have Tiana's name but not theirs?"

"That was a fluke. She turned out to be somewhat well known."

"How?"

"Her husband was a corrupt lawyer who ran a big scam. There's no evidence she was part of it but she did cite volunteering at various nonprofits in her personal statement so we wondered."

"That's it?" said Le Gallee. "Yes, it does sound low priority. Tiana was really helpful, Doctor. Different from the other volunteers but that was a plus."

"How so?"

"Our ladies are mostly in their sixties and up. Affluent, kind of old-school. You know, the typical volunteer."

"Tiana was younger and the residents could relate to her."

"Exactly," he said. "Music, clothes, she was more up to date. She was also able to help me with exercise classes. Fit and super strong. And always supportive."

"Of Lynne?"

"Of anyone who needed bucking up."

"Got it," I said. "You've been using the past tense. Tiana no longer volunteers there?"

"No, not for a while. Hold on and I'll tell you exactly . . . okay, here it is. For half a year, she came once a week, then she stopped a little less than two months ago. Says here she was stepping away to find full-time employment and now I remember her telling me she needed the money. Which isn't true of our other volunteers, they're pretty well heeled."

"Got it. Could I have their names, please?"

"Don't see how it could be of any use. These are older, genteel women."

"Like I said, just to be thorough, Dave. If it's a problem giving it to me, I can check with Detective Sturgis and if he thinks it's worth it, he'll get back to you."

Dave Le Gallee said, "No, that's okay, I'll email it to you. Feels a little less . . . official."

The file came through moments later. Single-page document, names, addresses, phone numbers.

For the most part, Safe Place volunteers listed private homes in Hancock Park, Pacific Palisades, and Beverly Hills. A scatter came from Pasadena and its rich cousin, San Marino, where Darren and Tiana Alberts had once lived like monarchs.

The address Tiana had given Safe Place was a steep drop from that. Multi-unit on South Holt Avenue. A map search put it just west of La Cienega and far enough south to be within earshot of the 10 freeway. An image search brought up a pale-pink, fifties stucco box with a deeper-pink bow tie decorating the façade. Someone's notion of whimsical, now just sad.

I forwarded everything to Milo, expecting a quick callback. It took him until five p.m. to connect.

"So she definitely worked with Lynne. Unbelievable."

"Worked well with Lynne, according to Le Gallee. Especially helpful during exercise classes. Quote unquote 'super strong.'"

"Muscles, tools, didn't like Martha . . . it still feels crazy but in a creepy not an impossible way. Unbelievable. Thanks. Reason you didn't hear from me sooner was Villalobos and I were getting eyestrain all day looking at crappy video. Just as we were about to call it a day, we caught a break. Of sorts. Actually, he picked it up. Front view of what we think is the same SUV driving away from the direction of that alley then heading west. The image is still too blurry to get tags but the car's definitely a Toyota Highlander, dark blue. And once Bryce

Meyers got a good look at the front, he narrowed it to six to ten years old."

"If Tiana had another set of wheels in addition to the Aston, it could've been hers all that time."

"Doubtful, Alex, she's never registered it. Given her financial circumstances, my bet is she picked it up cheap from a private party. Let me call Heck and see if he ever saw her in one."

Six minutes later:

"Nope, all he ever saw was the Aston and a limo service back in the good old days and after everyone collapsed, she Ubered. The limo thing got the idiot going. Fun times in the back, heh heh. Guy's obsessed. Anyway, I'm planning a drive-by at the place on Holt, later. Let you know what comes up."

"What time?"

"No need, Alex, it'll probably be a dud."

"Same question."

"Late. Ten-ish."

"Pick me up or should I meet you there?"

"What's with all the gung-ho?"

"The Zeigarnik effect."

"Oh, that."

A bit of psychology I'd described to him years ago: Tension due to unfinished business leads to increased mental focus. A feeling I like.

"You're all Zeigarnicked, huh?"

"Primed to go."

CHAPTER 39

He picked me up at ten fourteen.

I'd left Robin snuggly under the bedcovers, smiling and close to sleep. We'd spent the past four hours together. A bit of good food, a lot of romance, and that wonderful sense of serenity that follows. Then she asked about the case.

"A woman with tools," she said. "Giving the rest of us a bad name." She nudged me. "Does it make you nervous, handsome?"

"Notice I rarely get close to your bench."

"Phobic, huh?" she said. "We could do that desensitization thing. Use the bench for other purposes."

I said, "Long as the saw's off."

"Of course, darling. We do tend to move around a bit."

I was waiting outside when the Impala sped up and came to a sharp stop.

Milo sped downhill to the Glen and turned south. Sitting tall behind the wheel, jaw jutting.

On the hunt.

I said, "How's it going?"

"Peachy. You?"

"Great."

One hurtling minute later: "I finally traced her as Rhonda Cronin to Albuquerque using her Social Security number."

"She lived there before L.A.?"

"She was born there and got into trouble there. ADW when she was nineteen that landed her in jail for a month followed by another month of probation and an anger management class."

"Pretty light for a felony attack," I said. "What was the weapon?"

"Pool cue. She used it to smack another girl upside the head."

He rubbed his temple. "Not your usual drunk thing in a bar, this took place in the rec room of a community center. Rhonda and the victim were both beauty contestants—Miss some kind of chili—and were there to pose for photos. Words were exchanged and all of a sudden, boom, the other girl's down on the floor, out cold and bloody, and Rhonda's standing over her with the cue."

I said, "Pageant jealousy?"

"No, that's the thing. Rhonda had already come in second, the victim, third."

"Number One got away clean."

"Number One was on a tour endorsing a hot sauce. Albuquerque guy I spoke to, Dick Sanchez, remembered it because it was so weird. He called it The Beauty Brawl. They never got to the bottom of what caused it, other than Rhonda accusing the victim of being a mean girl and the victim leveling the same thing at Rhonda."

"Serious injury?"

"Concussion and hospitalization but full recovery. That and no priors is why Rhonda only got the month and Sanchez says they put her in a pretty quiet jail. He had no idea what happened to her after that but I managed to find her P.O. Nancy Odom, and she remembered Rhonda for the same reason. Gorgeous girl, no priors, just exploded, made no sense."

"Rhonda didn't give her an explanation?"

"Odom said she refused to talk. Then Odom got defensive, going on about caseload, meth dealers, other serious baddies."

"Rhonda got no scrutiny because she was low priority."

"Her sentence says she wasn't any kind of priority. The entire probation arrangement was one meeting at the beginning of the month and another on the final day. Both of which Rhonda showed up at. She also never missed an anger class. Odom did say she asked what her plans were and Rhonda told her she was going to college in Vegas. Odom suspected it was more like trying to break in as a showgirl because Rhonda had spent years in pageants, was all about her looks."

"Any information on her family?"

"Rhonda was an adult so Odom never met the family, relied on what Rhonda told her. Intact, no issues, Dad was in some kind of business, Mom was a stay at home who'd also done the beauty thing. Rhonda did show Odom a recent family photo with her in a tiara and the only thing that jumped out at her was all three of them were good-looking."

"Only child."

"Seems to be. Is that important?"

"One less relative to talk to. Are the parents alive?"

"Don't know and not gonna talk to anyone at this point, Alex. Intact families can get protective and I don't want her to know we're looking at her."

He took Westwood to Pico, turned left, passing through the Rancho Park district and the southern border of Century City where high-rises pretend L.A.'s a real city. Hooking a right on Beverly Drive, he continued through the original ranch houses and recent McMansions of Beverlywood, once a start-up neighborhood for newlyweds, now a final stop for the affluent.

As we continued south, the street got curvier, darker, quieter. Beyond quiet, the silence of slumbering suburbia. The trajectory gradually veered from affluence as big houses gave way to small houses, which finally conceded to blocks of apartments and the drone-buzz of the freeway.

Turning left on National, he made a series of GPS-directed turns, found his way to Holt Avenue, and cruised slowly before locating the address.

The building looked just as it had on my screen but for pink stucco darkened to an indecisive gray barely defined in the nocturnal haze. L.A. ranks architecture somewhere below slime mold, and the block was the usual mix of charmless boxes from various decades.

Milo said, "What's that, a bow tie?"

"Dressing for success."

He grunted, backed up, and parked in the only available space. Three buildings north and across the street, with a diagonal view of Tiana's.

Switching off his headlights, he worked his phone. "City has it listed as ten units, five on the first floor, five on the second. The Safe Place thing you sent me says hers is number eight, so she's on top."

Lights on in one apartment on each of the floors but that said nothing about rear units.

Milo thought for a while, said, "Stay here," got out, closed the driver's door softly, looked up and down the block, and crossed the street.

He was back moments later but remained outside the car talking through the open driver's window.

I said, "Nothing?"

"Nope. Door's security-coded. Gonna look around a bit more, stay put."

He was gone longer, returned breathing rapidly.

"Tenant parking in the back. God was merciful and it's open carports and in the number eight slot is a dark-blue Highlander. Expired registration, hopefully the plates haven't been switched."

He ran them, gave a thumbs-up. "Owned until a couple of years ago by an eighty-year-old guy in Woodland Hills. *He* kept up the reg and duly recorded the sale. But then the buyer—guess who?—notified DMV it was going to be junked so it was never re-registered."

I said, "Ghost wheels. Good way to avoid reg fees. Also helpful if you're planning something nasty."

"She planned for two years? Or maybe she was doing other bad stuff in the meantime."

"If she killed Martha and Lynne, we're talking a seven-year grudge, so two years doesn't seem like much."

He chewed his cheek, pushed hair off his forehead. "Good point. And going ghost is relatively low risk. Even if you do get pulled over, you can probably talk your way out of anything but a warning."

I said, "If you're a former beauty queen, highly probable."

"Little Miss Scofflaw," he said, punching a palm with a fist. "Finally I *have* something."

We watched the building for another hour. In all that time, three cars drove by and a single late-night dog-walker passed by with a trudging, older Lab in tow.

"Quiet night," said Milo. "Nice when I'm trying to sleep, crap when I'm working. Let's call it."

But ten minutes later, he pulled over on the southern tip of Beverly Drive and got on his phone.

Reaching the West L.A. duty sergeant and requesting as many drive-bys as the schedule allowed on Tiana Crown's block, giving her name and vehicle details.

"Yup, female. More important, Bob, she's a multiple murder suspect, otherwise I wouldn't bug you . . . three . . . exactly. Thanks. Something happens call me at home."

Next: texts to Alicia, Sean, and Moe.

Time for a new meeting. Seven a.m.

Resuming the drive, he said, "If you're busy or it's too early for you, sorry, can't delay. We need to get a plan going."

I said, "Oh, ye of little faith."

CHAPTER 40

Moe Reed said, "I know her but she doesn't look like that anymore."

He was the last to arrive in the big interview room, which this morning meant three minutes early.

Milo, Alicia, Sean Binchy, Hector Villalobos, and I went silent. We'd been drinking coffee, pretending to unwind. The young D's sharing the surprise that a woman might be a prime suspect.

Milo said, "Really."

Reed said, "No doubt. I've seen her in the gym."

He stepped up to the board. Several photos of Tiana Alberts, formerly Tiana Crown, née Rhonda Cronin were posted on the right side. The left was reserved for pictures of Sophie Barlow, Martha Matthias, and Lynne Gutierrez. Below those, the blurry image of the SUV in the alley and a clearer shot Milo had taken of Tiana's Highlander in her carport space.

At the bottom, some crudely built birdhouses.

"Which gym, Moses?"

"Fort Hard Knox, used to be near the 10 freeway, sometimes I'd stop off if I was going home that way. Never spent any time with her but did help her out once when she was bench-pressing more than she could handle and had trouble getting the bar back up. Her bench wasn't impressive but her deadlift sure was. I saw her do nearly three hundred. Bunch of guys stood around, watching. She's the one, huh? Crazy."

"She's a strong possible, kid. Pun intended. Sit down and tell us what else you know about her."

Reed took the empty seat next to me.

"Saw her maybe three, four times, always at Knox. A year or so ago. The place closed down soon after. Where does she live?"

Milo said, "South Holt, not far from the freeway. How different does she look?"

Reed said, "When I saw her she was obviously 'roided up. Big, ropy muscles, zits on her shoulders, and her face looked harder with bigger bones."

Alicia said, "Dare I say masculinized?"

Reed said, "You're allowed."

Laughter. Low and tense.

I said, "Did you ever see any 'roid rage?"

"I didn't, Doc. She was intense but most bodybuilders are."

"Focused."

"Very much so."

Milo said, "Obsessive?"

Moe smiled. "Guess you'd have to be when you're actually lifting but some of us keep our mellow going."

I said, "She didn't?"

"Never saw her blow up, Doc, but she did give off a stay-away vibe. Like the time I helped her. She got off the bench, mumbled thanks, and hurried away. Not hostile but clearly not pleased."

I said, "Embarrassed about needing help."

"That's how I took it. A lot of people are like that in the serious gyms. Come in thinking they're going to impress, overextend themselves and get into trouble. So yeah, she was probably embarrassed. And come to think of it, that was the last time I saw her there."

Alicia said, "Did she hold on to her looks at all?"

"She wasn't grotesque," said Reed. "Nothing like some people I've seen. I guess in clothes and with the right makeup, she'd still look good. But not like those shots on the board."

Sean said, "Losing her money and her looks. That could make you mad."

Alicia said, "So you kill three people? Saw the arms off one?"

Everyone looked at me.

I said, "Life circumstances getting worse and steroids could be a volatile mix. Especially for someone with long-festering resentment and anger control problems. Which we know Tiana had at nineteen when she suddenly attacked another beauty contestant."

Multiple note-taking.

"Walt Karski recalled that Tiana had a meeting with Martha and left looking unhappy. Mike Heck confirms that, though he describes Tiana as being angry. We may never know what transpired but here are some guesses. This was a woman who'd gone from conspicuous wealth and the chance to star in a reality show to being a pariah shut off completely from funds. What if she'd asked Martha for some sort of flexibility and Martha refused."

Milo said, "Martha had no control over the money."

"Tiana may not have been rational. If she was panicking, begged Martha for help, and was turned down that would've compounded the rejection. Especially if Martha was harsh."

I turned to Milo. "From what you knew of Martha would that be likely?"

He scratched the side of his nose. "Never saw her get nasty but she did tend to be business-like. And Heck describes her as unemotional and tough. So maybe."

I said, "Another possibility is that Martha called Tiana in for the meeting in order to accuse her of participating in the scam in the hope of getting a confession."

Sean said, "She could've participated."

Milo said, "No one was indicted except Alberts and he never served a day of time. The whole thing was a shitshow."

I said, "If something hostile did occur between Tiana and Martha,

Tiana may have stewed on it for years only to be triggered by meeting Lynne Gutierrez at Safe Place and learning she was Martha's daughter. To someone with serious psychiatric issues—like paranoia—that could've seemed like an omen. And we know steroids can foster paranoia."

Moe said, "If she combined it with meth, even worse."

"Any evidence of that?"

"No, but people do try to energize."

Alicia said, "She's there to volunteer and ends up bashing Lynne to death."

I said, "Not as Lynne, as Martha's daughter. She may have begun volunteering as a way to feel better about herself. She claimed to be helping sick kids but we haven't been able to verify that, so she could be trying to bolster herself. Then she's faced with a remembrance of things past and blows."

Milo said, "When Lynne walked to Martha's, it woulda been easy enough to follow her and learn where Martha lived."

"Or," said Moe, "she pretended to be a buddy and walked with her. Or gave her a lift."

"Evil," said Alicia. "If any of it's true."

Hector Villalobos said, "Going to do my darndest to get more footage, maybe we can finally get tags on the Highlander and confirm it as hers."

"Thanks," said Milo. "Great work finding the dumpster footage."

"Sacrificed my eyesight but if it turns out to be major, it's worthwhile."

I said, "I asked Robin what someone would use to make those birdhouses. She said it's pretty crude work that would likely entail hand tools including smaller saws. Jigs and the like."

More note-taking.

Alicia said, "Wow."

Sean said, "How does Sophie Barlow fit in with all this?"

Milo said, "Her murder doesn't rely on a years-of-rage scenario. Mike Heck dumped Tiana unceremoniously and took up with Sophie, so if Tiana's as volatile as she sounds, there's big-time insult added to injury. And in terms of the DNA staging, Tiana knew where Heck lived so no problem going through his trash and finding his cigarettes."

I said, "Something else to consider: A woman ringing Sophie's doorbell might have seemed less threatening than a man."

Moe said, "Excuse me, looking for apartment six, or my car broke down, can I use your phone."

"Or your bathroom," said Alicia. "A woman might be sympathetic to that."

I said, "Even if Sophie was careful and only cracked the door, Tiana could've taken her with a surprise blitz. Hand around the neck, propelling her inward and holding on until she's choked Sophie out. Then she staged the scene."

Another silence. Moe said, "So what's next?"

Milo said, "Find the Highlander and tear it apart. If Tiana used it to move Lynne's body, there's a high probability of transfer evidence. I talked to Nguyen and he said the right judge might go for it but we'd do better with more."

"Big surprise," said Moe.

Milo said, "We know where she keeps the car so let's watch her for a few and see what turns up."

He smiled. "Time to talk scheduling. The romantic side of ace detection."

CHAPTER

41

He came by to catch me up two days later but began by assembling a sandwich from the contents of our fridge.

Inch-thick, hand-cut slabs of rye-bread-encased roast beef, smoked turkey, Genoa salami, coleslaw, provolone, purple onion, red bell pepper. An anemic bit of romaine lettuce included as an afterthought "to keep it healthy."

I said, "Peppers have vitamin C."

"Whatever."

Blanche watched the construction project with slavering fascination and steadily quickening breathing. I took some roast beef, dropped a dried dog treat into my pocket, and carried her to Robin's studio.

What's a little drool on your shirt when you're in love?

Robin said, "Hi, babe. What's up?"

I bent and gave Blanche the beef. "Milo's feasting and she was working herself up."

She laughed, came over and kissed me. "The Humane Society is proud of you and so am I. Is he feasting out of joy or frustration?"

"He's not looking too joyful."

"Aw, too bad," she said. "Well, your timing's perfect, I was just about to bring you something."

She retrieved a folded sheet of paper from the far end of her bench.

One-page internet ad for a "mini-tool" woodworking jigsaw. Made in Korea. Six-and-a-half-inch blade in a U-shaped clamp, add four more inches of length for the handle.

Perfect for DIY projects.

Given the dimensions, the seller's claim that you could put it in your pocket seemed a stretch but not the suggestion that it would "fit in a bag."

Five-star reviews.

Nine bucks and some change.

Robin said, "Not high-tech but these cheapies can be surprisingly good and for those birdhouses you wouldn't need to get fancy."

"Would it be strong enough to . . ."

"Do what was done? Maybe not cut through bone. But tendons and ligaments? No problem."

I thanked her and kissed her.

"Aw shucks," she said and held my hand all the way to the door.

Blanche stayed in place, looking up at me.

"Oh, sorry," I said. Pulling the treat from my pocket, I gave it to her.

Robin said, "Look at that face. The definition of pleasure."

I said, "Easy when your priorities are sound."

When I returned to the kitchen, Milo had made his way through half of the culinary Everest and added a container of orange juice that I'd bought yesterday—now nearly empty—and a similarly drained quart bottle of fizzy water.

I showed him the ad.

"Nine bucks and it can sever limbs."

"Robin says yes."

"Okay . . . good, gives me something to look for."

"Even if you don't find it, you could see if Tiana bought one like it."

"I could," he said, "if I had access to her credit cards. Hector's been looking like crazy but so far, nothing else on the Highlander. John claims to be checking out judges but he just got distracted by a big gang thing. I'm thinking of giving a few I know a try."

He chomped, chewed, swallowed, drank juice, then water. Then juice.

"In answer to your unspoken question, surveillance has been unproductive. If she's volunteering anywhere, she hasn't gone there yet. She gets her food delivered and stays inside except for one trip yesterday to a gym on Sepulveda."

"Hard-core ironworks?"

"Nope, more like your typical L.A. narcissist palace. Alicia was the one watching and she managed to talk her way inside as a prospective client. No weight lifting for ol' Tiana, she was running like crazy on a treadmill. Alicia thinks she may have cut back on the steroids because she doesn't look that extreme. Though she has aged considerably since her lagoon days. Last night, Moe came on and watched her take out some garbage, which he swiped and brought back. We've got no crime scene DNA to match but he figured the contents might be interesting and was kind enough to save it for me."

He put the water bottle down, examined his palms as if they still needed washing.

"Food empties, beer bottles, used tissues and paper towels, a few of which held some minuscule wood splinters. I thought those might come in handy if the lab could find tool marks that could be matched to Martha's body. But Basia looked at them and said they were too small and even if you did pull up marks there's too much variance between human tissue and wood to say anything definitive. I'm on tonight and if it duds out, I'm going the gullible jurist route."

CHAPTER 42

When my phone rang at eleven forty a.m., I was downtown, walking to a municipal parking lot across from the court building, after an in-chambers meeting with a family law judge and two lawyers.

I said, "Found yourself a judge."

Milo said, "Yeah, but irrelevant. Alicia was watching the apartment from eight on, all of a sudden the Highlander leaves and gets on the 10 East. Alicia followed it to the Sixth Street exit, verified it's Tiana driving, no one else with her. They're stuck in traffic, which buys some time."

I said, "Downtown. Returning to the scene?"

"Why else drive there—hold on."

He was back a few moments later.

"That was Alicia. The jam eased and Tiana's driving around kind of aimlessly. Alicia managed to stay with her but a bunch of cars got between them. Hector was nearby so she called him in. Overall, Tiana's headed in the right direction if the dumpster is her destination but who knows? I'm almost there, let you know if anything happens."

"I'm ten minutes away from the dumpster."

"Why?"

"Court stuff."

"Oh. Well, keep your distance. Not that I should have to tell you."

A couple of years ago I was with him at a stakeout and got battered by a psychotic. No slipups by anyone; stuff happens. It took a few tense discussions for him to ease off sheltering me. But sometimes he still tries to protect and serve.

I said, "Good luck," hung up, and continued walking.

The Seville had merited free parking because my I.D. tag said I was a designated expert witness. That confused the attendant who felt he needed to consult with another attendant. Eventually the yardarm lifted.

Once out of the lot, I headed for the alley where Lynne Gutierrez had been treated like garbage.

CHAPTER 43

Normal cities revolve around a central hub. L.A. made a stab at normalcy for decades but then the freeways were built and everything drifted westward, leaving the hub to decay. Despite decades of nattering about revival, downtown L.A. remains more a concept than a reality.

A shaky concept; nowadays, the area's a bizarre mix of gloss and crud.

Government buildings, convention hotels, and office towers housing bankers, money managers, and the kind of lawyers who schmooze with politicians coexist with itinerant street vendors, mono-brand fast-food joints, once glorious movie theaters converted to discount emporia crammed with schlock, pawnshops promising to pay you handsomely for your gold, a stunningly violent Skid Row, overflow hamlets of homeless psychotics camped out and wandering the streets, the drug dealers who prey on them, the shelters that try to save them.

I found a privately run patch of ravaged asphalt three blocks from the alley in question and paid far too much to park.

Midday downtown light was hot, hazy, heavy. The air reeked of deep-frying, fossil fuel, human sweat, the occasional burst of too-sweet cologne. Men and women in tailored suits stepped around heaps of garbage and worked hard at ignoring the mentally tormented men and women who'd created them. The sidewalk was splotched dark where tall buildings combated the struggling sun, lighter where empty lots admitted glare, creating a strange pinto effect. Din alternated with inexplicable bursts of quiet. Then louder waves of noise began killing the quiet, as if a cosmic roadie was amplifying the city.

For the most part people went about their business, shunning eye contact. Paying no notice to what was obvious to me a block and a half in.

I spotted Moe Reed first, wearing a black leather motorcycle jacket and standing just left of the alley mouth, cleaning his nails.

To the right of the dim strip stood Milo in a black suit, white shirt, and blue tie, pretending to read a newspaper.

The suit was a valiant attempt to blend in but a close look at the fabric would tell you this was no banker or politically connected paper pusher.

Moe was able to take in his surroundings by shifting his eyes without moving. Using the paper as cover meant Milo had to lower it in microbursts and during one of those instances, he saw me.

So did Moe, who didn't react.

Milo did, glaring.

When I reached him, he said, "This is keeping your distance?"

I said, "Distance is relative. Where are the others?"

"The others," he said, "i.e. the people who *belong* here, are stationed at the other end. Except for Alicia who's still following the Highlander. Which seems to be going around in circles. Long as you're here, any wisdom on that?"

I said, "Could be she wants to go to the scene and is building up her courage."

"Or she's just nuts."

"If you want to get technical."

He began to smile. Killed it. "Seriously, Alex, you really don't need to be here."

"If she's mentally disturbed, I could help."

"Not from up close and personal. No way, not gonna happen."

"I have no desire for up close and personal."

He sighed. "Why'd you come? Really."

I said, "First time I've been downtown in a while. I took being so close as an omen."

Before he could respond, his phone played Mozart digitalized to squirts and bleeps. Turned to low volume and muffled by a suit pocket but still borderline criminal.

He answered, stiffened. "Got it."

I said, "She's here."

"Just turned in." Pointing up the alley. "The dumpster's right in the middle with half a block on each side. Hector and Sean have eyes on her. We'll wait to see what she does. If she gets out of the car, we approach from both sides. If she does a drive-by, we'll hustle and follow and do a traffic stop on those expired tags."

He sauntered across the alley entry, said something to Moe, who nodded.

The two of them shifted closer to the mouth of the alley and looked in.

I stood behind them, keeping my distance. Milo looked back to check, frowned and continued.

His phone rang again. "Okay, ready." To Moe: "She just turned in, is cruising slowly toward the dumpster."

Moments later, the Highlander appeared facing us, horizontal grille slats forming a strange, almost goofy smile. It stopped directly next to the dumpster. Inches away on the driver's side, just like in the body-dump footage.

Milo said, "For all we know she's gonna toss someone else in there—okay, she's out."

He and Moe began running.

I waited a few seconds before following. Able to outpace and overtake both of them easily but hanging back.

As I got closer, details clarified.

Trim, tall blond woman in all-black, carrying an oversized beige handbag. Black running shoes with red soles. She could've been shopping in Brentwood.

Milo and Moe were fifty feet away when Villalobos and Sean appeared, both vested. Black rectangles with glass eyes attached to the vests. Bodycams.

The woman was surprised and Sean used that to run past her so he faced her from the opposite side.

He and Villalobos, boxing her in.

She didn't move or otherwise react, complied when they told her to put her hands up. As she was turning toward Sean to be cuffed, her right hand swooped into her bag, brought something out, and made a quick, darting, almost delicate swipe at Villalobos's arm.

Villalobos managed to hold on to his weapon as he grabbed at his wrist. The moment it took to holster his Glock allowed red to drip on the alley floor.

Milo and Moe were thirty paces away, leaving Sean to face her alone. I thought of his near-fatal encounter years ago. Wondered if he'd overreact.

But he didn't. Merely backed away a couple of feet while keeping his gun on the woman.

She stood motionless again, then wheeled on Sean waving whatever she'd used to cut Villalobos.

Villalobos continued to squeeze his own wrist. The blood flow weakened but didn't stop.

The woman advanced on Sean swinging her blade slowly, horizontally. Sean kept his gun trained on her. Shouted hoarsely.

Gentle guy by nature. I'd never heard him raise his voice.

Now Milo and Moe were at the scene and Alicia, also vested and cammed, was running in from the opposite end of the alley.

Lots of guns aimed, lots of shouted commands.

I got close enough to hear Villalobos say, "I'm okay, stopped the bleeding," without much confidence.

Milo pulled out his phone and 911'd. Slipped out of his suit jacket, wrapped it around Villalobos's arm, and stayed with him, holding it tight.

Alicia moved closer to the woman. "Put the knife down now, or you'll be shot! *Down! Now! Now!*"

Tiana Crown, once beautiful, now hardened and coarsened with mad, water-colored eyes, shrugged and said, "Okay."

Smiling crookedly. Twice, she'd pretended to give up. I braced myself for a suicide-by-cop move.

Instead she dropped the metallic thing to the ground where it clinked, rolled, and settled.

Hobby knife with a tiny triangular blade.

A combine of arms moved in, pinning her arms behind her. Alicia cuffed her, arrested her, began Mirandizing.

Tiana Crown said, "I watch TV, not necessary, bitch." Husky voice.

She'd remained close enough to the dumpster to kick it. Dull thud.

Laughing, she said, "So much for nostalgia."

Alicia began Mirandizing her again. Knowing the cameras would pick up everything and wanting a complete recitation.

Tiana Crown talked over her. "Yadda yadda yadda yadda, bitch."

Just as Alicia made a third attempt, noise filled the space behind us.

Wailing sirens.

The red bulk of an LAFD ambulance.

EMTs rushed over to Villalobos, who said, "It's no big deal."

Ignoring him, they got to work. As Tiana Crown watched them, Alicia completed the warning.

Tiana Crown's eyes swung back to Alicia. "What's the magic word, bitch? Oh, yeah. *Lawyer.*"

Gloving up, Alicia inspected the bag. Smiled and pulled something out.

Small saw, identical to the one Robin had found.

Tiana Crown's eyes fluttered. "Big deal, I craft."

Alicia said, "Can't talk to you," and walked away.

CHAPTER 44

Tiana Crown ended up booked, re-Mirandized, and jailed as Rhonda Lee Cronin, the given name she'd used to collect nearly three thousand a month of assorted government assistance payments, some legitimate, others sketchy.

She was assigned a public defender named Wilf Mankell, young, inexperienced, slightly addled.

Or as Milo referred to him: "Space Cadet with a J.D."

John Nguyen called Milo to fill him in on Mankell. "Shit law school, no distinctions, he's lunch meat."

Despite that assessment, Mankell kept his client unavailable and proceeded to file assertively worded motions to dismiss that Nguyen termed "rectal ejecta but you still have to use up the toilet paper. One of them he's hinting at a diminished-capacity defense. Ask Delaware what he thinks of that, haha."

Eighteen days post-arrest, the evidence list was handed over to the defense. Two days after that, Mankell emailed Nguyen and asked for a meeting.

Nguyen told Milo and me about it over coffee in the court cafeteria.

"I yawn and ask him what for. He says I'll find out. I say no games, I'm busy, and if you're thinking of a plea bargain, forget it, this is a lock-and-load. Then I call him kiddo. Like you do, Milo. Except you're being nice and I'm letting him know I think he's a piece of shit."

We smiled.

Nguyen chewed on a cake donut. "He tries to sound authoritative but his voice goes all quivery and he says how about the chance of parole. I say in how long? He says ten and puts a rookie question mark at the end of it. Like, Mother, may I? I laugh, say see you in court, and he kicks it up to twenty. I say three murders and an attempted against a police officer? You auditioning at The Comedy Store? He immediately jumps to thirty. I say forty, he buckles. So, hell, Milo, if I can avoid going to trial, what do I care what happens in forty years?"

"I'm okay with that, John."

"Good," said Nguyen. "Not that it matters. And just to show you what a nice guy I am, I made it contingent on her sitting down with you and telling you why the eff she did it. Bring your pet shrink, maybe he can make sense of it."

Nguyen left and we sat there drinking coffee as I studied the blue folder Milo had brought.

Slim folder but potent.

Cellular tower tracking placed Rhonda Cronin in the vicinity of all three murders at all the right times. Three days prior to the strangulation of Sophie Barlow, she was pegged near the alley behind Michael Heck's apartment building, pointing to a DNA-collection mission.

Minute brown spots on the rear seat of the Highlander and huge brown splotches under the seat were confirmed to be Lynne Gutierrez's blood, ditto for the material in the treads of the Nikes that Cronin had on during her arrest.

The jigsaw Alicia had pulled out of Cronin's purse was new and produced nothing. But an identical tool recovered from her craft station—an old door on sawhorses situated in a spare bedroom—though well cleaned, yielded barely visible blood specks embedded between the teeth of the blade that matched to Martha Matthias.

Cronin's living room had been converted to a home gym and a

metal bar, hefty and capable of holding serious weights, produced more of Lynne's blood.

The last bit of evidence was unconventional but just as telling. Along with Cronin's pencil-drawn plans for an assortment of birdhouses in various stages of construction were rough sketches of a woman sitting at a table with a cord around her neck and another of a woman with disarticulated arms laid atop her torso.

Nothing commemorated Lynne Gutierrez's murder.

Milo said, "Why do you think?"

I said, "Collateral damage, like we said. Lynne had led her to Martha. Even if it was unwitting, she didn't want Lynne figuring it out."

"Intellectually challenged? Doesn't sound like much of a threat."

"Good point. When we talk to her, we can try to find out."

"Speaking of which, how does tomorrow look, say ten a.m.?"

"I've got appointments but I'll move them."

"That's different."

"So is the case."

"No kiddie welfare at stake."

"Just lawyers."

"In that case," he said, "you'll have more fun with me."

CHAPTER 45

Milo said, "Rhonda, Tiana, what's your preference?"

The woman, hollow-eyed, straw-like hair drawn back, jail complexion already settling in—pallor, pimples, wrinkles so deep they looked like black pen marks—smirked.

"My preference? Queen Asskicker."

I wrote, *Sufficiently mentally organized to crack wise.*

Milo said, "I'll go with Tiana."

"You go wherever you want."

"By the way, Detective Villalobos is okay."

"Who's that?"

"The detective you cut."

She shrugged. Shifted to me. Flashed a crooked smile. Batted her lashes. Stretched backward to showcase her chest.

Old habits.

My smile was intentionally bland and that tightened her jaw.

"You think you're cute," she said. "You think you can do what you want when you want. I met plenty of assholes like you at the mansion. In the lagoon, everyone's snorting, popping, drinking. Butt-ugly guys, real trolls, knew they'd score because the women were just hired holes."

Milo said, "You killed three women. We'd like to know why."

Tiana Crown leaned forward as if ready to strike out. Thought better of it.

Able to control herself.

"You've got a mouth on you, Fatso."

Milo said, "What I just said shouldn't come as a surprise, Tiana. Unless Mr. Mankell didn't explain the purpose of this meeting to you."

"*Mister* Mankell," she said. "When he goes through puberty, let me know."

"You do understand."

She corkscrewed her lips, looked everywhere but at us. "Yeah, I understand."

Still avoiding us, she crossed her arms over her chest.

Milo said, "Sophie Barlow."

"Her," said Tiana Crown. "Didn't know her. Not as a person."

I said, "You knew her as a vehicle."

"To where?"

"Getting back at Mike."

Pale eyes fluttered. She smiled.

Milo said, "Why were you so mad at him?"

Tiana Crown said, "Oh shit, don't make me work so hard, you know."

"If we did, we wouldn't ask you."

"He knows the answer. *Vehicle.* Shit."

We waited.

Tiana Crown said, "Why? 'Cause he's a total rat bastard. Claimed he didn't narc Darren out and I was stupid enough to believe him. Then, after all those years of me believing him and giving him what he wanted when he called, he tells me to get out of his life because he *found* someone?"

"Sophie."

"Skinny bitch." Another crooked smile. "That's when I saw him for what he is and knew he'd narced and brought the whole thing down."

"So you killed Sophie to—"

"To put a hole in his soul and then put him in jail."

She let her arms relax and seemed to deflate. "So now I'm in jail. But who cares? He'll get there one day."

"Why?" said Milo.

"Because he's a lying scumbag and karma's a bitch. You just wait and see."

Milo nodded.

Tiana Crown said, "Don't pretend you agree when you're just trying to squeeze the juice out of me."

"What we're trying to do is understand your motive—"

"I just told you, okay? Hole in the soul."

"Sophie Barlow was collateral damage."

"Whatever. Yeah. Call it what you want. Sometimes bad things happen to good people. If she was good, I have no idea, like I keep telling you, didn't know her and that's all I'm going to say about that."

Milo looked at me. I nodded.

Tiana Crown said, "What, Pretty Boy's the boss?"

Looking to the right. Back went the arms, forming an X across her chest. Drawn tighter. Rocking with each breath.

Regular breaths, on the slow side.

Relaxed. No remorse for what she's done.

Milo said, "Martha Matthias."

"Total bitch, okay?"

"What did she do to make you mad?"

"Just told you. Total bitch."

"Could you be a little more specific."

"A little more?" she said. "Total bitch with a hair up her ass."

Sitting up taller and drawing the crossed arms tighter yet. Wrinkling her top. Orange. In the women's jail that meant mentally ill. Mankell had pushed for it.

I said, "She did that to you."

"Did what?"

I crossed my own arms. "You went to ask her to release some

money during the investigation so that you could live. Not only did she turn you down, she stood there like this. So you cut off her arms."

Tiana Crown gaped. Her arms tumbled to her sides. "What is *wrong* with you?"

Milo said, "He's wrong?"

"No no no no," she said. "He's fucking *right* and that's fucking *wrong.* What *are* you, some sicko alien lizard invader mind reader?"

I said, "You don't do things randomly."

"Aw, gee. Thanks." Another lash-batting ballet was followed by lip-licking. "Now I get why you're the boss. And here I was thinking you were some rich guy's spawn in a nice blazer. Gucci?"

I smiled and shook my head.

"What, then?"

"Not important."

"Oh man," she said. "If I had you alone."

Milo said, "All these years and you suddenly decided to get revenge."

"You know what they say. A dish best eaten cold."

I said, "True but there had to be more."

"More what, Too Cute?"

"You think things through and plan carefully. In Sophie Barlow's case the trigger was Mike Heck treating you shabbily, which made you doubt he'd ever been honest when he denied ratting out the scam. So with regard to Martha, something else had to set you off."

Tiana Crown licked her lips. "Oh my. Oh my my my my my."

She moved to re-cross her arms. Dropped them abruptly. Fidgeted.

"Why do you need to know?"

Milo said, "We always want to know. And it's in your best interest. Letting us see you as something other than a cold-blooded murderer."

Tiana Crown burst into hoarse, too-long laughter. "But that's what I am."

I said, "You had grievances. You overreacted to them but if Mike had been honest and Martha hadn't been so cold, they'd still be alive."

Her mouth dropped open. "My my my my." Moisture collected in the corners of her eyes. Water flowing onto water. "You're right again. They screwed me. It's totally on them." Another bout of laughter. "That mean you're going to let me free?"

Milo said, "You really don't expect an answer to that, Tiana."

"Well," she said, "I would if it was the right answer. How about you, Boss? Think you can tell them whose fault it was and maybe shave off some time? Don't answer that, just foolin'."

I said, "What did Lynne Gutierrez do to you?"

"Nothing," she said. "I liked her even though she was retarded and talked funny. I showed her how to do sit-ups. I walked with her. For like the first block. To keep her company but also because I thought she might get into trouble out by herself. Even though they told me she was okay by herself. But I went the extra mile for her."

"So what happened?" said Milo.

"What happened? What happened was one day she said she was tired so I drove her and then she said it's here, I parked across the street and she got out. As I'm about to leave, *she* comes out from the side of the house. Older, scrawnier, totally had-out, a real scrag. But I recognized her right off because when someone does you like that, you don't forget. So now I knew whose kid Lynne was. Which made sense. Instead of taking care of her, the cold bitch had stuck her in a place. And then I saw how she treated Lynne and it fit. No hugs, no kisses, she turns and walks ahead and Lynne follows."

"Did Martha see you?"

"Uh-uh," said Tiana Crown.

"So you weren't worried about Lynne telling her mother about you."

"Lynne was retarded, she had no clue about anything."

I said, "Finding Martha when you weren't looking for her felt like karma. That was the trigger for killing her."

"That and everything," she said. "The way she treated Lynne. Sticking her in a place and then when she shows up not a hug, not a kiss, *nothing*."

Milo said, “Then why was Lynne—”

“You don’t get it, do you? How about you, Boss? Do you get it?”

I shook my head.

Tiana Crown leaned in and spoke in a suddenly soft, pliant voice.

“Her mother was gone. Who was going to pay for that place? How would she deal with being all alone? That’s a tough thing for anyone.”

Blinking.

“But when you’re retarded and talk funny,” she said. “Phew.”

Slow spreading smile.

“I put her out of her misery.”

Milo said, “Like a cat or a dog.”

“Exactly. It’s kind. I made sure it didn’t hurt. Couple of good booms.” Fingering the back of her own skull.

“Then you dumped her in the trash.”

“Big deal,” said Tiana Crown. “When you’re gone, you’re gone. And that’s all I’m going to say about it. About any of it.”

“Okay,” said Milo.

That surprised her. “That’s all you want?”

“Unless there’s something else you feel like telling us.”

“You know,” she said, “there is. You think you got me so you’re feeling real good about yourselves. But I’m going to a place where I’m going to be taken care of. Bed, meals, no forms to fill out just to get money to live on. So screw you. I won.”

Milo got up and opened the door. Two deputy sheriff jailers entered, cuffed her, and told her to stand.

As they walked her out, she craned back at us. “I won.”

But she faltered on the second word.

CHAPTER 46

Five months later, I received a letter from the Central California Women's Facility in Chowchilla. A sticker taped over the back said it had been examined by prison authorities.

Dear Doctor Delaware aka The Boss aka Too Cute For His Own Good.

Mankell told me who you really were and first I thought that was pretty low not telling me you were a shrink so to be honest I was a little peaved. But dont worry Im over it. LOL. So now I know you. Then I thought hey he helps people so he was there to help me. Which I hope is true. Anyway, I want to let you know it's even better here then I thought with 640 acres and all sorts of programs. Including a great crafts room and I been let to do my birdhouses but I cant sell them I just give them away to kids through this program they have here. So Im fine and I thought you might want to know because you have kind eyes.

Xoxoxox T

PS: I wouldn't mind if you visit me once in a while.

I re-folded the letter, slipped it back in the envelope, and dropped it in my office wastebasket. Then I removed it, found the file I'd created for the three murders, and dropped it in.

About the Author

JONATHAN KELLERMAN has lived in two worlds: clinical psychologist and #1 *New York Times* bestselling author of more than fifty crime novels. His unique perspective on human behavior has led to the creation of the Alex Delaware series, *The Butcher's Theater, Billy Straight, The Conspiracy Club, Twisted, True Detectives,* and *The Murderer's Daughter*. With his wife, bestselling novelist Faye Kellerman, he co-authored *Double Homicide* and *Capital Crimes.* With his son, bestselling novelist Jesse Kellerman, he co-authored *The Lost Coast, The Burning, Half Moon Bay, A Measure of Darkness, Crime Scene, The Golem of Hollywood,* and *The Golem of Paris.* He is also the author of two children's books and numerous nonfiction works, including *Savage Spawn: Reflections on Violent Children* and *With Strings Attached: The Art and Beauty of Vintage Guitars.* He has won the Goldwyn, Edgar, and Anthony awards and the Lifetime Achievement Award from the American Psychological Association, and has been nominated for a Shamus Award. Jonathan and Faye Kellerman live in California.

jonathankellerman.com
Facebook.com/jonathankellerman

About the Type

This book was set in Garamond, a typeface originally designed by the Parisian type cutter Claude Garamond (c. 1500–61). This version of Garamond was modeled on a 1592 specimen sheet from the Egenolff-Berner foundry, which was produced from types assumed to have been brought to Frankfurt by the punch cutter Jacques Sabon (c. 1520–80).

Claude Garamond's distinguished romans and italics first appeared in *Opera Ciceronis* in 1543–44. The Garamond types are clear, open, and elegant.